# GOTHIC

# GOTHIC

PHILIP FRACASSI

CEMETERY DANCE PUBLICATIONS

*Baltimore*

❖ 2023 ❖

*Gothic*



Cemetery Dance Publications special edition



Cemetery Dance Publications
132B Industry Lane, Unit #7
Forest Hill, MD 21050
www.cemeterydance.com



First Cemetery Dance Printing

Paperback ISBN: 978-1-58767-840-0
Hardcover ISBN: 978-1-58767-842-4

Cover Artwork and Design
© 2023 by Kealan Patrick Burke
Interior Design
© 2023 by Desert Isle Design, LLC

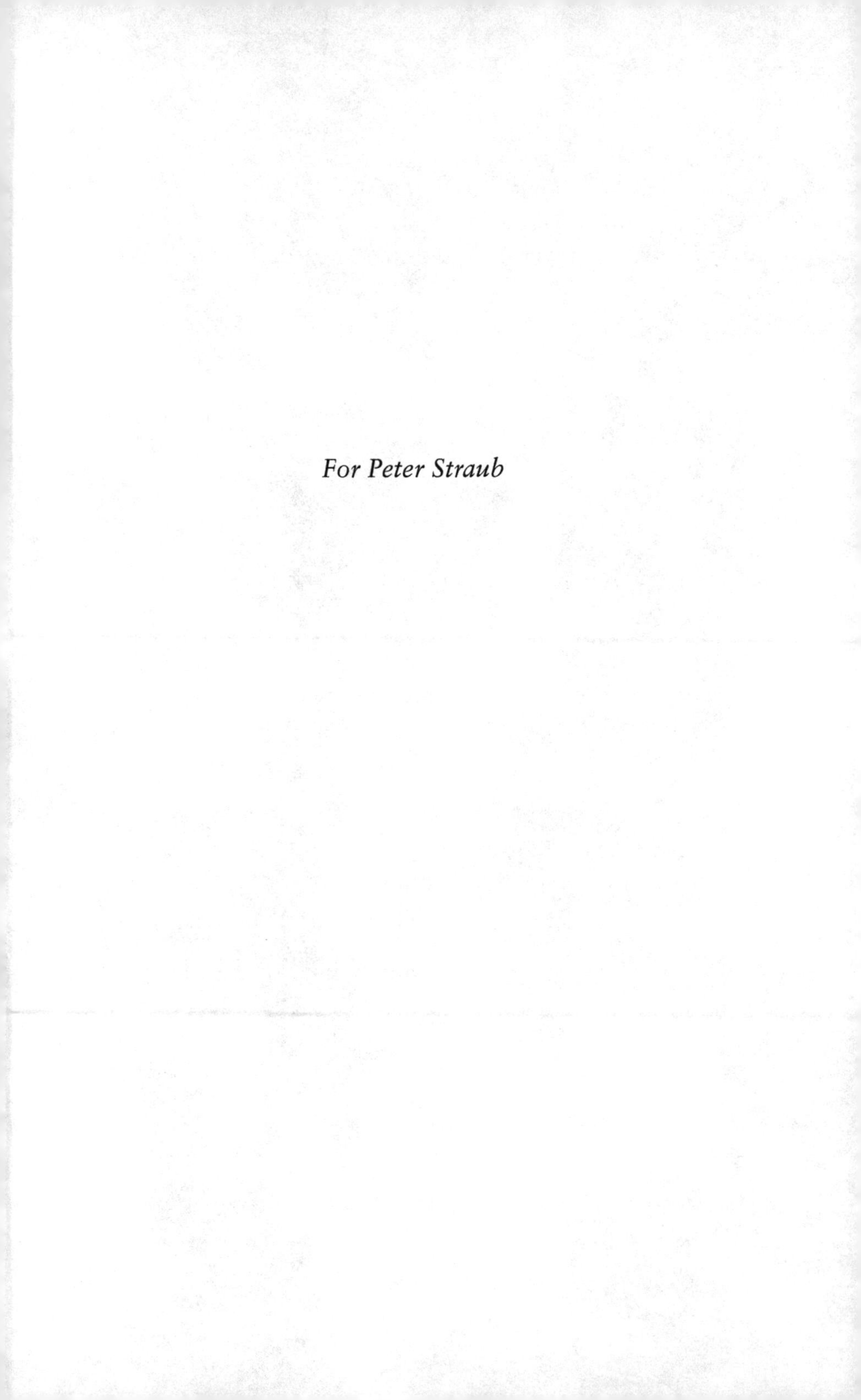

*For Peter Straub*

The Gothic castle or house... is a house of degeneration, even of decomposition, its living-space darkening and contracting into the dying-space of the mortuary and the tomb.

—Chris Baldick

This looks like a job for me, so everybody, just follow me 'Cause we need a little controversy...

—Eminem

# PROLOGUE

DIANA MONTRESOR opens her laptop, punches in a password to reveal the home screen, and brings up her mail program. She still wears sweaty workout clothes from her private yoga session. Her hair is pulled back, a black, silky ponytail draped carelessly over one shoulder, her youthful muscles pleasantly achy and warm from the strength work and stretches. The moment the instructor kissed her cheek and departed, Diana went straight to the freezer and pulled out a frosted bottle of vodka, followed by tonic and fresh lemon from the refrigerator. Cocktail in hand, she now stares blankly at the screen, pushing down a surge of anticipation that emails from this particular sender always bring to the surface. She's foolish to feel this way, but tries to stay positive, stay hopeful. It's an uneasy balance.

At the top of her Inbox are two consecutive emails, both from the American detective she'd hired to locate the relic.

The investigator is based out of New York City and has been on retainer for several years. She'd found him via a referral by the Montresor family attorney. Apparently, the American helped another family find a runaway girl, the heir to a massive pharmaceutical fortune who'd decided she'd rather live in a filthy hovel in the United States than a castle in northern France. The investigator had found the girl in some exclusive Chinatown opium den, where the spoiled and stupid went to die. His diplomatic recovery of the heiress earned him high marks, and the family attorney had vouched for the man's credibility, intelligence, and tactfulness.

Diana has similar investigators on retainer in strategic locations throughout the States: Los Angeles, Chicago, San Francisco, New Orleans, Miami. These are in addition to literally dozens of men and women positioned around the world, all of them paid a small monthly sum to do nothing but keep their eyes and ears open (albeit with the promise of a generous bonus for any information that led to discovery). Her global resources shape a net of eyes and ears that would have been impossible in her grandfather's youth; the enormous amount of information transmitted at the speed of electricity is a luxury her ancestors could have never dreamed of. An unfair advantage, surely, but one she plans to capitalize upon.

She will not fail.

Many years ago, when she first took over the search from her grandfather, there had been no trace—not a single lead—for decades. She hadn't even been sure what, exactly, she was looking for. What was its current shape?

How was it hiding?

After the death of her parents, Diana finished school and was taught all there was to know about the family's history and its intimate relationship to the arts, dark and otherwise. Her grandfather raised her, trained her. He instructed her, throughout all the years of her upbringing, about the importance of finding what was taken from them, the importance—the *need*—to correct the past. And, God willing, prevent a future darkened by evil, erase the threat of having murder and despair spread like a global virus.

The one thing in her favor is the knowledge that the relic needs a host, someone it can control, someone to spread the power that lies behind the portal, the hidden world on the other side of the stone, an all-consuming dimension located next door to Hell.

The host could be anyone, but it will need someone who will *listen*, who craves the things it can offer, who will sell their soul—wittingly or unwittingly, perhaps too naïve or foolish to know the difference.

She opens the first email, and her black eyes go wide.

Ms. Montresor,

I believe I have a lead on the object you're looking for. I hope I'm right, because with the amount of money you've been putting into my bank account, I was feeling downright guilty about the whole thing. Attached are a few photos taken by my guy at Howland Hook, one of the ports here in the city. Unless I hear different, I'm going to follow this thing and see where it ends up. Let's hope it stays local but, regardless, I'll keep you informed. Please take a look at the photos and give me your thoughts. They're not as clear as I'd like, but hopefully I'll have a chance to take my own pictures soon.

Based on your initial description, and what I was able to gather from my contact over a brief phone conversation, this could be what you've been looking for.

Fingers crossed.

Diana's breath catches in her throat. She takes a sip from the vodka tonic, lets out a held breath, and opens the first attachment.

The image shows a sealed crate, dangling from the hook of a crane, being lifted over a concrete deck.

She feels disappointment drain her energy like a wave. It could be anything inside that massive wooden crate. *You know better than to get your hopes up, Diana.* She takes another breath, focuses on staying detached, knowing damn well this will most likely lead to nothing.

She moves the mouse to the next file and double-clicks the icon. The computer thinks for a nanosecond, one that feels to her like an eternity, and then the second image pops open, covering three-quarters of the screen.

The crate, now resting on an expanse of concrete, has been opened and partially unpacked inside a large, empty warehouse. Surrounding the item are other crates, odd machines, bored-looking workers. The photo is a little blurry, as if the photographer had moved at the last second. She holds her breath as she leans in, eyes mere inches from the screen. A sign in the image's background reads CONTAINER TERMINAL, and one of the men in the photo seems to be inspecting the crate's interior. He wears a dark blue hat and matching blue vest. Diana thinks he looks like a policeman.

But none of that matters, because she knows what he is inspecting, knows despite only a portion of it being visible, despite the blurred image and shadowed lighting.

This was *it*.

"The bastard found it," she says out loud, and laughs lightly in dazed amusement. In disbelief.

There are more images to open, and she'll do so in a moment, wanting to delay any potential disappointment the other images might bring. Instead, she moves the cursor to the second email, wondering what else the detective has written.

> PS – the image you're likely stuck staring at is from a random inspection. I'm not sure what made them target that crate in particular. They must not have liked the looks of it. A cop once told me bad people give off a certain dark energy, maybe your artifact has a similar problem.

Diana smiles, mentally adding intuitiveness to the list of the investigator's traits.

She finishes her drink and makes a second before returning to inspect the remaining images. *I'm coming for you,* she thinks, clicking from image, to image, to image... each one reinforcing her knowledge that she's finally found what they've been looking for all these years...

*Time to bring you back where you belong.*

She closes the laptop and sits back in the chair, her dark eyes staring at the clear, moonlit night which fills the room's bay window, the Mediterranean resting below a sprawled field of stars like an abyss.

*God have mercy on whoever gets in my way.*

Part One

# THE PITCH

# ONE

"MR. PARKS, would you like a cup of coffee? I'm sure Harry won't be much longer."

Tyson grips the worn leather attaché case—and the new manuscript pages within—protectively, clutching it close to his gut. He figures he is one of the few writers who prefers to hand in physical pages versus digital bits when it comes to turning in a novel (or a partial novel, as it were), but he also sees it as an excuse to be here in person. He rarely visits the agency offices, and hardly ever sees his agent face-to-face, despite them both being in Manhattan. He carefully tilts his head toward the secretary, one of the hinges on his eyeglass frames so loose he's afraid if he moves too suddenly the damn things will fall off. To make things worse, the prescription is grossly out of date, giving the details of the surrounding office a *soft* look.

"That would be nice, thank you."

The blurred form of the possibly attractive (his glasses make it hard to be sure) young woman behind the desk smiles and stands. Because the office is narrow, she has to shimmy sideways to squeeze between his knees and the edge of her desk. Her skirt, he notices, is thigh-high, her bared legs the lean, muscular limbs of youth. Tyson studies her figure as she shuffles past.

He recalls some time he had spent on a Montana ranch while researching *Ne'er Do Well*, one of his more popular novels from the '90s, and how he'd been able to watch an Andalusian give birth. The horse lay on her side, calm as could be, as she pushed out a fully-formed foal sheathed in a bubble of milky-clear membrane. Within ten minutes, the foal's head and neck were free from the sac, its body surrounded with clean straw supplied by the rancher. Within an hour it was walking, the mother also now back on her feet, allowing the newborn to feed from her as they nuzzled inside the dirt corral.

He imagines the young, short-skirted assistant as that newborn foal. Naked and wrapped in a moist, milky casing, her slick body breaking through the membrane, those muscular legs wobbling as she tries to stand...

"Here's your coffee, Mr. Parks."

"Oh. Yes, thank you," he says quickly, not meeting her eyes. "It's cold outside. The chill hasn't left my jacket."

She smiles as she shuffles past once more, giving his jacket (and overall appearance, he supposes) a quick once-over. He knows better than to think her impressed, bundled as he is in old jeans and worn sneakers. A black dress shirt covered by a tan raincoat. A cheap wool scarf. The style-free haircut, the damn glasses. As she sits behind her desk, he takes a sip of the coffee and winces.

"Is it okay?" she asks, alarmed. "The coffee here is not the best. We do have cream and sugar. I'm sorry, I should have offered."

"No, no, it's fine."

But she continues to watch him, and he knows he can't fake it, not even for her sake.

"It's just... well, it's a bit cool."

*Ice-cold, actually.*

"Oh my gosh, I'm so sorry. I didn't... here..." She stands again, graceful and powerful, all blonde hair and skin white as cream. Clinging, deep blue blouse. Black heels. That skirt. Those legs. Tyson has the foolish desire to see her run, to see her *sprint*.

She reaches for the cup and he has the insane urge to fight her for it. "It's fine," he says, not understanding why he's lying to the woman.

"No, Mr. Parks, please, I insist..."

As she pulls the cup from his clutched hand, his attaché shifts and slides off his lap. It hits the carpet and papers pour out like a Chinese fan. "Oh shit," he says, and instinctively bends over, his gut impeding his progress.

The assistant kneels gracefully to the floor. "Oh no, I'm so sorry!"

Feeling a tremor of panic, Tyson glances toward the bullpen where the lesser agents are stalled at open-walled work areas. Even slightly out-of-focus, he can see that faces have turned to watch. "I... it's okay..." Shoving off the chair, he follows the girl's lead and drops to his knees, pride-be-damned, and begins scooping the papers back into the attaché. The assistant sets the cold coffee on the floor and helps him gather the pages. This close, he can smell her vitality, the length of her lifespan.

*So much time,* he thinks, and sour melancholy washes over him.

"Jesus, what's all this?"

Tyson looks up too fast. The hinge on his glasses gives way and they come apart, clatter to the floor. He hears the young woman say *oh no!* again and wants to slap her across the face. Instead, he squints upward toward the voice, but since the young woman has abruptly stood to greet the newcomer, he finds himself staring at the back of her thighs. Red-faced, he cranes his neck around her bottom to see her boss standing there, staring down at Tyson with confusion and a grimace of distaste.

To Tyson's blurred vision, the man's face is little more than a smear of pink and brown, yet still recognizable as being the person he is there to see (though he would have preferred it not to be from his knees).

"Oh," Tyson says tiredly. "Hiya, Harry."

# TWO

TYSON SETTLES deep into a leather club chair, black and seemingly brand new, the leather slick and smooth. He sinks uncomfortably into the plush cushion, feeling like a child despite his six-plus feet in height. "This is some chair, Harry."

Tyson's agent stands behind his desk, fingers templed on the slick surface, lips pursed. The floor-to-ceiling windows behind him show a drab view of New York City, the office high enough for the view to be partially obscured by misty clouds and the windows smeared with moisture, giving adjacent buildings the appearance of watercolors painted in shades of gray versus color. Streetlights dot the veins of avenues and streets below, fuzzy as underwater stars in a gloomy ocean teeming with life.

"Is that it?" Harry asks, pointing to the leather case in Tyson's lap.

"Yeah," Tyson says with a weak smile. "Can't vouch for the page order."

"Like I give a shit," Harry says, and comes around the desk. He leans against an edge, places his palms down on either side of his open suit coat. Harry's bright red tie screams like an inverted exclamation point, and Tyson shifts anxiously. He'd been able to tape his glasses together just well enough to wear them, albeit on a short-lived basis, but he still feels small in front of the younger man, who has a thing for standing over him when they meet. Harry has a presence that always feels *loud,* and *in charge.* Whereas Tyson, with his disheveled clothes and broken glasses, feels very, very *quiet.* Subservient.

He follows the upside-down exclamation point up to Harry's face: rugged and perfectly shadowed along the cheek and jaw, a thick black coif of hair nested above his forehead, the dazzling brown eyes. "Come on, man," he says, reaching a hand toward his once-prized cash cow. "Let me see the goods."

"Okay, take it easy, Harry," Tyson says, laughing loosely, and watches as Harry's smile flickers at the tips. "I mean, okay well, first, let me be clear. It's not a hundred percent finished."

Harry's flickering smile melts, his eyes darken like extinguished lanterns.

"Just... now just hold on," Tyson says, hating to already be on the defensive. "It's *good.* I mean, Harry... it's really damn good."

Harry's smile returns, but it's cautious now. Pensive. Tyson swallows and shifts his bulk for the tenth time, does his best to sit up straighter in the slippery, spongy chair. "I think this could be a big one, Harry."

Harry nods, rubs his jaw. Without a word, he walks back behind the desk and sits down, his face partially hidden from Tyson by piles of stacked books and piled contracts which cover the desktop like paper mesas on a mahogany desert. When he speaks, his voice is clipped.

Borderline aggressive.

"It's been six months, Tyson," he says. "Six. Fucking. Months."

"I know, but I'm telling you..."

"Just hold on!" Harry interrupts, loudly enough to be considered a rebuke, but smooth enough to not come off as *too* demeaning. "Look man, I've got to give them something, Ty. These guys gave us money. They gave us a nice advance..."

Tyson's backbone tingles. "Damn right they did," he says, his own voice rising. "I've made those cocksuckers a lot of money over the years."

Harry sighs, leans forward and adjusts his seat so he has a clear sightline to his client. "That's right, Tyson, you have. Hell, man, the same goes for me! And don't think for a split-second that I don't realize that. This corner office was built on your *words*, brother, and I will forever be your most humble servant and ardent admirer. I'm a goddamn sycophant, baby. I mean, you are preaching to the choir here."

"Okay, Harry..."

"Shit man, I'm the choir, the altar boy, and the minister's mistress all wrapped into one. I'm the motherfucking church janitor, buddy!" Harry yells, laughing. "But the truth, my man, the horrible *reality*, is that we need to give them what we promised. Contractually," he adds.

"I realize that, Harry, I do. Which is why I'm bringing you this." Tyson holds up the case as Exhibit A. "In person, I might add."

Harry sighs again and lowers his head, as if thinking. *Or praying*, Tyson thinks. Then he pops his lips, pushes himself back in his chair and taps the heels of his Berluti dress boots onto the desktop. "Okay, man. You're right," he says, spreading his hands and showing a toothy smile. "I'm a total dick. Lay it on me, brother. Confess your sins. I'm all ears."

Tyson touches the tape bump on his repaired glasses while his other fingers grip the worn leather of the attaché case hard enough to turn his knuckles white. "Okay," he says slowly, choosing his words. "Well... for one, I changed the title. It's now called *The Delicate Dark*. Brilliant, right?"

Harry waits, expressionless. Tyson feels sweat on the back of his neck and suddenly wishes he'd had that hot coffee. *The newly born foal breaks free from the membrane, breathes fresh air for the first time.*

"And, and... you remember the original pitch? The little girl possessed, running from the townsfolk who want to kill her? And then the mysterious priest..."

"Wait wait wait," Harry interrupts. He drops his feet from the desk, sits up and folds his hands in front of him. "What *townsfolk*, Tyson? Townsfolk sounds... folksy. Like, not modern. Please tell me you mean city, right? City folk? As in Los Angeles? In the pitch, the story took place in modern-day Los Angeles."

"That's right," Tyson says, touching his fingertips once more to the tape holding his glasses together, like a tic. Or a tell. "Originally."

Harry's face falls into open palms. "Oh please God strik
me dead."

"Just hear me out, Harry..." Tyson continues in a rush: "Okay, it's the year 1725, twenty-five short years after the Salem witch trials..."

"No no no no... please do not do this..."

"I'm telling you," Tyson says, voice rising. "If you'd just listen... it's *good,* damn it!"

Harry looks up with tired eyes. "I don't care," he says, exasperated. "I don't care if you've written Moby Goddamn Dick Part Two, dude. Tyson, we *promised* Morrow..."

"We promised them a novel based on a pitch..."

"That you are now changing!" Harry barks, emphasizing each word with a smack of one palm on his desktop. "*The Delicate Dark?* Is that supposed to be a joke? Possessed girls and priests and historical Salem witch shit? Dude, *please* tell me, please say it in a way dumb old Harry can understand. What the fuck are you *doing?*"

Tyson shifts forward abruptly, his case sliding off his knees and onto the floor. Pushing himself up using the padded armrests, he stands, his voice rough with emotion as he points a shaking finger at his agent. "My books were *New York Times* bestsellers, Harry! The *Times* once called me the new king of horror, for fuck's sake. You best remember that!"

Harry also stands, calmly meeting Tyson's eyes. "That's right, Tyson," he says, almost sadly. "They *were*. Twenty damn years ago they *were* bestsellers. Now they're clogging up the discount tables at every Barnes and Noble and Books-A-Million across the country. Your last two books didn't en turn a profit, man. They never broke even." Harry theatrically cups one hand to his ear. "That sound you hear? That's a death-knell, buddy." He places both palms flat on the desk, leans forward. "I'm trying to resurrect you, Ty, and you're digging the grave even deeper. Your career is in real trouble, man. Real trouble."

Tyson meets Harry's eyes for a moment, then he closes them wearily. He drops lifelessly back into the chair, suddenly exhausted. Defeated. He runs his hands through thinning hair. "I know that," he says quietly. "Jesus, Harry, don't you think I know that?"

"Then why are you giving me this?" Harry points to the forgotten attaché resting on the floor. "Why aren't you writing the book we told them you'd write? The one we *promised* them?"

Tyson stares back at his long-time agent, his supposed friend, with the look of a scolded dog. His glasses are tilted, the tape enforcement wilting, making Harry appear fragmented, as if Tyson were seeing him in multiple dimensions of reality. The trick of a mirror facing a mirror. The visual representation of the belittling of *self.*

"Okay... okay, Harry. I'll do it," Tyson says, fighting back the army of tears that want to follow their advance scout. *Out the eyes and down the face, off the chin in pure disgrace.* He holds them at bay, a weakened general staving off a mutiny, the desperate horde born of exhaustion and defeat, built up during months of failure, months of staring at the great void of the hopeless future and watching blankly as it stared right back, empty, futile, and all-consuming.

He removes his broken glasses, turns them in his hands, studies the rushed tape job, the scratched lenses. "I'll need some time."

Harry turns his back on Tyson and stares out the windows toward the gray clouds, the eruption of concrete and glass, the staggered skyscrapers of the city that judged, and judged, and judged. "Good galloping Christ," he mumbles.

After a moment, he lets out a heavy sigh. "I can probably buy you a month..."

"A month!" Tyson cries, dropping the worthless glasses to the floor, where they land on the leather case holding his even more worthless manuscript.

"...to finish the book." Harry lowers his head, as if studying the cars and people far below. "The *right* book."

*Or perhaps he's only staring at the tips of his thousand-dollar shoes,* Tyson thinks.

"You need to change your style, Ty," Harry says, addressing the city below instead of the man behind, his tone almost apologetic. "You need to modernize... keep up with the times... If you don't, this world will step right over you like you're a dying animal, then just keep on going, leaving you behind to bleed out."

Tyson says nothing, but instead stares languidly out the large office windows, as if searching for answers in the mist; a man awaiting a verdict from the ominous gray buildings of the unforgiving city.

# THREE

As TYSON approaches his townhouse on Riverside Drive, he feels a sudden pang of emotion towards the old brownstone. He'd purchased the property a smidge over twenty-five years ago. Paid cash. Now it was worth almost five times the amount he'd paid for it, and if it wasn't for the fact that he'd been forced to take out a fat, high-interest mortgage against it a few years back, that might have actually made him feel good.

He steps through the creaky iron gate—a feature he'd personally added to the property during the height of his popularity in the late '90s—takes the four rising steps slowly and unlocks the heavy wooden front door. Three locks later he's opening up and stepping inside.

The late afternoon sun pushes silvery light through the lace white curtains Sarah had fashioned over the windows, giving the room a leaden luminescence. The place is spacious for the city—three bedrooms, an office, a ground-floor patio off the kitchen in the back, another two-chair patio off the master bedroom accessed via French double-doors. It has three floors but the third is essentially nothing but a large guest room, a half-bath, and a storage closet. The rooftop, although convertible to a deck, has never been modified, so a bare rooftop it remains. Useable, but not elaborate.

"Honey?" he calls, knowing in his bones the place is empty. The lifeless space and gray light make the room feel cadaverous to Tyson, which does nothing to improve his mood. He drops the beaten leather attaché (and the unserviceable manuscript it contains) onto the couch, hangs his raincoat on the hook by the door. He walks to the kitchen, pours himself a scotch—hesitates a fraction of a second—then pours himself some more.

*Two fingers is a handshake, buddy. I need a hug.*

He smiles, recalling the line from a short story he'd written a few years ago as the scotch gurgles into the glass. It was a story he liked very much, and one that had paid okay. Sadly, anthologies are a dime a dozen in the horror world, and he isn't holding his breath for any royalties from that particular book. The story was about a man who purchases a vintage suit and, upon wearing it, is shown the previous owner's mysterious, and grisly, death. Tyson's attempt at a more mainstream thriller, which seems to be all the publishing world wants to see nowadays.

Personally, as he hobbles into middle-age, he prefers to read "quieter" tales from the horror genre. The historical pieces.

The mysteries. He's grown tired of monsters and demons and maniac killers. Those tropes are a young man's game.

Still, like it or not, he must find a way *back*. Back to the hardcore horror he'd penned during his 30s and 40s. That's what the public wants. What they expect of him. Publishers, too. At least the ones who still buy horror, that is. Change isn't welcome in the publishing world. Too hard to market.

Sluggish and depressed, Tyson walks down the hall to his office and opens the door. At the far end of the room sits his desk, the docile laptop resting closed on top of it. He thinks about taking another look through the manuscript he'd shown to Harry (well, *tried* to show to Harry), debates giving it a once-over.

*Yeah? To what end, champ? You gonna modernize it? Good luck with that. How about you get a smartphone first, then we'll talk.*

Tyson's free hand brushes the air as if he can bat away the negative thoughts like a buzzing fly, but he decides against the exercise. He's tired—and hell, deep-down he knows the thing is garbage, so what would be the point. He knows he'd reached and fallen short, gone for something different only because the familiar was elusive. Lost, perhaps. Like old dimes and spare keys.

So, instead, he drops his broken eyeglasses onto the desktop and pulls his old prescription pair from a desk drawer. He gives one last forlorn look at the computer, takes a swig of his drink, and shuffles defeatedly back to the living room, where the soft couch waits, begging to be napped upon.

Feeling untethered, lost, and emotionally battered, he waits to feel tired enough to lie down, but his nerves are agitated and his mind churns with anxiety. Instead of sleeping, he sits quietly amidst the hazy late afternoon light, numbly watching as the gray windows transition from pewter to charcoal.

At some point he starts to weep, but for the life of him can't remember when it started, or if it is ever going to stop.

# FOUR

SARAH OPENS the door expecting to hear the usual sounds: classical music flowing from the living room stereo, the tapping of keys from Tyson's office. She also expects to see the place better lit given the late hour and somber weather.

"Like a tomb in here," she mumbles as she begins clicking on lamps. She shivers and, after setting her purse on the kitchen counter, goes immediately to the gas fireplace. She flips a wall switch and there's a soft *fwump,* followed by the delicious flicker of orange and yellow flames dancing upon charred stone logs. She puts her hands to the fire, enjoying the warmth and vitality. She's glad she badgered Tyson into having the gas switch installed, so much nicer than getting down on hands and knees to ignite the flames.

*And where is Tyson anyway? He should have returned from seeing Harry hours ago.*

Sarah walks to the office, sees the door slightly ajar, and pushes inside. She doesn't expect to see anyone, and at first the dark room seems to confirm its vacancy.

She begins to reach for the standing lamp in the corner...

"Hi, Sarah."

"Sweet Jesus," she gasps, planting a hand to her chest. She turns and sees the slumped shadow of Tyson behind his ratty, broken-down desk, the same one that's been with him for more than thirty years (and looking every inch the part—one of the legs having been chipped away during a move, impolitely replaced with an old John Grisham novel, two of the six drawers are missing handles, and one drawer has stopped opening altogether). The old desk is too small for a writer. It can barely hold a laptop and a stack of paper at the same time, never mind reference books, notepads, and all the other things writers like to have nearby while working on a project.

*Well, we won't have to look at that eyesore much longer, will we?*

Tyson stands and strides around the desk, comes toward her with open arms.

For a moment—probably caused by a trick of the dark and shadowed room—she feels a pang of fear at his approach. A feeling horribly akin to revulsion. It's the *speed* with which he'd suddenly moved, after being so stagnant there in the dark, like a creature who had been lurking and has now sprung toward her, ready to clutch her tight in its long, scaly arms...

She shakes away the ill feeling, cursing herself as she does so. She puts on a smile and goes to him, to the man she loves more than anything in the world. He embraces her tightly and they hold each other a few moments, feeling the comfort and warmth you only feel being held by someone you deeply love. Such an embrace can also be a truth serum, a way to pass information from one body to another without speaking aloud. Sarah, for example, realizes (after only a few moments, and without him saying a word) that the meeting with Harry had gone terribly wrong.

She pushes him away gently, reaches past him to the desk and twists the knob on the nickel-plated Anglepoise lamp he keeps there. His eyes—*those pretty blue eyes*—pinch at the sudden brightness.

"New glasses?" she asks, looking up and into his sad, weathered face.

"Oh, uh, no..." He touches the wire frames with his fingers. "Old. My other ones broke. I really need to get back to the eye doctor. Can't see a damned thing..."

"Not in the dark, anyway," she says. Then, delicately—oh so delicately—she asks what she already knows. "Tyson, what did he say?"

Tyson looks at the floor, then a bookcase. Anywhere but at her, anywhere but into her lie detector eyes. "Doesn't matter," he mumbles, his breath heavy with the smell of scotch. "Let's start dinner, I..."

"Tyson," she says more sharply, cutting him off and placing her hands on his cheeks, turning his head so his eyes have no choice but to meet her own. "Tell me what happened."

He steps away from her hands, turns his back to her, then completes the circle to face her once more. "Well..." He rests his chin in his palm, the elbow nestled into the other hand, a posture he sometimes takes when pondering a problematic plot construction, or considering how to turn a phrase. "It didn't go great."

Sarah's face twists with a sudden rage.

She spins away from him, storms across the room and through the open office door, moving fast toward the living room. "That... that... hypocrite *bastard!*"

Tyson follows her out, hands up in a warding-off gesture, his rumpled clothes and disheveled hair giving him the look of an apologetic beggar. "Sarah, relax, please."

She looks back at him, points an extended finger at his chest then, as if realizing he isn't the one who's actually done anything wrong, recalibrates the accusatory digit toward the upper corner of the room, in what he assumes is a symbolic gesture of pointing toward Harry's high-rise office. "Did he even listen to your pitch?"

He shrugs, looks away. "Yes and no. He didn't like the title..."

"Oh, oh," she says, eyes wide, palms pushing outward like an angry mime stuck in an invisible box. "Let me guess. The genius probably wanted to call it something like 'Hollywood Teenage Virgins Bare Big Bouncy Boobies While Sacrificed to the Great God Cthulhu'."

Despite her anger—and, oh yeah, there was plenty of that—Tyson can't help but appreciate her fury, relish the feeling of having someone in your life that will always defend you, always have your back and support you. Always love you.

Even when you're wrong.

"Hey, I like the sound of that," he says.

She ignores him. "Nine! Nine, Tyson. You know what that number is?"

"Yes, but honey..."

"*Nine* bestsellers. Most of which hit number-fucking-one on the *New York Times* list. You've made more money for that... that scumbag than... my God, Ty, he should be kissing your ass! Not treating you like a first-time novelist. It's disgusting. *He's* disgusting!"

"Honey, he's not. He's trying to do his job. The reality is that I *did* promise a book based on a specific pitch, and the publisher did pay me based on *that* pitch. The switcheroo is not very professional on my part, and... hell... I've put Harry in a bad spot, that's the truth."

Sarah takes a couple deep breaths, and when Tyson sees she has calmed down, he rests his hands gently on her shoulders, offering his best who-gives-a-shit smile. "Let's not worry about it, okay? Let's have a drink and eat something. I'm starved."

She returns his smile weakly, her eyes still a brewing storm. Not convinced, but willing to concede. For now. "Fine," she says, letting out a breath that carries away the bulk of her frustration. "So, what are you going to do? Write a whole new book?"

"Something like that." He's already moving toward the wet bar in the corner, eager for the numbing, sweet burn of the Dewar's. "It'll be fine. I have a plan."

"Uh-huh," she says, and he senses her step closer, feels her breath on his back as she wraps her arms around his (rather pudgy) waist and presses her body against his. She kisses the collar of his shirt and, shit-day or not, the monkey in his pants gave a life-affirming twitch. "I'm sorry I blew up," she says softly, warmly, and stands on tiptoes to kiss behind his ear, right where she knows he likes it.

"Don't apologize, baby, I appreciate it. And hey, don't think I'm not upset. It's just... well, you know, it is what it is."

He goes slow on the drinks, letting her feather one or two more kisses on that special spot, then turns and hands her a scotch, with two rocks the way she likes it. They clink glasses and drink. Well, he drinks. Sarah sips. Gratefully, Tyson can see her moving past it, which is the same thing he'll have to do. What choice does he have?

She sets her drink on the wet bar and places her hands lightly on his chest, stares up at him with those knockout green eyes. "Listen, I'm sorry to change the subject..."

"Please do."

"Okay, I just want to make sure you're still having dinner with Billy tomorrow night? Your annual birthday steak?"

"Yeah, of course. You know Billy..." He pours more scotch into each of their glasses (more into his) and hands hers back. "Hard to believe I'll be fifty-nine. Good lord, that's almost sixty. Then seventy. Then, you know, ka-put."

"Charming," she says, taking the glass. "Now I know what to get you for your birthday. A tombstone."

"Hey, that'd actually be pretty badass."

"Yeah yeah, so I'll see you for dessert after Billy's done with you, right? I might meet Linda and Barb beforehand, and I want to be sure you won't be alone on your special day."

"My special day can shove itself up its own ass, but no, I'll be fine."

*Just gotta get through this birthday bullshit and figure out some way to knock out 80,000 words in a month. No problemo. Fine and dandy. Right as rain. Four on the floor and the engine is rumbling, daddy-o...*

Sarah kisses him warmly on the lips and presses her fingers lightly to his crotch (momentarily shutting down his trickle-down thought associations), then leaves him for the kitchen, scotch still in hand, hips moving like an old blues song, to find fixings for dinner. Tyson watches her go, hoping that this amazing woman will forever find it in her heart to love an old, out-of-shape, beat-to-death failure like himself.

He downs the last of the drink, lets out a shaky breath, and pours himself another.

He makes it a hug.

Part Two

# THE SURPRISE

# FIVE

PALE SUNLIGHT streaks through splits in the bedroom curtains; dust-motes float through the slanting beams like untethered spacemen drifting through golden space. Radiant spills of the morning light melt on the cherry-stained hardwood floor, glow butter-yellow against the gray-blue walls and the stark white duvet draping the king-size bed, and the tired man who lay on it.

Tyson had slept little, up half the night thinking about his dilemma, racking his brain for ways to write the book he needed to write, to find an *opening* for a new story, a gap to shoot through. He couldn't get his mind around the tone of the thing, the presentation, the style. At 3 A.M. he'd gotten out of bed and gone to his office, wearing only boxers and a ratty white T-shirt that featured an image from Junji Ito's *Uzumaki* across its chest—a smiling young woman whose entire head was a spiraling vortex pointing into oblivion, only her curled lips and straight teeth still present on what had once been an attractive human face.

He pulled one of his older titles from a shelf, his best-selling book ever, *Dangerous Dreams*. The big hit of his early career. There'd been a major movie produced the year after publication, and a limited television series two decades later that was not as reverential as the film had been, picking and choosing elements, the characters kept in name only, their personalities plucked from the outcome of multiple focus groups.

*The check still cleared though, didn't it?*

Tyson opened to the first chapter and began to read. He searched for a tempo, a language, something he could decipher like a code, recreate in a new story with new characters. It was *his* work for God's sake, why couldn't he replicate it? Why couldn't he repeat his own success?

But his creation betrayed him, sinister and secret were the words, the phrases, the flow of the plot. It was a locked box. A mystery his tired—*stressed, old, worthless*—mind could not solve.

He shoved the book back into its spot on the shelf and debated trying to work right there and then. He stared at the laptop, closed and lifeless, on his desk. The thought of writing even a sentence was enough to suck the life from his chest and slow his heart. His shoulders slumped and a small groan escaped his lips.

*Failure! Phony!*

Tyson left the office and made his way back to bed, to his loving partner's warmth and unflagging love. He curled into her and tried to make his mind a blank page. Tried to traverse the jagged mountains of worry, the eternal desert of his thoughts, to reach the land of sleep and dreams.

And he did.

But now comes the morning, and all the thoughts and fears and anxieties rush back into him like an avalanche of despair. He forces himself up and out of bed, wincing as his knees pop like broken crackers while he kneels for the robe he'd dropped to the floor the previous night. He flaps it around his ever-expanding waistline (what those in the business call a "writer's belt," ha-ha) and shuffles to the bathroom.

The mirror over the sink is large and—quite rudely, he thinks—shows all of him. Mordantly curious, he takes off the robe, the Uzumaki shirt, the boxer shorts. He studies his flab-ridden body, the thinning hair, his tired eyes and slack-skinned face. His flaccid dick slumps between his pale thighs like a frightened child hiding beneath a black bush, and he feels a surge of contempt for the useless thing.

Sighing, he takes two steps toward the mirror, leans in, intently studies his own blue eyes.

As a child, Tyson liked to imagine that the gold flecks among the cool blue cornea were maps, and if he could only figure out what part of the world they represented he could find treasure at each golden freckle. Later he extended the idea, thinking them a star map, something he could look up into the heavens and trace, leading him back to the planet from which he'd been sent. When he was much older, he read that gold flecks in your eyes meant you'd seen evil in your lifetime, and he often wonders if that were true.

"You're a right evil bastard," he growls, making a terrible face into the mirror, a mask of what an evil man might look like. “Happy Birthday, you nasty, worthless old fuck. I hope you die.”

He stares himself down another moment, imagining himself a gunslinger, waiting for the reflection to back down (or perhaps provide an even more frightening visage). When nothing happens, he straightens and practices his best smile, the one he’ll offer to Sarah when she wakes.

Self-flagellation complete, his next grand decision of his special day is whether to make coffee, take a shower, or try to shit. He counts off the options on his fingers, and finally decides on the order. “Shower it is,” he says, and takes one step in that direction when he catches his gaze in the mirror again.

The blue eyes in the reflection stare back at him boldly, feverishly.

DARING him.

MOCKING him.

*There are no discovered treasures for those who do not seek them out,* those eyes say.

*OK, fine. So coffee, then shit, then... what?*

*Then?* the reflection answers, and Tyson watches helplessly as it smiles. *Then you go write that book, you filthy cunt.*

*Or I’ll cut out your heart.*

# SIX

TYSON STARES at the words and the white, blank vista beneath them:

CHAPTER ONE

He sips his coffee, already cooling, grimaces and shakes out his hands. A magician preparing for his most delicate trick.

"Staring at a fucking blank page. What a damned cliché I am," he says aloud, and, without thought, furiously begins typing.

The fat lady went ot the moon on a rocket built by Poe, she stepped onto ARmstrong's corpse and stubbed hr big-ass toe!

Tyson is snickering at his prose masterpiece when the office door pops open. Startled, he looks up to see Sarah, and quickly deletes the sentence. "Oh, hey babe."

"Hey yourself," she says. "How's it going?"

"Fine, fine. The words are literally bursting from my fingertips," he says, and purposely avoids eye contact with the empty screen. He notices Sarah is wearing her lululemon down jacket and clutching her bone-white Gucci shoulder bag—both the results of a recent shopping trip with her mother. "You, uh… going out? I thought you'd taken the day off work."

"I did, but I've got some errands to run."

Of course, Tyson knows as well as Sarah that her "work" is really more of a "volunteer" situation, helping out a few days a week at an old-timer's antiquities shop on the recently hipster-dominated Orchard Street in the Lower East Side. She enjoys the benefits of her employee discount, but otherwise the job is simply something to keep her busy. *Such is the life of a daughter born from incredible wealth*, Tyson thinks, fighting off a stab of envy.

"When are you meeting Billy?" she asks.

"I'll leave at five. Hopefully get to the restaurant around six. It's Friday rush hour, so…"

"Keens again?"

Tyson laughs, and means it. It feels good to feel carefree and happy, if only for a fleeting moment. He nods. "You know Billy, Mister Tradition."

"Well, I'll probably just see you after. I'm looking forward to a quiet night together," she says coquettishly, giving him a sly look. "I think you're gonna like your present," she teases, then waves and steps out, closing the door gently behind her.

Tyson watches the door for a moment, his smile melting into a lined frown.

*Trapped again,* he thinks. *Come on! Do some tricks, you old bastard.* The last of his good vibes flow away as his eyes focus once more on the screen and the traitorous, treacherous cursor. *Blink... blink... blink...*

The door bursts open again and Tyson nearly shrieks.

"Oh shit!" Sarah says, beaming. "Happy Birthday! I nearly forgot to say it. Kisses."

She blows him a kiss and then she's gone once more, the door slamming shut behind her. Breathing heavy, heart thumping, Tyson waits a few moments, unsure if she's going to pop back in one last time and scare the devil out of him. He keeps his eyes on the door—giving his heart time to slow, waiting until he hears the muffled sounds of the front door opening and closing, the house silent and empty once more—before he turns his attention back to the screen.

*Okay. Okay, big guy. No more interruptions. No more excuses. Just... tweak what you've already done. Think* modern.

He eyes the pile of notes to his left, the printed outline of the novel he'd presented to Harry stacked neatly beneath it. "Well, I suppose instead of an 18th Century witch, she *could* be a Hollywood fortune teller," he says, scratching his chin. "Yeah yeah... that's not so bad."

Tyson tilts his eyes to the ceiling for a moment, murmurs silently to himself. He waits for that "switch" in his head to flip, the one that clicks his mind over from an analytic, problem-solving brain to the wide-open sky, creative one. He turns his stare to the window, his pupils dilated, and lets out a held breath. Almost unconsciously, he picks up the small remote control off his desk and clicks on the stereo behind him, which begins the carousel of his compact disc set, *The Complete Rachmaninoff.*

Then slowly, methodically, but with a growing sense of rhythm, he starts to write.

# SEVEN

SARAH DECIDES to drive the Mercedes rather than take the subway. Despite it being a Friday, the traffic isn't so bad and, truth be told, every now and then she likes to drive her own car and listen to her own music. Especially when running an errand like this one. One that makes her happy, one she wants to *savor* a bit. She smiles, ignores the honking taxicabs surrounding her, the poor souls trying to reach the Lincoln Tunnel so they can get home to the Jersey suburbs before the late afternoon rush kicks in.

A nervous excitement crawls beneath her skin. She knows how much Tyson hates surprises, how much—especially lately—he hates birthdays. There comes a time, she realizes, when birthdays are less something to celebrate and more something to dread, less a celebration of a blossoming life and more a recognition of a life slowly terminating. It didn't help that money is tight, and Tyson would absolutely *detest* the idea of her spending her own money on him with any great flourish.

And this will certainly be a flourish. Even for her (and her parents' wealth), this is a solid chunk of change. A serious purchase. Or, as she prefers to think about it, a significant investment. An investment in art. *Tyson's* art. She knows, deep in her heart, that he just needs a *nudge.* One push in the right direction and he'll be back to his old ways, creating fiction like he used to, the kind that kept her up at night as a younger woman, and was a part of why she'd fallen in love with him in the first place, if she were being honest. He'd been a celebrity in her mind. A magician. A brilliant, terrifying, shining man. And even though he's older now, and not as wealthy and perhaps not as... *prolific...* she knows the desire to create still burns inside him. She means to try and fan that flame if she can, because she wants it for him, yes, but also for herself. She wants to see those brilliant, burning eyes look into hers once more. If she can reignite that flame, perhaps it will reignite the flame of their relationship, as well. New work—good work—will mean more money, more confidence. If everything goes perfectly (and at this thought she smiles) he may even be self-assured enough to finally marry her.

Sarah muses on this idea of marriage. She wonders why it's so important to her, why she feels it to be such a void in their relationship. After all, it's a modern world and, in many ways, the church-and-state institution of official coupling seems almost old-fashioned. Almost trite. Is she so desperate for reassurance from her partner that she needs a ring and a "Mrs." before her name to prove it? Or is it simply the little girl inside of her, the one who once dreamed of a big wedding, of telling all her girlfriends how her *husband* this or her *husband* that.

Besides, Tyson's ideas on marriage after the death of his first wife were clear: Not interested. In years past they'd had the occasional fight about it, usually ending in tears (her) and slammed doors (him). Lately, though, he'd been less hostile if the subject came up, and she did her best not to push it. Sure, it made introductions to new acquaintances awkward from time-to-time, and if she heard herself referred to as his "partner" one more time she might scream, but she'd live with it if she had to. She loved him, after all, and that's what mattered.

Regardless, it didn't stop that little girl in her from the occasional online window-shopping of wedding gowns and engagements rings, and where was the harm in that?

*But I'm not a little girl, anymore. And I'm not defined by my husband. So what's the big deal? Am I so pathetic that I crave... what? Assuredness? And from whom? Tyson? The public? Do I really care what people think?*

Sarah lets that train of thought linger for a bit longer. She isn't used to feeling independent, isn't comfortable with extreme feminism or some of the modern ideals surrounding women empowerment, and that depresses the hell out of her. What, she wonders, is wrong with her? Is she weak? Needy?

*No, darling. Just poorly raised.*

The thought rings true as a dinner bell. But it's a balled-up, tangled thought, one that needs to be picked at and unknotted at some point. But not now. Not today.

She mentally stores the subject away for future perusal and focuses instead on her mission, desperately hoping she is doing the right thing.

As she nears her destination, however, she begins feeling more and more confident, more and more *right*. Relief smooths her anxieties, and she begins singing along to the radio as she makes a turn onto 14th, then a left on Washington. The Whitney looms ahead, the Hudson River to the east. The sky is overcast, the air sodden and chilled, but she doesn't let it drown her rising spirits.

By the time she pulls into the small parking lot of the tidy brick building that serves as a central office to the large, attached warehouse of *Le Fanu Antiquities*, she's singing rowdily along with Billy Joel, the Piano Man crooning *She's Right on Time*.

"And by gods, look at that, she actually is," she says, happily noting the dashboard's digital monochrome clock flipping to read 11:00.

**"SARAH, DARLING!"** Anton cries from across the small showroom floor, the antique furniture displayed within a glistening array of curved walnut, mahogany, oak and kingwood atop a polished floor of cream marble; the neatly hung, ornately framed oil paintings bursts of warm color splashed against pristine white walls.

Anton is as dapper as his showroom. Raven hair slicked back, dark suit tailored snug to his long, trim form. His shoes reflect the track lights high above, his pearly teeth shine white as a bleached skull on a pirate flag. He puts his arms on her shoulders lightly and brushes both cheeks with his lips. His breath is clean peppermint and Sarah, for all her own sense of style and primness, can't help feel like a dumpy slouch standing beside him (self-consciously straightening her posture and checking to be sure her suede jacket doesn't have any stray hairs or smudges).

"Anton," she says warmly, genuinely thrilled to finally see the gift she purchased so many months ago. "Tell me it's here. Tell me I can see it," she says, knowing he would have never called her out here if that were not the case, but it felt good to pose the question, like a child double-checking that Santa had come despite knowing full well their parents had stockpiled gifts beneath the tree the previous night.

"Of course it's here!" he croons, his tone rising. Then his face falls slightly, a delicate frown turning his pursed lips downward. "However."

"Uh-oh," she says, but Anton only puts his arm around her, begins walking them gently to his office.

"Relax, relax. Just letting you know that it's still in the transport packaging. We've removed the crate, but as you can imagine it's thoroughly well-wrapped." They reach his office and, without asking, he pours two flutes of champagne from a recently opened bottle.

*You'd think I was buying a six-figure painting,* she thinks. *But I'll take it.*

He hands her a glass, and they clink a silent toast before each takes a sip, Sarah nearly gasping at how delicious it is. "My God... Anton, you shouldn't have, hon. You're going to blow your commission on champagne."

He gives a disarming laugh and perches on the edge of a satin-upholstered tub chair as deftly as a cat. "Nonsense. This is a wonderful thing you're doing, and I'm a big fan of your partner in crime. Plus, I just *love* a surprise. Not to mention, your family has done business with us before, but that's a footnote, darling, a footnote."

She sips again, knowing he's right. Her parents are indeed quite wealthy, and it was Mother who referred her to Anton when she bounced the idea of a special gift for Tyson. "Well, you're very sweet, and this champagne is delicious."

"I will have a bottle brought with the piece. No arguments. You two can toast to its arrival, or his next book, or whatever. Smash the damn thing against the side, Lord knows it can take it! Now, are you in the market for a little something special for you? I have a gorgeous mid-century bureau that'll make you gasp. And, if I may be so bold, I noted the perfect location for it while doing my measurements."

"Oh, that's sweet. No, not today. Maybe down the line. Today is about Tyson."

"Well, you're a dear to think of him so highly. I applaud you." Anton offers his best soft clap to go with a reverent head bow.

Sarah laughs, feeling a bit giddy. She isn't a woman who flaunts her family's wealth, and certainly never around Tyson, who is always horribly embarrassed by any show of flair (*especially in the last few years... with the mortgage...*), but at times like this she misses it; misses big purchases in fancy places with handsome salesmen fawning on her.

*And this* will *make Tyson happy*, she thinks, *even more so if it cures his writer's block.*

"So," she says, setting down her emptied glass. "May I?"

Anton, eyebrows arched, stands, and sets down his own glass. "My my, we are excited, aren't we? I *love* it! Yes, dear, of course. They should be loading it to the dock now for transport. I'll have them cut free the wrappings and you and I can both have a long look at the beast."

---

IN THE massive, industrialized warehouse, some of Anton's well-spun enchantment falls away, deadened by fluorescent reality. There are no marble floors here. No art on the walls. No champagne flutes. Just crates and boxes, dollies and fork-lifts. Mounds of stagnant furniture and décor mummified in bubble wrap and furniture pads. It smells of plastic and burnt coffee, with a trace of cigarettes.

Away from the track-lighting and slick trimmings, even Anton's polish seems to lose some of its luster. Standing on concrete, he appears much more human. Sarah can even notice the pocked remains of old acne scars on his cheeks, brought to the surface by the harsh, unforgiving industrial lights.

For his part, Anton seems not to have noticed the change in atmosphere. He holds her wrist gently, his eyes searching the interior. Then he grins and turns to her, and for a moment he recaptures that salesman razzle-dazzle with his infectious smile, igniting the charm one more time, giving her a taste of the old magic that only money could buy.

"There it is," he says, pointing to the far end of the warehouse, where she can make out an elevated shape moving between the stacks, shelves and crates. "Shipped via freighter straight from the Pyrenees and the manor of the late Signor Fornasini who, after a century of living a rather secluded life, left a lovely and crumbling old fortress near Roussillon to the bill collectors and estate hawks, such as yours truly." He slides his hand from her wrist to her elbow, gripping it lightly.

"Come on, love, they're moving it to the loading dock now. Let's go have a look at your prize."

He begins walking briskly, weaving between unidentifiable objects waiting to be claimed, bought, or sold. Hundreds of pieces that will be scattered into the city like seeds, taking root in living rooms and kitchens, dens and bedrooms. *They all have a story,* Sarah thinks, and would have found it fascinating to consider was she not overwhelmed by the sheer *size* of the object being driven slowly toward the dock, hoisted up on the thick tines of a forklift.

"Good lord, is that... it?"

Anton nods, his smile turned boyish by the thrill of a strange, rare object. "Don't worry, it's not as big as it looks. Remember, it's carrying about a foot width of baby fat in the form of protective padding."

"Yes, but still... Anton, are you sure that will fit into the house?"

Anton nods again, assuredly, in a way that does not permit further questioning. "Trust me, Sarah. This is what I do. We'll get it there, don't you worry. I've measured every inch of your home and there is no doubt in my mind about it, so please don't worry. *You* just worry about making sure hubby isn't around, right?"

Sarah ignores Anton's slip, reminding her of her internal debate on the drive over.

"Oh yes," she said, "that's on me. I'm on it, don't worry," she says, practically gawking at the massive crate floating through the air. It isn't just the size of the thing that gives it a sense of largesse, she realizes, it's something *else,* something she can't quite put her finger on. It's almost as if it has an aura about it, like a chest you know is filled with gold and jewels, or a piano-sized Pandora's Box.

Three warehouse workers stand waiting on the loading platform as the forklift driver eases the piece high above the dock, which rises about five feet from the warehouse floor. Along the far edge of the dock are three industrial roll-up doors. Beyond the doors, a transport truck waits for its payload.

"To be honest, I've never seen anything quite like it," Anton says as they watch the lift move into position. "The Victorian Gothic period isn't really known for making things of that... *size*. And certainly not so well adorned. The mythological aspects of the carvings are breathtaking, and I've only seen the photos. I'm sure they'll be doubly-glorious in person."

Sarah agrees. "It certainly fits the bill. It was fortuitous timing, isn't it? Me needing something like that, and you having just heard about it."

"Well," he says airily, "that's just how it works, love. Something's always coming in and something's always going out. This one, however, is unique. I'm glad it's going to a good home."

"Me too," she says. "Inspiration is needed." Sarah takes a breath and lets it out. *Please let him love it,* she thinks for the thousandth time.

Anton is turning back to say something further when there's a *POP* loud enough to echo against the concrete walls. There's a firecracker flash of white as a burst of sparks shoot from the controls of the forklift. The driver curses (Sarah thinks it's something like "DAFUCK!") and throws an arm in front of his eyes to shield himself.

"Oh no," Anton says, and then there's a gusting *SHPIFFF* as the hydraulics pump bursts and the tines of the forklift click and break free, dropping the massive object in a freefall from a height of eight feet, unobstructed, the great thing riding the pikes down like an elevator with the cables snapped toward the concrete dock, and the men caught beneath.

It lands not with a crash, but a *crunch.*

Two of the men are able to jump clear. The third is less fortunate.

From her perspective, Sarah can see the worker's leg trapped beneath the thing as it falls. The bottom half of his leg bends like a bow, there's a *snap* and the man screams louder than she's ever heard anyone scream in her life. A shard of bone punches through the pantleg above his knee and blood spurts from his thigh like the hard spray of a crimped water hose that's suddenly been let loose. The stream of blood creates a slick, jagged trail ten feet long from where he's collapsed. He bucks once, like a dying bronco, then drops flat onto his back, the unimaginable weight of the thing still resting atop his destroyed leg as he convulses.

Sarah clamps a hand to her mouth and her vision goes momentarily spotty, as if she'd been caught staring into a bright light before looking away. Her stomach curdles and she tastes champagne-tinged bile rising in her throat. As if through the veil of a dream, she hears Anton yelling, sees him running toward the dock. The other two workers are desperately trying to lift the massive crate off their co-worker, who isn't screaming anymore, but now lies quiet, arms splayed, his face pasty as warmed-over cream cheese.

"LIFT IT!" Anton screams, thrusting his own hands beneath the armpits of the downed worker. The driver of the forklift jumps onto the dock and helps as they all raise one corner, allowing Anton to slide the downed (now mercifully unconscious) worker out from beneath.

Later, when a second forklift once more raises the crate, neither Sarah, nor the workers, nor Anton himself—given their heightened state of stress and panic—notice that there isn't a single drop of blood on the concrete beneath the object.

As if it had been magically wiped away.

Or absorbed.

---

AFTER THE ambulance has come and gone, Anton gives Sarah every assurance that the piece will still be delivered on-time and as promised. "I feel terrible for that poor man, of course," he says, "but the medics assure me he'll survive, albeit without much future use of that leg."

"Oh my God..."

"But that's why we have insurance, Sarah. I promise you he'll be taken care of, okay? Accidents happen all the time and if we let it interrupt business, hell, we'd have been washed-up fifty years ago."

Anton navigates Sarah back to his office, where they both steadily finish off the very expensive, but no longer very tasty, bottle of champagne. He's even loosened his tie, and she tries not to stare at the drying stains on his sleeves and the cuffs of his pants.

Blood from the man he'd pulled to safety.

"Don't worry, dear, I'll take care of everything," he says again, as if to himself, before downing the last remnants of champagne from a trembling flute glass clutched within white-knuckled fingers. "And I'm so sorry you had to see that. But listen, think on it no more. We'll be heading over in the truck shortly and will be long-gone before Tyson enjoys even one bite of his juicy red birthday steak."

# EIGHT

TYSON HUNCHES inside the subway car heading toward the Upper West Side. A taxi would have been faster, but he's in no hurry, and money is always an object these days, a very tactile and real thing that needs to be well-guarded.

Feeling shriveled and inept, curled like a worn-out worry in the plastic molded seat, he stares blankly at his stupid hands; the useless, unimaginative fingers. He silently curses those fingers. Curses his tired old brain, his inept imagination.

*How have I fallen so far?*

Seeking distraction from his self-loathing, his eyes roam the subway car interior, resting on a young woman reading a paperback. The sight brings up a memory, one that fills his mind like a sudden, sunbaked breeze. He smiles what his brain registers as a happy smile, but what a passerby might consider a smile drenched in melancholy, twisted in loss. Instead of the young woman—a bespectacled blonde with well-worn pumps and an out-of-fashion suit—he sees a younger version of Sarah.

In his memory, it's Sarah sitting there, ten years younger, reading a hardcover edition of his second novel, *Blood Moon,* the novel that put him on the map, the one that proved he wasn't a one-hit-wonder. He'd watched her as the train rocked, as the hard lights softened on her skin as if melted by her beauty. Feeling his stare, her eyes had flicked up to his own—once, twice—the first time in passive annoyance (he was, he recalled with giddy shame, essentially leering at her by this point), the second in amused recognition. She closed her book and smiled at him, but said nothing. He smiled in return, waiting to see what she would do, what she would say. He'd heard it all by then—every mumbled, stumbling request for an autograph, every exuberant line of (mostly) false praise.

She turned the book over, stared at the black-and-white author photo covering the back of the dustjacket, the one he hated because he felt it disingenuous to the tone of what lay within. His grinning, well-groomed countenance was a lie, a deceit to the reader who picked it off the shelf at the bookstore or library, saying to themselves that the handsome young man in the photo could *never* write something so dark and foul as to make them squirm, cause them to leave the nightstand lamp turned on when falling asleep at night, check under the bed and in the closets for serial killers and boogeymen before feeling *safe.* Feeling *sane.*

"The photo doesn't do you justice," she'd said, and his eyes had gone wide with surprise.

"Oh?"

"No..." she said cattily, then opened the book up once more and continued to read, as if he'd asked her the time and she'd given it. The end.

"May I ask..."

"It's very good," she replied, not looking up at him, a smirk curving the corners of her lips. "I doubt I'll sleep well tonight because of you."

"I see," he replied. "I'm sorry."

"Oh, don't be. It's what they pay you for. What I paid for."

"And what's that?"

Then she looked up at him again, and his heart quickened. Her smile was genuine, but her eyes were troubled. Troubled, and beautiful. "To frighten me, of course. After all. It's what you do best, isn't it? Frighten people?"

He'd rubbed at his temple and pulled at his ear, searching for the right words, the ones that not even the greatest of writers came by easily: the words that bring a child-like embarrassment, a sudden warmth to the cheeks, a tremble to the fingers. The words most simply, and honestly, stated as a kindergartner's note: *I like you. Do you like me? Check one box for YES, the other for NO.*

He'd found the words before 96th Street and asked her to have a drink with him. "I promise not to give away the ending," he'd said, and she'd accepted.

*I'm Sarah.*

The train rumbles to a stop, the doors opening with a gasp, closing with a whisper. When the train starts once more, it leaves the past behind, puts the present back into motion. Tyson hears his exit called and stands to stretch his legs, gripping an iron post for balance and trying not to think about how he got here, or the glories of years long gone by.

*Three cheers for the illustrious fucking past. May it rest in peace.*

He sighs heavily, wondering what happened to that confident, successful man. That *young* man. The one eternally smiling on the back of a book cover that sold more copies than his last six books combined. The man who would ask out a pretty girl on a train. Not this tired, old, hunched beast, weighted down by a swollen gut clenched in writhing anxiety, the creative mind muddled by worries of just what the hell he was going to do.

*A month.* He lets the word—the idea as a structure of space-time—bounce around in his head. He sees it as a dark cube floating in hazy gray ether. It seems so small, and yet it *ticks*. From deep inside that black cube comes a soft, successive, *ticking* sound.

*Like a bomb,* he thinks, frowning. *Like a motherfuck...*

"Yo, man."

Tyson watches the cube bounce lazily away, vanish in the thick haze.

"Hey, you're Mr. Parks, right?"

Tyson scans the car's interior. With his broken glasses stuffed into the pocket of his raincoat it's hard to make out much of anything further than ten feet away. Luckily, he knows his stop by heart. Hell, he'd been getting on and off at this station for nearly two decades.

"Yeah man, sure. Hey, Mr. Parks. You're taller than I would have thought. Dang, what are you? Six-four?"

Tyson turns around, locating the source of the voice: A young man in jeans, an oxford dress shirt beneath a black raincoat, and a ridiculous fisherman's bucket hat sitting nearby, holding a copy of *Deep in the Night*. A crappy paperback with library stickers on the spine.

*Admittedly not one of my better efforts.*

*Deep* was written in the fall of 1995 while he was on deadline with his editor, who had demanded a second book be submitted by the end of the year. Hollywood was a big part of the game in those days, and he'd been busy trying to piece together a script, but screenwriting was tricky for him, a different beast that he'd never been able to...

"Mr. Parks? You okay?"

Tyson breaks from his reverie. "Huh? Sorry, son. Daydreaming, I guess. And no, I'm six-three, actually." *An inch shorter than King.*

"Hell, I was close though!" The young man laughs, then, almost apologetically, pushes the paperback book toward Tyson. "Sorry to ask?"

"Of course," Tyson says, smiling and taking the well-thumbed paperback.

"Oh man, thank you so much. I am such a fan. I've been reading your books since I was, gosh, like ten years old."

"Better you than your mother," Tyson mumbles as he pulls a Bic from his inner coat pocket.

"Sorry?"

"What's your name, son?"

"Oh, I'm Ben. Ben Howard."

To Ben,
Who once rode the rails with me.
Best, Tyson Parks

He hands the book back, a little unsettled at the young man's intense gaze. "There you go, son. Enjoy it. Not one of my better books, I admit, but there's still some life in those pages."

Ben takes the book back, smiling in an infectious way that makes Tyson forget his discomfort at the boy's scrutiny. "Not wanting to be rude, sir," the kid says after staring at the inscription a moment, "but what's someone like you doing riding the subway? I figure you'd be chauffeured around in one of those Town Cars I always see white folks in. No offense."

Tyson notices his stop approaching, secretly hopes Ben isn't getting off at the same place. It can be awkward to casually break away from a fan.

"You riding much longer?" Tyson asks.

Ben smiles again—a different smile this time—as if saying, *Don't worry, white man, I ain't following you home to steal your grandma's silver.* Even asking the question makes Tyson flush with mild embarrassment, but Ben gives a little laugh, dispelling any tension, imagined or otherwise.

"No sir, just a few more stops now. Meeting up with a friend at the Flatiron market. Craving some good Italian."

Tyson nods, trying to hide his relief. "Ah. Well, have fun. And enjoy the book."

The brakes of the subway car sing their hideous, screeching song as the coach rolls to a stop. Tyson sways with the inertia of the train, gripping the post tightly. The train finally stops and the doors hiss apart. He steps toward the gray platform, the monotone speaker announcing Herald Square Station, a few short blocks from his lunch date.

He passes through the doors with the small spattering of other exiting riders.

"Oh, hey, thank you!" Ben yells after him, then adds, "And I hope you feel better!"

The subway doors shush shut before Tyson gets a chance to ask Ben how he'd known he isn't feeling just fine and dandy. As the train rumbles away, he shakes his head and starts for the stairs, the street, and the cloudless gray sky above, with all the enthusiasm of a man leaving one purgatory for another.

BEN WATCHES Tyson disappear along with the departing crowd. Tracks him until he starts up the stairs into gray daylight.

The train roars through a tunnel as he shoves the small paperback into one coat pocket. He takes a cheap ballpoint pen and a small, worn spiral notebook from the other. He pulls the pen's cap off with his teeth and thumbs the notebook open to a semi-blank page. Struggling to write with the jerk and sway of the train, he makes a note in his neat, efficient hand.

Ben blows out a sigh as the train slows for the next stop. He replaces the book and pen in his coat pocket and readies himself to exit at 28th Street.

He has a phone call to make.

# NINE

THE BULL'S glassy black orbs stare down at Tyson. Its thick neck is fastened to a gold square plate, which is itself fastened to the dark wood paneling of the wall. Slick black horns curve up and out, taper to pinpoint tips. Tyson swears he sees one of the hairy beast's ears twitch before he quickly looks away, unsettled.

He and Billy sit in one of the red leather booths lining the wall of Keens Steakhouse, the same restaurant they've been coming to on Tyson's birthday for the last decade (and then some). Two neat whiskeys have already been placed in front of them, and the server didn't bother with menus or briefing the men on specials, knowing perfectly well what they want, how they want it, and what the occasion is. After all, she's been serving them on this same date, at this same booth, for as long as they'd been coming.

"What a little bitch Harry is," Billy says in his proper English accent, his long hair smoothed back from his forehead in waves, his dark eyes glittering, his camelhair sweater and navy slacks accentuating his fit, trim figure. The inevitable wrinkles that simply age so many others only make Billy's face that much more handsome. Tyson always thought him a bastard for his looks and his accent and his charm and his success (it isn't without reason that Tyson nicknamed his best friend 007), but loves him more than a brother for his kindness and loyalty and unwavering friendship. He knows he's lucky to have a friend like Billy in his life, and hopes he provides at least some modicum of reciprocity. He doesn't have most of Billy's qualities, but in one he is assured: he loves his friend dearly, and his loyalty to him will never waver.

"So, you don't think he has a point?" Tyson answers, testing the single malt, savoring the warm, sweet burn on his tongue.

"Far be it from me to offer career advice..."

"Oh, please..."

"... much less *creative* advice, Ty."

Tyson gives him a scalding—but not unfriendly—glare, which Billy appears completely oblivious to. "Billy, we both know you're the better writer at the table. Shall we discuss that Edgar award?"

"I'd trade that Edgar tomorrow to have a few bestsellers, my friend."

"I wouldn't be too sure about that. You have revered anonymity with your work. You've earned trust and praise to the point where you're untouchable. You write what you want. I'm... hell, I've become this vending machine that publishers think they can just, you know, *push* a damned button and a bestselling book pops out. Oh, and God forbid it's not the *exact* same book I've already written ten times over."

Billy lifts a hand to catch the attention of the waiter, then shows two fingers.

*Jesus, order the bottle, already,* Tyson thinks, the idea of tying one on good and proper increasingly appealing.

"Okay," Billy says evenly, meeting Tyson's eyes, "let's look at this from Harry's perspective, just for a moment. Here's a guy who's used to pressing the... what'd you call it? The vending machine. Yeah? And bam, out comes a Tyson Parks bestseller. Wonderful news. He punches it again, what comes out? Historical fiction about a nun and a priest with mommy issues that's scary as a Harry Potter book."

"Hey..."

"You know it's true," Billy says quickly. "I mean, maybe if you'd used a pseudonym like they asked, you know? A little distance between the historical books and the horror stuff... I don't know. But tell me, old chum. Tell me what happened to your recent historical thrillers? Were they bestsellers?"

Tyson sulks as the new drinks are set down. "Of course not. They bombed, as you well know. And they aren't thrillers, they're still horror..." he adds weakly.

Billy's eyebrows twitch up, but he continues with a wave of his hand. "Point redacted. But they all bombed, is what I'm getting at. So, what do you do? You write another... and another. And your sales dip... and dip... and dip..."

Tyson glances up at the bull, feeling old and frustrated. "Look, Billy, everything can't be... blood sacrifices and men in black robes, serial killers and demon possession. I feel that I have more inside me. More... I don't know, range, I guess." He sighs heavily, slugs the last of what he knows is a pricy drink.

"You want my advice, mate?" Billy says after a moment, his tone stern enough that Tyson's afraid to look at the truth in his dark eyes. "Give the man what he wants. Get back to what made you popular. Just for a bit. Knock a couple out of the park, show you still got it, get your advances up. Then, when the ship is righted, go back to your witch burnings and cathedral cults and no one will bother you."

"God damn it! Don't you think I fucking would if could?" Tyson yells, the outburst surprising even him. He slams a fist onto the tabletop. "I CAN'T DO IT!"

Billy's eyes go wide, and he perceptibly eases back in the booth. Tyson, breathing heavily, spares a look around the room, which seems to go quiet for a beat before settling back into its rhythm, albeit with something further for its patrons to discuss.

*That crazy writer has had a few too many. Which one is he again?*

"I'm sorry, I'm sorry," Tyson says, lowering his voice to a near-whisper. "The point is... I've *tried*, Billy. For fuck sakes, don't you think I've *tried?* I've been keeping a motherfucking *dream* journal, for the love of God. I... did you know this? I went on a damned *retreat*, thinking the old remote cabin in the woods routine might grease the wheels."

"And... what?"

"And *nothing,*" Tyson hisses. "Empty. Blank. Nada. Nothin'. Bupkis. Et cetera, et cetera." Tyson slumps, rubs his unshaven cheeks, picks up the empty glass, looks at it with strained eyes, puts it back down.

Billy doesn't offer to order another.

"Let's face it, Billy. I've lost it. I've lost it, and it's not coming back."

The waiter arrives with two rib-eye steaks, medium-rare, a platter of beans, another of au gratin potatoes. She also sets down two glasses of ice water. "There you go loves," she says, and exits quickly, as if afraid the two men might order that bottle after all.

Billy sighs, drops a napkin into his lap. "Sounds to me," he says, eyeing his meal steadily, "like you need a new muse."

Tyson cuts into his steak, suddenly ravenous. "That and a half-million dollars should do the trick."

Billy looks up sharply. "What do you mean?"

Tyson looks around, then leans in, voice low. "It means I'm bloody broke, Billy. I owe back taxes. I have a massive mortgage. And, in case you haven't heard, Brown isn't cheap."

"Wait... I'm lost. Since when are you broke? What about the advance?"

"Gone," Tyson says, and pops a large chunk of steak into his mouth, chewing out the juices, shivering with pleasure despite the grim conversation. "Spent. And if I don't produce a new book in a month, not only will I not get the remainder of the payment, but they'll want their advance back. I'm totally, and thoroughly, *fucked*."

"Jesus. Does Sarah know this?"

"Don't even say it," Tyson says, pointing the business end of his fork at his friend. "Sarah's money is *her* money, hers and her family's. I want no part of it."

"I'm just saying, she lives with you, has for years. You're partners. It makes sense for her to contribute."

"No. End of discussion." Tyson stabs another piece of meat and shoves it into his mouth with such force the tines of the fork scrape his palate. He winces but goes on chewing, as if the steak were a proxy for his problems, to be chewed up and devoured. "I'm ruined, Billy, that's the truth," he says. "I hope Violet forgives me, because she'll be going to a community college next year."

Billy stares at Tyson another moment, deep in reflection, then slowly begins cutting a small piece off his own steak. "It won't come to that," he says calmly, factually. "If push comes to shove, I'll loan you the money. I have a healthy reserve. We bachelors, as you can imagine, don't worry about things like sending kids to college."

Tyson pauses, sets down his fork, the meat in his mouth partially masticated, his eyes suddenly wet. "You'd do that?"

"It's done," Billy says, and daintily chews a small bite of his own steak. "Not the whole five hundred, obviously, I'm not James Patterson just yet. But consider yourself bankrolled for up to, oh, let's say a hundred grand. Market's going to crash soon anyway, I'd rather put it to good use. At three-percent interest, of course. I'll simply begin thinking of you as an investment."

A fat tear streams down Tyson's cheek, salting his lips and flavoring the steak before he finally swallows it down. He wipes away the wet trail with a sleeve.

"Oh, now stop it," Billy says.

"I'd never accept it. Not ever. But you're a good friend, Billy. The best."

Billy raises his water glass, and Tyson does the same. "Enough of this weeping and bullshit. To my best friend on his birthday."

"And to new muses, may they fuck our rotting corpses dry," Tyson says, too loudly, but happily, and the men laugh as they click glasses.

"Hear, hear!" Billy replies, catching the eye of a silver-haired old woman staring from the next booth, her face twisted into a disgusted snarl.

"It's okay, love," Billy says in his most charming manner. "We're writers."

# TEN

THE YELLOW Cab pulls to the front of Tyson's townhouse.

"You should come up," Tyson says, drunk and full and momentarily happy. "Sarah would love to see you."

"What, and spoil your romantic dessert?"

Tyson opens his mouth, closes it.

"That's right, buddy boy. I know that you and Sarah have your own birthday tradition. Let me see if I have this right. First, she gives you your present, which is always a rare book. Then it's champagne, strawberries, whipped cream, and lingerie. Am I near the mark?"

Tyson only smiles and shrugs. "I'm a lucky guy."

"That you are, now get out you bastard."

Tyson stumbles loosely onto the sidewalk, then turns back, puts a hand on the roof of the sedan. "No, come on. I insist. One nightcap before the lingerie show."

Billy sighs, nods. "Fine, fine. Let me pay the driver and I'll come in for *one* drink."

Moments later, Tyson and Billy are through the iron gate and Tyson is digging out his keys. After a few near misses, he unlocks the door.

"Wait a moment," Billy says, and adjusts Tyson's disheveled tie.

"What the hell you doing that for?"

"I'm the fashion police, didn't I tell you? Now open the damn door, it's freezing."

Tyson huffs a bemused laugh, shrugs, and pushes open the door, into the dark. "What the... it's pitch black in here. Hold on..." He takes a blind step into the living room... before being blinded by a burst of light.

"SURPRISE!" Tyson jerks backward at the riotous cheer of nearly fifty of his closest friends and peers. The room is bursting with decorations, streamers, party hats, and smiling faces. Tyson's jaw hangs open.

"Oh my God..." he says, and then starts to laugh. Sarah runs up and kisses him on the mouth. Billy pats him hard on the back.

"Surprise, sweetheart," Sarah says. "I love you."

Tyson is still catching up, catching on. "I can't believe this..." he says, looking around the room, seeing so many friends, the familiar faces of men and women, some of whom he hasn't seen in years. He spots a smiling Harry across the room, who raises a glass and waves.

Sarah pulls Tyson into a hug as the room continues to buzz. "I have two presents for you this year," she whispers in his ear. "I'll give you one now." She winks at him, tilts her head to the ceiling, theatrically cupping a hand to her mouth. "Come on out, dear!"

Two hands wrap around Tyson's eyes from behind. *No...* he thinks excitedly. He gently takes the hands from his face, the ones he knows better than his own, and turns, filled with hope and bright, overflowing joy.

Smiling up at him is a sly-looking brunette wearing a black dress, her upper lip pierced with a neat silver hoop, her ears studded with the diamonds he'd given her on her 16$^{th}$ birthday.

*Violet!*

For a moment he only stares, lost in the total shock at seeing his daughter, here, in person, on this strange night. She's so beautiful, so young. And she's *home*. "Oh my God!" Tyson cries, and hugs her fiercely. "You told me you were going out of town for winter break..." he says, laughing at his own gullibility.

"I am!" she says. "To New York City, of all the dumb places." Then, "Daddy... can't breathe." She kisses his cheeks again and again until he finally relents. He puts one arm around her, the other around Sarah's waist, taking a moment to look up at the expectant faces of his guests. "I don't know what to say. I... I'm..." He chokes up, then hugs his family to his chest, unable to go on.

"I know *exactly* what to say," Billy says loudly, saving his friend. "Turn on the music and give this man a drink!"

The crowded room cheers once more, the music from the room's stereo pops on, and Tyson Parks is happier than he will ever be again.

Part Three

# BURYING THE DEAD

# ELEVEN

THE MONTRESOR line has a proud but haunted lineage.

Diana stands in the cold, the slate gray sky matching the grim coloring of the large mausoleum rising from the earth before her, the limestone weathered to a runny charcoal, the apex guarded by a marble-cut angel, sword raised as a symbol of defense, or vengeance. Her waterproof black leather boots keep the moisture rising from the graves from reaching her skin, and the hooded shearling coat keeps the damp air off her body, but the chill of the past is not so easy to defend against and, unlike the weather, it sustains.

The mausoleum is by far the largest in the sprawling cemetery, the grounds located along the eastern border of the port city Boulogne-sur-Mer, her grandfather's birthplace, and home of the Montresor family for over three hundred years. It's one of the few mausoleums raised above an enclosed crypt, a necessity given that it houses more than a dozen members of her ancestry. The makeshift chapel built into the ground level is but a speck when compared with such garish monuments as the city's Notre-Dame cathedral and the massive crypt housed there, but it's a rare family who rests centuries of ancestors together, and she hopes her flesh will one day lie down among them for whatever eternity awaited. Her flesh and, most likely, no more. Unless she ever decides to have a family of her own, an idea so foreign and bizarre she can't imagine it.

Diana makes a point to visit the crypt once a month, timing the trip with monthly check-in visits of her grandfather, who lives in a nearby villa, surrounded by round-the-clock nurses and servants catering to his every need, every whim. She knows Jean doesn't have long to live, and the clock is ticking on her succeeding where he—and the ancestors who came before him—had failed. She's desperate to return home with the artifact before he passes away, his corpse brought to rest with their ancestors.

Another stone for her to speak to, another placard to ask for guidance.

A strong gust of frigid wind strokes her face, and she waits no longer. She treasures these visits but also feels urgency to get back home, find out what new information the American detective has discovered. Impatiently, she works the heavy key into the old lock, pushes open the heavy iron gate, and disappears inside.

The chapel is simple. Spartan. A plain cross stands on a carved Rossa Francia marble pedestal (the coloring of which always reminded her, disgustedly, of rare beef) below a narrow, arched window. The window's wavering old glass is stained a pale rose, giving the room a surreal tint, the stone walls and small benches stained the color of sin. She crosses herself and walks down the aisle, alongside which three pairs of benches sit empty, waiting for the next Montresor death before they can be used again.

*It won't be long now,* she thinks grimly, wondering again how long her grandfather has left, how frail he'd seemed on her last few visits.

She reaches the top of a twisting stone stairwell leading down into heavy dark. With a steadying breath, she presses gloved hands against the rose-stained stone walls for balance and starts slowly down the narrow stairs that lead to her ancestors, waiting for her with an eternal patience in the lightless crypt below.

As she reaches the bottom, she uses her cell phone's flashlight to find the rusted metal base of the battery-powered floodlight set into the corner and switches it on. It lights immediately, filling the narrow chamber. The strength of the light, however, is dimmer than she remembers from her last visit, and she makes a mental note to have the groundskeeper replace the battery before she returns next month. She has no wish to share the dark with the dead.

The crypt is long, extending underground to match the full length of the structure above, and heavily shadowed at the far end where the light's weak glow does not reach, giving the narrow crypt the effect of extending into infinity. The short wooden stool still sits where she'd left it, midway down the bumpy cobblestone aisle that separates the sealed tombs on either side, each marked with an aged placard. The last

Montresors—Jean's parents—had been brought to rest here more than fifty years ago.

Her own parents, long dead, had their remains housed in Spain. They'd been killed in a historically tragic disaster while on holiday, trapped in a theater and burned alive with over three hundred others while attending an opera. Despite the best efforts of officials to sort out the numerous charred corpses and body parts, it was finally determined there wasn't enough of them left to entomb.

Feeling morose, Diana sits heavily on the stout-legged stool and studies the placard before her. The notched bronze plate is badly aged but still legible, even in dim light.

Julianne Montresor
1777-1865
Les Survivante

Diana leans back against the rough, cool wall, the dull brown illumination giving the room a feeling of timelessness, of ancient memories ground deep into the stones that surround her, resting heavily in the earth—memories waiting to be shared, voices wanting to be heard.

She can almost hear the screams coming from inside the tomb before her, echoes of a dark history that will never see the light, along with an artifact bequeathed to her like a curse, a trap disguised as an heirloom.

The altar.

An unholy grail dripping with the blood of her family name.

Hers, and one other.

Federico Croce.

A man whose own history she has followed like bread-crumbs through generations, using whatever means necessary to continue the search: study, bribery, threats. Or sometimes, in the Montresor search for truth, a form of persuasion known only to the women in her ancestral line. A form of old magic taught to her as a child, a magic that changed her eyes forever, twined to a rare skill she has long-since perfected. Part hypnosis, part persuasion. Always effective.

Frowning, and fighting off the despair breaching her thoughts, Diana reaches out to place a gloved hand on the worn metal grooves of Julianne's name. She closes her eyes and lets her mind pull up the memories, the hard-won knowledge.

The ancient horror that is her burden to avenge.

# TWELVE

*FRANCE. 1725.*

...trumpets blare in the frigid dark outside the castle's stone walls. Men shout at the night—some in victory, some in death. Signor Federico Croce, along with his mad horde, has arrived.

And for Etienne Montresor, and those closest to him, time has run out.

Etienne was able to escape by pricking a guard's throat with a thorn-sharp fingernail, recently dipped in the hidden hollow of a ring (accessed by sliding the ring's lone cut ruby) that held a secret store of liquid death. The other soldiers had been distracted with the massacre of Etienne's poor family: his proud wife, Marianne, beaten, stripped, and raped on the cold floor of the great hall; his six-year-old boy Raymond repeatedly stabbed in the back, legs and stomach, taunted and beaten by Croce's men before having his throat opened by a fat man's black dagger. Etienne didn't know the fate of twelve-year-old Julianne, his only daughter. She'd been pulled from the room on Croce's orders, bound and carried away, her screams crashing against the walls, her high-pitched wails for help—for salvation—fleeting, unanswered.

It was just an hour prior that the castle's meager guard had been caught unaware by the sudden attack, and quickly overrun. Etienne knows some still fight at the outer gate, but it matters not. The vanguard, the tip of the spear, had struck deep, the group which initially pierced the castle's belly overwhelming his personal guard before stealing his family from their sleeping chambers and dragging them to the great hall to be murdered before his eyes, leaving him to stand helpless while his wife and child died, screaming for mercy while he wept out his love, begged the invaders to make it *quick*, to take him instead...

Marianne must have found the time—likely the moment the invaders broke in her door—to swallow the belladonna-laced capsules he'd hurriedly thrust at her before running for the front gate, the cries of alarm sounding through the halls, his worst fears realized. It was the third in the line of soldiers desecrating her who finally, mercifully, spat out a curse, one that simultaneously soothed and shattered Etienne's aching heart. "This bitch is dead!"

It was at that moment he struck, piercing the exposed neck of his nearest captor. As the soldier dropped, clutching his throat and foaming at the mouth, Etienne ran for his life down the hallway leading toward the library. Once there, he drew aside a tapestry bearing the image of Joan of Arc, pushed on a seamless door to reveal a narrow dark corridor ten paces long, terminating in downward-spiraling steps.

Now, he hears shouted curses closing in. Stomping feet nip at his heels as he pushes through the narrow opening and into the lightless corridor. His black cape flows around his tall, pale form like smoke as he hurls himself onward, laughing hysterically—*madly*—bootheels clapping against the dusty stone floor as he flees into the dark, toward the steps that lead downward, into the depths, far below the foundation of what has been the Montresor family home for over a century.

Despite the night's horrors, Etienne is well aware that the family name of Montresor will be extinguished tonight if he doesn't act quickly. The altar can possibly, just possibly, allow him a type of escape, a way to continue *beyond* this life, to find safety—even *immortality*—in another world. Perhaps one day he will come back, somehow save his daughter, who he fears Croce has plans for other than a quick death. He doesn't know, can't think clearly, the complicated spells already filling his mind, clouding his reasoning.

He isn't prepared, isn't ready... but he has no choice.

It's the only way.

Etienne reaches the underground chamber, enters the cold dark, and slams the heavy door shut behind him. He slides the door's thick, rough metal bolts into wall-mounted iron sheathes.

It will hold for a time.

He prays it will be enough.

In the absolute black of the sealed chamber, he stumbles forward blindly until finding his workbench and, resting upon its rough surface, the tinderbox. His fingers fumble with the box before reaching flint and steel. With a surge of relief, he retrieves the items and strikes a spark to the black metal basin of brimstone-laced coals which stands next to the bench. The basin ignites with a familiar and satisfying *whoomp*, the room coming to life in a burst of red light which quickly simmers to a flickering glow, smearing the walls in leaping orange and climbing yellows. Shadows dance in the corners like hell-trapped jesters.

A thunderous pounding batters the door. Etienne curses. They'd found his trail faster than he would have hoped. Sweating and frantic, he turns his attention to the massive slab of stone laid upon blackwood bracers in the middle of the room. Reflected firelight from the basin gently strokes its smooth dark surface, the face of which swirls like a gray storm, as if sensing what is to come.

Moving with dangerous speed, Etienne dips a thin torch to the flames and carries it to a wall of deep shelves crowded with sacks of powder, crystal vials harboring liquids of indescribable color, clumps and crumbs of scattered, glistening stones. Dried flora hangs limp, their strange scents of earth and spice perfuming the room.

He snatches a small gray sack of powder and a vial the deep red color of blood. He has just begun his way back to the altar when a thunderous *CRACK* splits the air. The heavy chamber door splinters beneath the force of swung steel—most likely a broadsword. Or worse, an axe.

"Damn them," he spits, spinning back to the shelf to clutch a larger sack. He smiles grotesquely, fingers curved around the coarse base of the torch, as he shuffles back to the eager, flickering surface of the altar.

He murmurs enchantments as he goes.

# GOTHIC

WITH THE final chop of a brute's axe and the merciless kick of a heavy boot, the door finally breaks inward. Croce pushes past the men with a curse, demanding he be first to enter. He searches the room, eager eyes darting side-to-side, and sees that damned Montresor sprawled, naked, atop the very object he'd come here to claim.

The altar is slick with blood, as is Etienne's pale flesh.

Croce strides across the room as his men rush in behind, the clamor of scraping of weapons and armor tearing apart the silence of the rounded chamber, their raised voices intrusive and coarse, spoiling his victorious moment. Glass shatters and he spins, face red with fury and wet with perspiration, pink rivulets run down his cheeks, his sweat mixed with the blood of the murdered family spattered on his brow. His eyes are wide whites in the dim room, his pupils dark droplets of ink in puddles of spoiled milk. "Fucking fools! Touch nothing!"

The men freeze and eye him warily, their grizzled, sun-charred faces frowning. But they obey, albeit sullenly, like feral wolves held at bay before a bleeding sheep.

Croce walks to his rival's body lying atop the stone tablet. He hears a steady *plink-plink-plink* as the man's blood runs off the altar's edge, red drops flowering in the porous stone floor beneath. He's staring down at Montresor's face, looking for signs of life, when the old man's eyes flutter open, shimmering white amid the thick blood covering his skin—the fountainheads of which are deep, self-inflicted gashes in his forehead, wrists, and neck.

One of his legs has disappeared into the stone, as if dipped in a bath of ink.

The dying man's lips move to speak, and Croce clamps a gloved hand over Etienne's wet mouth, shaking his head.

"Too late, too late," Croce says, pulling his eyes away from the swirling black surface, already congealing around the warlock's white knee like lips sucking clean a chicken bone, the spell defeated. "You won't succeed in finishing the spell, I'm afraid." He looks pointedly at the leg, half-submerged, stuck partway between this world and the other. Smiling in grim victory, he removes his hand from the man's face. "Go on, say your last words, fool, so I may mock them in your own banquet hall, over wine and spirits, for decades to come. Perhaps your daughter, who I will make my concubine, my *whore,* will one day delight in the retelling of your pitiful end."

Croce studies the altar, then strokes the blood-soaked flesh of the last Montresor with his fingertips. He wipes the blood on the stone, almost laughs when it is immediately absorbed into its black depths. "It has a taste for blood, yes? It drinks you like wine," he says reverently, eyes gleaming. "Your body is the first of many meals I have planned for this sacred object. In time, I will tap its true power." He licks one finger, savoring the cooled blood of his enemy as if it were honey. "I have much to do with this relic, much to do… and I thank you for the bequeathment. Now, please Etienne, hold my patience no longer and speak. Is it mercy you wish for? If so, I will have my man put a dagger through your heart."

But Montresor does not speak. Instead, he lifts a clenched fist to his mouth and, with one last breath, blows the concealed palmful of powder into Croce's shocked face.

The powder scorches like acid, dissolving skin as his mouth and eyes burn and bleed. Through his own shrieks of unbearable pain Croce hears the dying warlock's laughter all around him, as if he is surrounded by a hundred dying madmen instead of one.

As Croce screams, Montresor's death mask transforms into a blood-slick smile—relishing a sad, small victory, buried in loss.

He has failed. The passage was closed, the way sealed. He will die in a world of failure and pain.

These last grim thoughts dissolve along with the last of his hope as the final spark of his brain is snuffed out like a candle. His eyes roll into his head, his weary heart pumps the last drops of his life onto the stone, where it is consumed.

A soldier pushes past his shrieking employer and plunges a dagger through the dead man's heart, thinking him the threat, but when he turns and sees what has been done to Signor Croce, he gasps, crossing himself.

The great man's face is cracked like a shattered egg and bleeding from every split. His lips are dry and shriveled as a rotting corpse, the skin of his face pulled hideously back from a tight-jawed grin. His hands press hard against his eyes, as if trying to keep them from spilling out of their sockets.

"The fool! The mad fool!" Croce cries as he stumbles drunkenly across the chamber, waving his arms and shrieking curses at the air before collapsing into a shadowed corner. His wails fill the room with such heart-wrenching agony that several of the soldiers push out through the broken door—wanting away from this room, from these screams. They do not stop until they pass through the cursed castle, many fleeing into the night.

One remaining soldier, a mercenary who has seen much of death, goes to Croce and kneels before him. "Signor, what's happened to you?"

The grizzled mercenary crosses himself when Croce pulls his hands away from his face to stare back at him, bulging eyes now wide and empty as pale sky. Tears of blood run from their corners, flow down poisoned, cracked cheeks.

"The demon has blinded me," Croce whispers.

And then he begins to laugh—a sputtering rasp that grows into great, bellowing howls that carry through the vacuous halls of the near-empty castle like wind through a black ship's sails, freezing the hearts of any who hear it, heralding death, and madness.

# THIRTEEN

*ITALY. TWENTY years later.*

...the scribe slides the parchment across the stone, dabs the trembling quill in the inkpot, and waits for his master to begin. Sweat runs from his face, dotting the parchment and stone alike, glistening like beads of amber in the flickering candlelight. It has been several weeks of transcription labor, and he prays the task is nearly complete. The stack of unbound parchment to his right, at the edge of the table, is prodigious: fifty pages of madness scrawled in his hand.

For Signor Federico Croce, the forbidden, long-lost altar has been everything he hoped for, and so much more. And while his blindness has prohibited him from doing most of the necessary work alone, he's been able to compensate with the many assistants who have come through his doors over the years. Some of whom, it's true, have left mad. Some have departed in the middle of the night, forever hiding their bizarre, physical deformations—missing limbs; black, melted skin; eyeless, tongueless.

Many, of course, never leave at all.

This current scribe, however, Croce takes great care with. Scribes are not common in Genoa (although the port brings artisans and skilled laborers of all kinds), and he cannot risk an extended gap in his work, in his craft: the recording of history, his knowledge of the beyond...

His *stories.*

Already there are rumors in the village of witchcraft, black magic, murder. He knows one day they will come for him, and he needs to be *finished* with the work before that day arrives.

Finished... or hidden.

Yes, he will hide. Hide, and be ready to rise once more when the moment is right.

"Are you ready, damn you?" Croce huddles on a heavy chair in the corner of the dim chamber, a room deep beneath the gentler, more ornate lodgings of the ground level up above. Since his accident, he can no longer see the light (Montresor's devilish powder made sure of that), but his flesh, also, is now overly sensitive to the sun. The slightest warmth of sunlight on his skin curdles his guts as if poisoned. The very *idea* of being under the sun's wide eye makes his skin crawl, the hairs on his neck stand on end. No, he prefers the cool, earthy chambers below his castle, adjacent to the tombs of his ancestors, where the air is cool, and the sun has no place.

He thinks the altar likes it better here as well. He can almost feel its *contentment,* the way its energy, its lifeforce, squeezes his heart *oh so gently*, caresses his blind eyeballs, tickles his wizened cock with mischievous, invisible fingers. He removed the slab from atop the rustic base that fool Montresor had created and had his best carpenters build ornate supports inlaid with Boulle marquetry and featuring fat, golden caryatids, the female forms flowing along thick rosewood legs—heavy clawed feet at the base, iron-plated supports at the top strong enough to support the stone slab's immense weight. Although he cannot see it himself, he knows its beauty is without equal.

It's told him so.

Croce sighs, searches for the words, waiting... focuses on nothing but the final scenes of the story playing out in his mind. The last act is about to commence, and he doesn't want to forget a single moment, have the scribe miss a single letter. Staring into the unceasing void of blindness, his mind still *sees* the tremendous power of the altar (which, to a layman's eye, is now nothing more than an ornate stone table), its swirling power saturated with impossible colors. He hears it whisper into his ear, telling him such wonderful things, opening his mind to words and ideas that will one day populate the world via underground channels, back-alley word-of-mouth. The altar shows him how the transcriptions of each page will be composed—multiplied—in foul rooms across Europe, handed out for consumption by any vile mind that craves it. They will learn from the tales—learn of death, of what lies beyond. What waits there.

"I'm ready, Signor," the scribe says, and Croce hears the fear in his voice, can *taste* the madness already infesting his blood, scratching at the back of his throat like a cockroach.

He realizes, of course, that he will soon need a new scribe, one who knows Italian and Latin, perhaps French and English as well. Someone to write the new texts, and translate the ones already completed.

"There are… so many stories to tell," Croce mumbles to himself, to the dark.

"I'm sorry?" the scribe says, unsure of whether to transcribe the words, but Croce only laughs from his shadowed corner; cackling like a witch, wide white eyes shining with reflected firelight, as if floating in the dark.

---

TO THE scribe, Croce's firelit visage is eerily similar to the faces he sometimes sees within the surface of the stone table, the ones he continuously tries to convince himself are the fantasies of a tired mind, illusory deceptions of a poorly lit chamber; the faces that appear to be simultaneously laughing and screaming, as if relishing the pain they feel. Once—just once—he allowed himself to focus on the stone, on the faces swimming within its depths, to try and decipher whether it was really, truly a portal as he'd been told, a gateway to another world.

*Impossible geographies. Landscapes beyond imagination. Something, creatures… alive.*

The scribe looks down at his trembling hands, at the shifting blackness of the stone beneath his pale skin, angry as a storm beneath the parchment, the voices telling his fragile mind all the horrible, grotesque, painful ways he can end his own life.

If not this very night, then soon.

Once the work is complete.

He shuts his eyes tight, takes a deep breath. When he opens them once more, they stay focused only on the parchment. The parchment, and nothing else.

Signor Croce, from the corner, is speaking. Dictating. Without hesitation, without further thought, the scribe lays his pen to parchment, writes down the story he is being told.

# FOURTEEN

A*ND FINALLY, in the end...*

...he almost made it.

Federico Croce watches the flames lick the walls of the sanctuary, the last hiding spot he'll ever use during his exodus from his home, from his country.

From the inquisition.

Croce has been driven from his castle by the Pope's monkeys, charged with heresy, with necromancy. With nothing more than a handful of servants and two wagons of belongings, he's been chased and tormented, forced into the wild like an animal.

He was barely able to escape the clutches of the Inquisitor's soldiers these last few hectic, and exhausting, weeks. But now here, in Turin, just miles from the French border, he's been stopped in his tracks.

This will be his burial site.

The church is nothing more than an old chapel that couldn't hold fifty congregants on Easter Sunday. It is under the pastoral leadership of Federico's distant cousin, a man he's known since they were children growing up outside Florence, a man who opened his doors to a pariah, a fugitive, a heretic. This gracious older cousin, Giovanni Battista Croce, now carries an arrow in his heart for his kindness. He was the first to go outside, to plead with the men on horseback—their shields decorated with crosses, their weapons eager for blood—to inform them that the church means sanctuary for any who seek it. He demanded the soldiers disperse peacefully.

Instead, they shot an arrow into his chest.

Before he hit the ground, a second went through his eye.

Croce's servants scramble to fortify the lone chapel door—thick, heavy oak banded with iron—as the soldiers fire more arrows into the church, killing men and women. How many of his people have died Croce did not know, or care. He knows only that he is doomed, and that time is short.

Fortuitously, as a precaution, he ordered the altar carried inside prior to the soldiers' arrival. Now it is his only means of escape.

"Boy!" he screams into the darkness that is his entire world, his living curse left like a mark from that demon Montresor, a man he vows to track down in hell and murder all over again with his bare hands.

"Signor?" a small, scared voice.

Croce reaches toward the voice, tugs the harsh fabric of a servant's tunic toward him, close enough that he can smell the child's fear mixed with the sharp odor of the onions he'd eaten that morning. The boy is parentless, but quick and worthy. A servant who comes in handy when small hands are needed. Keeping one hand on the boy's shirt, Croce shoves the other into the pocket of his lined coat and pulls out a sealed envelope, a letter he hoped not to send.

"I care not where my body may take me..." Croce mumbles, feeling a burst of self-pity. Then, shoving the letter at the boy's chest, thinks of another phrase from the great Alighieri.

*The path to paradise begins in hell.*

He laughs at the idea, nods, then turns his milky eyes toward the child.

"Now, listen. There are catacombs beneath this chapel, where a sewer runs. There are entryways to the sewer you can find if you take a torch and do not turn off the main path. Keep going to the end, behind the last tomb, then through an iron gate. From there you will find the sewer, and the way to freedom. Understand?" Croce shakes the boy hard enough to procure a whimper, which pleases him.

*Yes, be frightened. It will make you fleet of foot.*

"The last tomb," the boy says softly.

Croce offers a horrible smile, exposing two rows of blackened teeth rotted by decades of dining on strange roots, tasting alchemical powders, eating diseased meat and poisonous herbs—the diet of a mad occultist gave him teeth to match a dark heart, twisted as a dead Juniper tree.

"Yes, yes." Croce smells smoke, hears the first crackles of flame already eating the outside of the church. They'd set their torches, and he needs to hurry. "Once you are free, find your way back to Genoa, seek out a merchant named Fornasini. He does business at the port, you hear me? At the port. Ask for Fornasini and give him this letter. He will reward you. Gold and food and shelter... it's all in the letter. Can you do it?"

"Si, signor," the frightened voice replies, and Croce hears servants screaming, panicking as smoke fills the room, as flames lick at the walls, as the heat grows.

Croce pats the boy on the head. "You're small, thin. You can make it through the sewer, which will lead you away from these men, these soldiers of Christ who wish to murder you. Tell me the man's name."

"Fornasini, by the sea," the boy says, confidence building, eager to run. To flee.

Croce nods tiredly. "Then go, bastard, get out or burn with the rest of them."

He hears the boy's feet patter away and rises slowly to his feet, his lungs immediately filling with hot smoke. He moves his blind eyes around the room, hands held out from his body, reaching, searching for the stone. The crackling of the fire grows more urgent, and he knows the blaze is eating away the walls, the chorus of flames singing loud, alive as rushing water. A soldier chops with eager strokes at the chapel's great door—perhaps to save those inside, perhaps to bury his axe in them before they burn.

Everyone is shrieking and crying out, praying, but there is no one to help them, nor him. Not anymore. Then, finally, in his dark inner world, he sees it: the pulsing violet shadow of the stone slab. The portal.

Escape.

He is shoved hard from behind and falls to his knees. Afraid to stand, he begins to crawl, palms flat on the dirty stone floor as he shuffles forward, mumbling incantations as he goes, hoping there will be time to do what must be done.

Unlike Montresor, he *will* complete the spell.

Moments later there comes a splintering crash, and new voices join the terrified screams of his servants and their families. Loud, angry voices. Shouts of blood and death. The hissing whispers of arrows, the dull thud of punctured flesh. The fire roars savagely now, and it becomes harder to locate the power of the stone, but still he crawls, desperate, feverish, chanting louder and louder as he draws near...

A body falls on top of him, lifeless and heavy. Croce is driven flat to his stomach and feels a brittle rib snap beneath the force of it, stabbing his chest with a deep, broken pain. The air is punched from his lungs, which burn from breathing the hot smoke. The fire surrounding him is so great that he feels his exposed skin baking like bread in an oven, the air so dense with poison there is nothing left to breathe.

Holding his breath, ignoring the pain, he slides toward the altar, the energy from which pulses faster, more vibrantly, as he gets within feet, then inches. His searching hand slides into liquid fire and he screams, the pain so sharp, so intense, that his blind world momentarily flashes bright white.

*The gold,* he thinks, sickened by the sensation of his own burning skin. *The gold engravings have melted, and now I wear them as jewelry.*

Whimpering, he reaches upward, high as he can with his remaining hand, and rests one palm on the surprisingly cool surface of the stone. He immediately feels the raw power, the brute *rage* of its spirit, and from one heartbeat to the next the terrible pain—in his chest, his lungs, his deformed hand—blink out and disappear, as if cut away with a knife.

In this moment, the force beyond the stone takes over his mind, shuts out the sounds of death… it *whispers* to him. Instructs him.

Nodding, grinning madly, he begins to remove his clothes with the one good hand remaining to him. Coat, shirt, shoes, pants, undergarments, all the time waiting for the fatal blow of an axe, an arrow through the back, for the flames to tug at his hair and melt his scalp.

Once free of the garments, he chants quickly under his breath, a rhythmic incantation. He leans on the stone… and feels a shocking cold run up his arm, an icy liquid sensation, as if he has lowered his hand into a bucket of cold water.

"Oh!" he exclaims, just once, as the realization comes to him.

He is moving through the portal.

Laughing loudly—as all around him come cries of pain and shrieks of murder—Federico Croce lifts one bare, bony white leg onto the surface of the altar, and feels it sink.

A rage-filled bellow comes from nearby and his head snaps backward as something impossibly large and heavy slams into his skull. There's another white flash in his brain, and he knows something is terribly wrong. Groaning, unable to think, he uses the last of his energy to roll his body onto the great stone, dropping through its surface and into its cold depths, forever leaving this world of screams and fire and death, and entering another.

To live in what lies beyond, eternally entangling his spirit with madness.

---

**SEVERAL WEEKS** after the burning of the church, and the massacre of those harbored within, a large wagon pulled by four great horses clambers up the hill toward the structure's remains. A handful of riders follow the wagon, tools and weapons strapped to their saddlebags.

The rubble of the church no longer smolders, but lies broken and black, a charred skeleton exposed to the sky. The rooftop has collapsed onto the corpses—the only burial they will receive.

Fornasini calls a halt to the wagon, climbs down from his horse and orders his men into action. The men leave the wagon and horses, unstrap tools, pull on coarse leather gloves and approach the ruins. The merchant is paying well to retrieve the artifact believed to be buried here, entombed within all the death and horror, and they will not return empty-handed.

Hours later, the bodies that can be salvaged are taken from the wreckage and laid out on scorched grass. The object of their search is also pulled free, lifted by six strong men and set gently near the bodies.

Fornasini studies the remains of the dead. There are nearly a dozen young men, women... even a few children. The tiny corpse of an infant burned to the bone.

He sees no corpses matching his friend, and so turns his attention to the stone. Its base had burned away—only charred stumps of thick wood, spattered in melted gold, remain. Fornasini smiles, knowing it hardly matters. The stone will be part of a new shape soon, one designed by a very select group of craftsmen, a guild of the dark arts who worship the same God as he does, as Croce had, when of this earth.

The Dark One. The Mighty Serpent.

"Load it into the wagon. Pack it well, or I'll take your heads," he barks. The men scramble to obey.

He glances one last time at the jagged row of ashen bodies, warmed that his friend, the great warlock of his time, is not among them. Nor, he knows, is his body buried in the rubble of the damned church.

Federico Croce is nowhere on this plane of existence.

The transfiguration is complete.

# FIFTEEN

AS DIANA drives away from the cemetery and the memories contained there, she focuses on what her next steps will need to be, and what those steps will potentially mean for her immediate future.

Just how far is she willing to go?

The question is tainted with doubts, the answer laden with fears—because she will do whatever must be done to reclaim what rightfully belongs to her family and, if needed, put a stop to anything that has already been put into motion, using whatever means necessary.

It's this thought that allows fear to slide beneath her skin and distort her focus, dilute her willpower. She mustn't be weak, not now. Not when she is so close.

Rain splatters the Mercedes' windshield, the sudden shower pulling her abruptly from her deep thoughts. The gray day has grown dark, and she clicks on the headlights, forces herself to reduce her speed on the water-slicked road. She glances at the passenger seat where her phone lies face-up, deathly silent.

*He'll call, Diana. You need to be patient.*

Forcing herself to take a breath, she pushes the audio button on her steering wheel. A Brahms concerto fills the car's luxurious interior, massaging the brittle silence. She feels herself slowly relax, longing for home, a hot bath, and a stiff drink. She needs to center herself, prepare her mind and body for what lies ahead.

When the time comes, there will be much to do.

She fears none of it will be good.

---

THE PRIVATE investigator sits on the shadowed steps of the empty townhouse, currently featuring a realtor's sign tastefully posted on the street-facing brickwork. Part of him is curious what the asking price is for the place, that morbid curiosity most people get tickled with when they see the availability of an object far beyond their means. He doesn't have millions in the bank, unfortunately; he most likely couldn't afford the ten percent needed for down payment.

Still, money isn't everything. He's grateful that the night is not too cold for his long watch, and is pleased he'll be able to call his client soon with some good news. He knows she's anxious. And even though he still doesn't fully understand the nature of the job, or the rationale behind its urgency, what he does know is the money arrives like clockwork the first of every month, the installments wired from an untraceable overseas account. He also finds spying on a chunk of furniture a lot less stressful (and morally dubious) than a cheating husband.

It doesn't stop him for being cautious, however. Doesn't stop apprehensions from nagging at the back of his brain, nibbling at his thoughts like subway-sized worry-rats. His instincts are almost always right—he'd come to trust them as much as any photograph, any piece of evidence—and currently they're telling him that something isn't right about this job. As mundane—as downright *dull*—as it appears on the face of things, there's an undercurrent of real danger he can't put his finger on. He figures it might be that he hasn't met his client face-to-face, and that's certainly part of it. He prides himself on his ability to read people, it's one of the things that makes him good at his job, better than most, in fact. But you can't *read* a person via email, or text, or even over the phone. Not really. Not like you can when you're sitting across from them, staring them in the face, watching their eyes, their mannerisms, their tics. He wonders how much of this situation Diana Montresor has divulged to him, and how much she's holding back.

A hard cold breeze blows across the steps and the man, nearly invisible in the gloomy, dimly lit street, pulls his coat tighter around his tall, narrow body. He makes a note of the time and jots it onto the page of his small notepad. He'll need to hang around a few more hours at least, until the shindig is wrapped up and folks go home. He wants to have a record of when everybody leaves, the party over. Probably unnecessary, but it's important to be thorough.

Earlier, he'd watched from afar, with great interest, as the moving truck unload its cargo into the house. Despite having seen the entire process, he's still not entirely sure how what came out of the truck's belly fit through the doorway of the writer's townhouse.

Before he could overthink it, however, he was caught off guard by the line of taxis that started to arrive at the residence a few hours after the truck and its miracle-working movers had departed. Twice he'd had to circle the block to ensure he wasn't noticed, at least not in any way that drew attention. The writer himself finally arrived some hours later, chaperoned by a friend. The detective could hear the loud cheer when they entered and smiled to himself from his hiding spot. A part of him was happy to see the old dude getting a warm welcome. It's a hard world, and you have to take whatever joy it offers, accept it with gratitude, and hold onto it tight.

All things considered, he would rather be inside with all those people, having a drink, eating a slice of birthday cake, rubbing elbows with a bunch of authors and publishing folks.

But the cold steps will have to do. The steps, and the shadows.

So instead he studies the night, his senses wide open, noting the small things as a way to keep himself sharp: how a dog barks on the next block, a neighbor arriving home holding the hand of a young child, a car double-parked at the end of the street, how one of the old streetlights on the corner occasionally flickers, as if haunted.

And so, the night wears on, and the man watches.

In the brownstone across the street, the festivities continue unabated, oblivious to him, to the surrounding activity of the neighborhood. The windows are bright, the music and conversation giving the night a cheerful throat.

Of course, lodged deep in that throat is the thing he'd finally tracked down after months of searching, followed by a week of hard investigation—illicit photographs of manifests, cash payouts for shipping information, stolen photocopies of purchase orders and invoices before he tracked it to a Riverside antique dealer. From there it made its way to here, where it now sits quietly, somewhere within all that temporary happiness, a mysterious guest holding unknown value to some distant client, an innocuous object that calls those worry-rats to nibble at his brain, to jangle his intuition that something isn't *right* here, that somehow—in a way he can't yet fathom—those nice folks enjoying their night of celebration might just be in danger.

And so, he will sit, just a little while longer, and watch the night.

Part Four

# A NEW MUSE

# SIXTEEN

THE PARTY is magnificent.

Tyson swims drunkenly through the group of friends. He's touched and delighted to see a few writers he typically only sees at the occasional horror convention, and a couple others that even an old veteran like himself is a bit star-struck to have attend his little party. He'd heard Joyce Carol Oates stopped by but, due to another engagement, had left before Tyson's arrival (which makes him feel a bit guilty about ordering that nightcap with Billy). Some new blood showed up, however, and it warms his heart to see younger writers in his home, celebrating *him*, his achievements. Respecting his work, acknowledging they're standing on the shoulders of giants. *Even if the giants are a little tipsy,* he thinks, chuckling to himself.

And yes, it does his heart good to see his baby girl, but to see her in the kitchen chatting with some of the "fresh faces" in the field makes Tyson feel simultaneously old and youthful. He can't help viewing the young bucks as competition, even if they haven't accomplished a smidgen of what he has, even if they would *kill* to have the career of Tyson Parks. He decides to let go of any nascent resentment of these new faces, of their youth, their theoretically bright futures still so vast and unmarred by error. Life's too short, and besides, the horror must go on, right?

Tyson finishes his drink, grimaces, and makes the conscious decision to stop worrying and just enjoy his party, let all his petty thoughts go by the wayside for now, for just one night.

Feeling proud of himself—downright magnanimous, actually—he's just starting for the bar and a fresh drink when Sarah tugs at his elbow. He spins to look at her and is mildly surprised when the room continues around another quarter-turn before snapping back to Sarah's beaming face.

"Whoa," he says, a bit unsteadily. "This might have been my last drink tonight."

"You having fun?" she says, a wry smile on her face.

"Oh hell yes, you bet. This is amazing. *You're* amazing!" he says, slightly garbled and a little too loud.

"Are you ready for present number two?" she asks, giggling and taking his hand.

Tyson carefully sets his empty glass on a side table. "I am," he says, then hugs her roughly, his hand finding the slope of her breast, and whispers into her ear. "But please don't tell me it's another daughter!"

She laughs, removes his hand from her chest and kisses him. "No, but that *would* be quite the surprise. Honey, let me get you a bottle of water, then I want to show you, okay?"

"Yes to water, yes to the lingerie show," he says.

A passerby he doesn't recognize pats his shoulder, says *Happy Birthday* and shakes Tyson's hand before moving on into the mingling crowd. By the time Sarah comes back holding a chilled bottle of Evian, he's already forgotten what it is they're supposed to be doing.

---

SHE LEADS him through the partygoers—the bulk of which have begun to thin out as the party presses on past midnight—toward his office. "I was going to wait until everyone left," she says over her shoulder, "but frankly I've been terrified all night that you might walk in here with one of your writer buddies, wanting to show off your book collection."

"Wait for what?" Tyson says, intrigued. "And why do I get the feeling it's not a book this year?"

Sarah can't figure out, given Tyson's drunken state, if he's disappointed or merely curious. She squeezes his hand and opens the door to his office. It's far enough down the hall from the main room that conversation and music are muffled, the office itself dark and quiet as a freshly-dug grave. She leads him inside and closes the door behind them.

"Hey, wait a second," he murmurs, breath hot on her ear, "I think I know what the gift is..."

Sarah laughs and slaps at his hands as he gropes her ass and hips, runs his palms up the inside of her cashmere sweater, fingertips slipping beneath the silk cups of her bra. "Wrong!" she says, and steps quickly away, leaving him alone and untethered in the dark. "Although, maybe we'll call that present number three. But that's for later..."

Tyson tries to follow her voice as it drifts through the unlit room. He's become slightly disoriented, and suddenly can't figure out which way he is facing. *Is the door that way?* he wonders, and feels sweat break out on his forehead. He squeezes the cold, perspiring water bottle, takes a long sip.

"Sarah?" he says, and thinks his voice sounds shaky. There's a tremor in his throat he doesn't much care for. "God, honey? It's so damned dark in here... I, uh..."

"Just hold on," she says, so close that he jerks back a little. But when her familiar hand slips into his, all the pressure leaves his chest, and he feels anchored once more. He exhales gratefully. *A horror writer afraid of the dark. That's a good one, all right.*

Sarah pulls him a few feet forward, momentarily lets him go, then slides both hands gently onto his face, her skin cool and soft against his stubbled cheeks. She tilts his head down to look at her, but all he can see is emptiness.

"Don't move," she whispers, and her hands fall away.

Before the anxiety can return, he hears the *click* of the floor lamp, the one that stands next to his reading chair, and the room snaps into existence around them. Tyson finds himself facing the back of the office, staring at a wall of books that make up a chunk of his most prized possessions, shelves filled by some of the greatest genre writers of the century, their pages inked with inscriptions that could never be replaced.

Sarah steps in front of him. Tyson thinks she looks nervous.

"So?" he says, trying to smile away her tension, and his own. "Now what?"

Sarah pats his chest, firmly grabs his hips, and turns him around.

"Holy Christ," he gasps, as the water bottle he's been holding drops to the floor.

# SEVENTEEN

W*HAT A beautiful monster you are.*

Tyson's old desk is gone, the very same one he's had since he was a pimply-faced freshman at Suffolk University. *I screwed Holly Pages on that desk the day I turned twenty-one,* he thinks, a footnote he's kept from his current partner. There's a distinct feeling of emptiness at its disappearance, and he can't help feel a momentary stab of pain in his gut. That old piece of shit went from his dorm room at Suffolk, to a shared apartment at NYU (where he'd first met Billy). Over the last few decades, it had been hauled to three additional apartments all through the Midwest and East Coast as Tyson moved from New York, back to Boston, then to Maine, Detroit (briefly), and then finally back to New York and this office, in this townhouse. *My final resting place,* he thinks morbidly. But that's what loss does, he figures: brings on morbid thoughts. Loss, death, the infinite beyond. The end of all things.

And so that is his first thought when Sarah turns him around: the foreignness of not seeing the familiar.

In its place, however, is something even more difficult for his mind to process.

A *new* desk.

*Or is it a table?* he thinks, as the beastly thing's got to measure six-feet-by-four-feet without breaking a sweat. The side facing them is a slab of slick black oak so polished it looks wet, as if freshly oiled. Tyson imagines that if he *did* touch the surface, he would pull away his fingertips to find them smeared with rich black fluid, as if he had dipped his fingers into an inkwell. As he studies it more closely, he notices the wood is also densely engraved, and he finds himself stepping toward it, as if in a trance, then crouching slowly before it, as one might approach a wild beast, one that's eyeballing you as a danger (or a hot meal).

Across the top edge are heavily sunken letters forming words carved nearly four inches in height and sprawled horizontally, end-to-end:

**DO THIS IN REMEMBRANCE OF ME**

Surrounding the words, woven within a densely layered twisting ivy pattern that runs the entire circumference of the massive desk, are strange symbols—stretched cherubic faces, bizarre images his mind cannot, or will not, translate. He doesn't think the symbology is religious—or occult—and finally dismisses it as artisan design, something altogether original. He walks slowly around the thing's substantial bulk, taking in every facet of its unique, complicated design. He's reminded of the Ray Bradbury story, *The Illustrated Man.* Every inch of the black wood is covered with intricate patterns, symbols, and beautiful, haunting imagery. The work is so delicate, so smooth, that it seems to almost *ripple,* as if the intertwined vines of ivy are sliding just below a thin skin, like a dense cluster of snakes roiling beneath the surface of an oil slick.

The top of the desk is made from a solid, polished, charcoal-gray stone. *Granite, perhaps?* Tyson thinks. But it's unmarred by any natural veins, and he concludes it must be dark sandstone, or possibly something like basalt. But it's also smooth as glass, as if diamond-cut, shining like a black pool beneath a pale sky, windless and deathly still. His laptop, the small lamp, and the assorted stacks of papers set on the slick surface seem trivial, lost among its vastness. Tyson notices his chair has been replaced as well, with something newfangled and ergonomic, but he hardly spares it a second glance as he slides it away in order to study the rest of the desk.

It's dark on this side of the desk, the drawers and cubby space lost in deep shadow, and he reaches for the desk lamp, clicks it on. The drawer faces are wide, and intricately carved. The knobs are not knobs at all, but faces, or masks, with bugged-out eyes and wide-open mouths, snarling and filled with sharp teeth.

Numbly, he pulls the chair towards him and sits down. He spreads his fingers across the cool stone top, feels an unmistakable energy flow from the stone and into his hands, like touching metal that has a weak electric current running through it.

From far away, someone is speaking. But the words are white noise, the chitter of a tree-nuzzled bird, the rumble of distant traffic, or an oncoming storm.

"...over two-hundred years old... if you hate it, we can bring the old one back..."

Slowly, not even fully realizing he's doing it, he turns his head and lowers it to the desktop. When his ear is about an inch above the black stone, he closes his eyes and audibly gasps, then releases a long breath, one that carries the weight of all his anxiety and doubt and despair away with it, out of his lungs and into the air, where it dissolves, and is no more.

"...not even sure how they got it in here... Tyson, please... speak to me... I'm sorry..."

Tyson ignores the distant voice, because there's something else coming from the desk's cold surface... something that demands all of his attention.

*Whispers.*

For a moment, he wants to laugh, but quickly stifles the idea.

But there's no doubt now, no doubt at all. As his ear hovers just above the desk's surface, he can absolutely, undeniably, hear *them*.

Yeah, sure... he can hear them all right, just fine and dandy.

*I'm listening. And yes, yes, I understand...*

"Tyson!"

The whispers stop. His meditative, almost fugue state blows apart like a crushed walnut and reality pours in: the room, the smell of his own body—booze and sweat and age—the light, and her. Sarah. She studies him anxiously, hands wringing. Her face is as forlorn as a small child waiting for her parents to return after being left at the side of a deserted road, watching as the speeding car becomes a puff of brown dust in the distance, not yet realizing she's been forever abandoned.

He notices she's softly crying, and this realization both surprises and disgusts him.

"I'm so sorry, Ty..." she says. "Do you hate it?"

Tyson presses his fingers to the desktop and stands. He walks around the desk, *feeling* its presence at his side, his legs. Feeling it hate his leaving.

He puts his hands over Sarah's own, squeezes them warmly, and looks deep into her anticipative eyes.

"Honey," he says. "I could kill you."

Her face goes pale, her lips quiver, and fresh tears spill from her eyes.

"I don't..." she says, confused and... *afraid?*

Then he smiles broadly and moves his hands up her arms to her face, gently wipes the tears from her cheeks.

"For spending so much damned money on me!" he says, then bursts out laughing. It's a young man's laugh. A joyful, almost unhinged, laugh. "This thing must have cost a fortune!" He pulls her into a tight embrace, smiling wildly toward the ceiling. "Oh my God, Sarah. Oh my God..."

She pushes him away, puts a hand to her forehead, simultaneously incredulous and hopeful. "Wait. You mean you want to keep it? You *like* it?"

"I do, I do..." he says, and Sarah squeals with delight, hugging him back fiercely, breathing heavy sighs of relief into his chest. "I don't deserve you," he says, and kisses the top of her head.

From behind him, something reaches out and tickles the back of his leg.

"I've never been so happy."

# EIGHTEEN

THAT NIGHT, after the guests are gone and Tyson's daughter is fast asleep in her third-floor bedroom, Tyson and Sarah make love amidst slanting bars of moonlight, the bed's coverings cast away, long-since kicked off, now slumped in jagged heaps on the carpeted floor.

There are moments during sex when he surprises her.

There are other moments—filled with unrecognizable touches, like those from a stranger—where she becomes a little frightened at his tenacity, his almost alarming passion that borders, at times, on violence. But she *knows* this man, and is able to stay with him, guide him, slow him when necessary.

For the first time in their decade-long relationship she has to tell him *No,* and that's all right. That's okay. Because he listens, and she even enjoys it once he's calmed down.

Regardless, she's relieved at his final grunt and gasp, the offering of hot fluid inside her signaling the end of her night's work.

Afterward, she's sore but content, fighting away any feelings of being annoyed, or upset.

*Or ashamed,* a quiet part of her mind says as he snores next to her, where he lies naked and sticky with his own sweat and semen, sprawled like a bear atop a sun-warmed rock.

She wipes a tear away from an eyelid, and smiles to herself.

*I suppose I should be grateful he likes the desk. Mission accomplished, right?*

She steps out of bed to put on underwear, a comfortable bra, and a thin T-shirt. After a brief hesitation, she pulls on a pair of cotton sweats she hasn't worn in years.

Dressed, she crawls back into bed. Dragging the comforter up from the floor, she pulls it up to her chin, buries the side of her face in a pillow.

After a while, she sleeps.

---

**SARAH DOESN'T** wake in the middle of the night as Tyson slips out of bed, silently takes boxers, khakis, and a T-shirt from his dresser drawers. Dressed, he moves stealthily out of the bedroom and down the stairs, toward the office.

He's whimpering as he goes, scolding himself in wet, harsh whispers.

Had Sarah wakened, she might have asked him why he was crawling on all fours.

If so, he would have answered: *Because that's what bad dogs do.*

# NINETEEN

WHEN SARAH enters the kitchen the following morning, it's already filled with the incredible, heartbreakingly wonderful aroma of freshly brewed coffee. Violet sits at the breakfast table, wearing a Brown University T shirt and black leggings, reading the *Times*. She looks up at Sarah, bright-eyed and beautiful. Sarah, tired, hungover, and sore (and most likely looking like hell warmed over), allows herself a moment to hate all twenty-one years of the vibrant, gorgeous young woman, then loves her all over again.

"Coffee?" Violet asks, already moving to the cupboard to pull down a mug.

"Does the pope shit in the woods?" Sarah replies, then sinks into a kitchen chair. "Black, please."

Violet tops off her own mug and brings a fresh one to Sarah, who smells it first, savoring the rush to come, then sips slowly.

"Oh yeah," she says. "That's the stuff."

Violet laughs and goes back to her paper. Sarah looks behind her, toward the disaster area of the living room. Billy and a few others had helped dispose of the empty bottles, cups, and paper plates lumped with half-eaten cake squares, but the place is still only a high-death-toll shy of a war zone. *Plus it stinks like scotch and cigarettes,* she thinks. She turns her back on the mess and sips again at the cup of coffee, much stronger than Tyson normally made (*this is a college kid's cup of coffee,* she thinks) and relishes the burst of flavor and caffeine, lets it smooth over the most brittle edges of her hangover.

"A cleaning service is coming at ten," she says absently, and Violet nods from behind the paper, offers a mumbled, *Oh good.*

It isn't until her third sip of coffee that Sarah finally realizes what's off about the morning:

No Tyson.

And then, soft, barely audible, she hears it: the tapping of a keyboard.

*My God… I'm sitting here barely able to keep my head elevated and Tyson's in there… what? Writing a novel?*

Sarah leans back so she can look at the office door, just visible from her seat at the kitchen table. Now that she's heard it, it seems obvious. The clattering *tickety-tack-tackety* of a writer at work.

*And by the sound of it, he's on quite the roll,* she thinks, surprised to feel herself frowning. "How long has he been in there?"

Violet shrugs. "Been at it since before I got up at six for my run. So at least a few hours, I guess."

Sarah takes a deeper, steadying drink from her mug. "Think I'll check on him."

She starts to rise when Violet's head tilts up, her deep brown eyes wide, and full of warning. "I wouldn't do that if I were you."

Sarah pauses, then sits back down, astonished. "Why not?"

Violet glances toward her father's office, as if to make sure he hasn't snuck out and into earshot of their conversation. He hasn't, of course (the steady rhythms of *tack-tack-ticketytick* a dead giveaway), but she leans in anyway, speaks softly. "I stuck my head in there about an hour ago and nearly got it ripped off. I'm telling you, he's a man possessed right now. A regular writing machine."

"Wait, did he actually yell at you?"

Violet shrugs again. "More like a snarl, actually. Like a dog protecting his bone. To be honest, he looks like shit. I mean, he's never been a morning person, but still." Violet sets down the paper, clutches Sarah's hand across the table. "Hey, after the cleaners leave, how about you and me go to the Met? There's a Hartley exhibit I want to check out."

"Yeah... let me think about it." Sarah's astonished, and worried. Even the pleasure of being invited on a date by Violet is subdued by her concern for Tyson. As far as that man was concerned, Violet is the epitome of one of heaven's angels walking the earth, mixing with the common and damned. He cherishes her more than *anything*, and in ten years she's never once seen him so much as raise his voice to his daughter, even in reprimand.

She sighs inwardly, thinking of the previous night. Apparently, he isn't enjoying being one year older.

*I'll give him some space,* she thinks, then gets up to fix herself breakfast and pour a fresh cup of coffee. Given the state of things, it was making out to be a long day.

# TWENTY

STANDING ON the sidewalk outside the museum, Violet checks her phone one more time while waiting in line for what will be her fourth cup of coffee that day. Jennifer hadn't yet texted her back about meeting up, and Violet now doubts that she will. After high school, Jennifer had stayed in the city to attend Barnard, and Violet has the sense her friend never got over her own decision to leave New York for Providence. This latest brush-off is likely another passive aggressive measure to punish her former high school bestie, a series of torments that started after Violet rebuffed the pass Jennifer made at their graduation party, when they'd both crashed drunkenly in a guest bedroom at Andrew Peter's house. Violet hadn't been interested, but she'd also been hurt that her friend hadn't confided about her sexuality for so many years. The fragmenting cracks made in their friendship that night (and the awkward morning that followed) had only just begun to heal when Violet moved away, albeit only a few hours by train, to attend Brown.

And since Sarah hadn't been feeling up to the museum, and now Jennifer was (apparently) blowing her off, Violet feels a sullen depression creeping in, an unfamiliar and uncomfortable feeling of loneliness, a sensation she clinically thinks of as being very adult, an analysis that only depresses her even further.

*Fuck it,* she thinks, and forces herself to ignore the tempting influx of dark feelings trying to claw into her mind. Straightening her posture, chin high, she puts away her phone and decides she'll take on the museum by herself. Besides, if she does it alone she can see whatever the hell she wants, linger in front of whatever catches her interest and not have to worry about someone else's boredom, or schedule.

Feeling better, she orders a coffee and begins mentally planning her route through the Met, knowing she won't be able to resist starting with the Impressionists. Van Gogh, after all...

"Oh!"

Violet feels a hard shove, then the slosh of hot liquid as it slops through the loose lid of her cup and onto her hand, burning the exposed skin.

"Ow! Shit!"

The man who has knocked into her takes a full step back, flinging spilled coffee off his own hands. "Damn that stings!"

"Are you... I mean, did I..." Violet says, her words stumbling as she sucks the now-cooling coffee off the back of her thumb. "Who hit who, here?" She says it smiling, unable to help herself when seeing the stunned reaction of the guy she'd run into (or who'd run into her), charmed by his somewhat amusing—and okay, *cute*—facial expression. It doesn't help that he wears a sort of retro black raincoat and fisherman-style floppy hat even her father wouldn't be caught dead with. "Are you okay?" she asks.

The man raises his eyes to her (Violet pegs him as being grad-student age), seemingly relieved that the girl he'd run into is amused versus totally pissed off, and offers his own cautious smile. "I'm fine. And I think I'm the antagonist here, making you the young heroine."

Violet's smile expands into her cheeks. He *is* cute. "Oh man, you've lost me," she says with a small laugh.

"It was my fault, I mean. I wasn't paying attention to where I was going. I was heading to the museum and got lost in my thoughts." He brushes beads of coffee from the lapels of his coat.

"The raincoat's come in handy, I guess," she says, then winces internally. *Oh, that's a good idea, Vie, why don't you insult the guy. No wonder you're still single.* "I'm kidding. It's cool. The coat, I mean."

"No, no, it's fine. I realize I look like my mother dresses me—she doesn't by the way—but yeah, it does come in handy given my knack for spilling stuff on myself. As you can see, I'm no Baryshnikov when it comes to coordination."

"Who?"

Raincoat guy looks at her with wide eyes, feigning shock and mild outrage. "Oh dear, not even *White Nights*? Gregory Hines?"

Violet blinks.

"Oh, well... that's just sad. What about *Stormy Weather*? *Top Hat?*"

Violet shakes her head. "Sorry, you've lost me again."

"Yeah, I get that a lot," he mumbles. "Look, I'm Ben. Sorry about the rude bump."

He holds out his (now dry) hand, and she surprises herself by taking it and giving him a firm handshake. She should be more cautious, she knows, and even though her instincts are telling her that this encounter is mildly too convenient, she also can't help feeling that the guy—Ben, that is—is harmless as a turtledove. It's partly the raincoat, the ridiculous hat... but mostly it's the eyes. And his smile doesn't hurt.

*Easy Cinderella,* she thinks, but allows herself to be a little daring, nonetheless. "So, you're heading to the Met?"

He nods sagely, as if considering. "There's a new exhibit I want to see, and I found myself with a rare afternoon free, so..." He shrugs, and Violet senses him receding from their encounter, likely eager to head inside.

*What the hell. We only go 'round once.*

"The Hartley. Yeah, I'm here for that, too," she says. "I'm not a superfan or anything, it's more of an excuse to visit the museum again. I mean, I tend to lean toward contemporary versus modern, you know? And Impressionism, which is my favorite, so I'm not really... well, I guess he sort of dips into that, right? Or at least with *The Ice Hole*, which I love, but he's overall more cubist, or whatever, right?"

Violet forces her mouth shut, cutting off her incoherent (and thoroughly uneducated) discourse. Her sole experience with this painter consists of seeing a print on a friend's wall (that she'd initially thought was a Van Gogh).

Art connoisseur she is not. Babbling idiot, on the other hand...

"Anyway..." she says, drawing it out, feeling more ridiculous by the second.

"You know," Ben says, pursing his lips, oblivious to her reddening cheeks. "If you want, we can walk through together? Unless you're waiting for someone?"

"No! No, I mean. No, I'm not. Yes, that would be fun. I'm Violet, by the way." She puts her hand out awkwardly and they shake a second time.

"Cool," Ben says. "You want to get that?"

"Huh?"

Ben points to her coat pocket, where a soft, repeating *vrrrrrmmmm* sound is coming from her phone. She pulls it out, sees a missed call and a text of regret from Jennifer.

Violet puts the phone away, suddenly not in the least disappointed at her friend's stupid grudge. "I'm good. You want to go in?"

Ben nods and they walk toward the museum entrance, each sipping what remains of their spilled coffees.

---

AS THE afternoon wears on, Ben begins to feel badly about the deception. He's surprised how quickly he sets aside his initial motivations for meeting the young woman, finds himself engrossed by her company and the beautiful surroundings.

They spend hours talking about art and books and whatever else courses through their easy, almost familiar conversation as they stroll through the museum's many exhibits.

He realizes that he actually *likes* Violet, and, in a different world, he would probably ask for her number, pursue the possibility of a more personal, less deceitful, relationship. While their meeting at the Met is of course no coincidence, his feelings toward her are a surprise, one he keeps carefully in check as he asks her, with as much innocence as he can muster, about her father.

"A famous writer, huh?" he says casually. "I think I've heard of him. I actually do like horror."

"Well, I don't. I've never read his books. They're awful. And he hasn't been much of a writer lately, to be honest. I probably shouldn't say anything..."

"Oh, please, my lips are sealed."

"It's just... he's been struggling these last few years. He's sort of become a shell of the guy he used to be. Could be writer's block, or maybe he's just getting old, who knows. But my stepmom thinks the new desk, the weird one I told you about, will inspire him. I sure hope so, he needs something to go right. Needs a win, you know?"

They stop in front of *Corridor in the Asylum,* one of Van Gogh's more obscure, and oddly disturbing, paintings; the artist's depiction of the asylum he'd lived in near the end of his life. The image he'd chosen to paint is a relatively innocuous corridor of arches that seem to go on for eternity, as when two mirrors face each other, creating a light clock, an infinity of images traveling though space-time, forever.

"Creepy," Ben says, feeling dwarfed and intimidated by the painting's massive size, the way it bursts from the white wall in torrents of mustard yellow, crimson waves, and pastel green smears. *Only a masterful artist*, Ben thinks, *could make something so dead seem so alive.*

"I love it," Violet replies, chin tilted, eyes fixed on the canvas.

And so, for a while, they stand before the painting, side-by-side, saying nothing; temporarily allowing their deceptions and motivations to abate, to flow endlessly through yellowed corridors toward a mysterious, unseeable, end.

# TWENTY-ONE

VIOLET RETURNS home in the early evening, as the clouds hovering above the city burned scarlet and apricot, reflecting the dying day's red sun.

The townhouse is still and shadowed. A chemical-tinged tang of lemon scents the air and Violet notices the tables have been wiped to a shine, the floors mopped spotless, the upholstery fluffed, pillows perfectly placed. No lights are on, but she sees well enough to make her way toward the stairs. As she passes her father's office, she stops, tilts her head toward the door.

*My God, he's still going?*

She clearly hears the sounds of the keyboard; even through the closed door it's easy to hear the keys being pecked at mercilessly. Violet looks at her watch, sees it's just past six o'clock, and wonders if he's even taken a break, or a nap.

Perhaps he stopped, took an hour off, and then went back to work. That makes the most sense, otherwise it means he's been working for... what?

*Nearly twelve hours straight? Is that possible?*

Walking to the second floor, she peeks into the open door of the master bedroom, sees Sarah asleep, fully clothed, atop the smooth white bedspread. Sarah had considered going to the museum, but Violet could tell how worn out she was from the last couple days, and when she suggested her stepmother stay home and relax instead, Sarah hadn't argued.

Violet steps silently into the bedroom, crawls onto the bed beside Sarah, nudges her shoulder. "Yo."

Sarah spins as if she's been poked with a hot iron, her eyes wide and wild, her face so strained and ghastly that Violet pulls back, holding up her hands in a defensive gesture. "Whoa! Sarah! It's me..."

When their eyes meet Violet realizes Sarah doesn't recognize her... doesn't even *know* her. Then, after a moment of internal processing, her face crumples. "Oh God," Sarah whimpers, and puts a hand to her mouth. She rests her other hand on Violet's cheek, then pulls her close to hold her.

Violet feels warm tears on the curve of her neck where Sarah has burrowed her face, crying openly, sobbing, shaking in her arms. "Sarah?" she says, trying to sound soothing but scared, not comprehending. "What's wrong? What happened?"

"Nothing... nothing. I'm so sorry," Sarah says, voice muffled, her breath hot and panting. "I had the most awful... I can't even believe it was a dream. I can't..."

"Okay, it's okay," Violet whispers, doing her best to comfort this woman who'd she come to think of as her mother, even if she's never said as much out loud. Sarah had raised Violet since she was a child, after her biological mother had passed away, but they've always connected more as friends or, perhaps, sisters. Now, though, seeing her so upset, Violet loves her as a child does a parent, with an almost naïvely passionate sense of protection, and aches to have whatever this pain is inside her go away and never return.

Sarah pushes herself back, wipes her face. "Oh my God, I'm a fool," she says, and attempts a smile. It's wan and phony, but Violet reciprocates as best she can, despite her fears and concern. "It's just... you know what they always say. It was so *real*, you know? I've never, not *ever*, had a dream seem so real."

"Do you want to talk about it?" Violet says quietly, cautiously, unsure whether she really wants to hear about a dream that would do this to a grown woman.

Sarah shakes her head, her smile more genuine now, the glimmer back in her eyes, the horror momentarily erased. "Fuck no," she says, and they both laugh, and then Sarah cries a bit more from having been so afraid of whatever her subconscious had conjured while she slept, and for having survived it.

---

LATER, WHEN Violet has gone upstairs, Sarah sits slumped at the edge of the bed, eyes vacant, trying to recall the horrors of the dream, hoping that reliving it while awake will soften the sting of the experience.

*It was the desk. But also... not the desk. An altar. Covered in dark blood.*

*SO MUCH BLOOD.*

*A massive cage, a desert of gray sand, a bruised, starless night. Piles of torn flesh, a line of... children... babies... waiting their turn, held by cloaked figures... and then Sarah's turn, pulled onto the altar, naked, laid out on the slab, wrists and ankles gripped tight by hard, cold hands as she screamed for help, for her life... and the robed figure held the long blade, his face in shadow but she knows... she KNOWS him.*

*Tyson.*

*There's a glimmer from deep in the shadow of his face and that streak of white in the dark is teeth. A smile. The blood beneath her is so cold and she fights and squirms but they hold her too firmly and they chant indecipherable words as an ice-cold blade slides into her side... pierces something deep within her. A puncture. The air is sucked from her chest and her eyes roll and she feels the cold steel move inside her, cutting...*

"Stop it," she says, mumbling the words into the empty room.

She doesn't know what caused such a vivid nightmare, doesn't know why things suddenly feel so... *wrong*. It's as if their lives have tilted. She can almost feel the stomach-emptying sensation you get when a ship lolls on a rogue wave, an unsteadiness which pervades throughout your body even after you reach dry ground, long after the rocking stops.

*Come on, Sarah. Time to get a grip.*

Sarah decides she's moped and fretted long enough. Dream or no dream, she needs to get up, get out of this gloomy room, and get her head straight.

Feeling better, she makes her way to the bathroom. A hot shower will do wonders.

It isn't until she's beneath the water that she wonders, with a pang of annoyance, just where the hell Tyson has been all day.

# TWENTY-TWO

TYSON'S FINGERTIP is bleeding.

He isn't sure how it happened, and he didn't even notice until he saw the H-J-U-N keys turning sticky red. For the first time in what feels like days, he stops typing. His breathing is heavy, strained, and a faraway voice informs him that other parts of his body are also begging for his attention; trying desperately to tell him *something's wrong.*

He ignores it all.

But the *finger* is a problem. Yessir. Because the fucking thing is *slowing him down.* He stares at it dumbly, trying to understand how it even happened.

*How do you cut your finger tapping plastic keys?*

Upon closer examination, he notices that the bloodied nail is badly chipped, split at the crescent. The skin beneath is puffy, inflamed, and chafed. He squeezes the tip between two fingers of his other hand, watches in numb wonder as a bead of blood pushes through a crack in the skin. "Damn," he says. Whether caused by excessive dryness or the rough edge of his fingernail he doesn't know, or much care. What he *does* care about, what is absolutely PISSING HIM OFF, is that the injury has stopped him from working. From *writing.*

And oh, how *glorious* the writing has been! How inspiring! What an incredible relief it is to feel the words FLOWING through him once again.

*Cockadoodie finger,* he thinks, and smiles, the Annie Wilkes vulgarism bringing him a few mental steps back toward the here and now, toward reality.

Tyson cradles his sore hand gingerly, now feeling the dull throb of pain from the damaged tip rising to the surface of the present. He pulls in a deep breath, lets it out, and takes a moment to look around the room, surprised that he can hardly see a damned thing.

*When the hell did it get dark?*

The windows glow a dull crimson, but most of the office is hidden in dense, stretched shadows. He looks back to the computer screen and feels a chill run up his spine. He realizes, with a sort of dull terror, that he has absolutely no memory of what he's been writing.

None at all.

As the spell of his writing marathon dissipates, he begins to become aware of other things besides his finger, besides the dark. The constricted muscles in his legs, for starters, *howl* angrily at him. The back of his neck is pinched and taut as a steel cord, his back twisted and knotted at the spine, and his hands... his *fingers*...

"Owww!" he cries, staring in disbelief at his curled, cramped fingers. He winces at the hot, deep throb of overexertion in his wrists and forearms.

"What the hell?" He tries to piece it all together. When had he started writing? Was it *last night?* Is that possible? And what time is it now? Past morning, that's for sure. Late afternoon?

He looks at the clock in the upper corner of his laptop's screen. It's almost 7 P.M.

"Sweet Jesus."

*I haven't stopped working in... twelve hours? Or no, more than that... since three in the morning... my God...*

He pushes the chair back and begins to stand up, then his right leg cramps sharply and his bladder lets go. Hot urine runs down his leg, soaking his khaki pants. "What the FUCK?" he screams, horrified, and more than a little frightened.

A loud knock comes at the door. He stares across the room in panicked terror, then down at his stained crotch in a state of mild shock, confused at what exactly is happening to him. *I must have been in a fugue state,* he thinks, nodding feverishly as cooling piss seeps into his sock, drips into one of his favorite blue house slippers.

"Uh, hold on please," he says, and slowly, gingerly, sits back down. He gives the laptop screen a quick glance, thinking he should pretend to be working, but the blood-smeared keys and his gnarled fingers force him to forgo attempting this deception. He opts instead to rest his hands atop the desk, but avoid the keyboard, as if he were only pausing a moment to reflect. *Good, good. This works,* he thinks, fighting the urge to pull at the fabric of his sodden crotch.

"Yeah, come in."

The door opens and Sarah walks slowly—*carefully*—into the office. "Hi babe," she says, sounding almost nervous. "You good?"

"Yeah, yeah, I'm good. Geez, day got away from me I guess."

Sarah laughs a little, and the strange tightness in the room lessens, some of the old familiarity, the warmth, slips back into the air. "I guess the desk works," she says.

"I'd say so, sure. I mean, I've been in a real trance here... uh, I mean..." He turns his gaze toward the window, and the last of the daylight, then looks back toward her, the room so dark he can't even make out her face. She's nothing but a shadow among shadows.

*And what must I look like to her? A troll beneath the bridge. Stinking of piss and sweat and blood.*

"Listen, babe, let me finish up here and then I'm gonna take a hot shower. I really stink. Don't come too close, huh?"

She nods, as if grateful. "I'm gonna start dinner, if that's okay. Just wanted to let you know."

"Perfect, I'm starved," he says, meaning it. His stomach is clenched, gurgling in frustration, pissed-off and ready to be fed. "Give me twenty minutes to clean up and I'll be there."

"Sounds good." She starts to turn away, then stops. "Sorry, honey... but I've gotta ask. What are you working on?"

His eyes flick to the screen.

The witch bent backward, arched and taut, her pale breasts moonlit; dark hair spilled like ink over the smooth stone. She burned hot inside, wanting the blade, *needing* the blood and the pain so the sacrifice would be complete. The robed figure approached. A hooked knife appeared like magic in his curled palm, a glittering needle among expanses of flowing black robe. Without a word he thrust it into her side. She gasped in a sort of ecstasy as he let it glide up and through her, the soft flesh separating...

Tyson swallows a lump in his throat, winces at the sight of blood on the keyboard. *Clean up in aisle five,* he thinks.

"Oh, you know, the overdue novel. Tick-tock, tick-tock..."

"Sure, I figured. Well, that's good, right? See you in a bit." Sarah leaves the room, closes the door behind her.

Tyson lets out a held breath, looks down at his mangled fingers, sucks a smear of blood from the split fingertip—his pack leader. He flexes his hands, gasps at the immediate surge of fresh pain, then sighs with relief when he feels the muscles and tendons loosening, relaxing. He turns his attention to the laptop once more, momentarily forgetting the gurgle of his stomach, the calls of pain from his body, the urine cooling against his balls, leg, and ankle. Oh, the sweet *shame* of it all.

He runs his eyes over the words again, praying for some recognition.

"It's not *bad*," he says, but the words sound false even as he speaks them.

Meanwhile, the part of his brain that mans the giant red *Emergencies Only* lever goes into action, yanking down on the handle to let beautiful disillusionment pour into his thought cells, soothe any unwanted emotional upheavals caused by the inexplicable. Filling his mind with much-needed rationale.

*Oh yeah, sure... NOW I remember. OF COURSE. Boy, ha-ha, I'd forgotten I'd written that part, but oh yeah, it's all coming back to me now. Sure as rain on a gray day, you betcha.*

Feeling more assured, his eyes drift to the lower-left corner of the Word program, where the word-count number resides. Disbelieving, he lowers his head closer to the screen, as if the number might change; as if his eyes have tricked him, or he's misread...

**54792 words**

"I'll be damned," he says quietly, as if not believing.

As if afraid.

Grimacing, he hits the command-S key combo twice, making doubly-sure the work is saved. As he stands, desperate to shower, praying the coast from the office to the bedroom is clear of girlfriends and daughters, he wonders just how much of the book he has left to write.

He is only mildly concerned at the realization that he has absolutely no idea.

# TWENTY-THREE

ON SUNDAY, Tyson does his best to stay away from the office. He's still sore from yesterday's marathon session, and the split skin of his fingertip stings annoyingly. His hands are sore and tight, riddled with cramps.

To force himself away from the desk, he agrees to chaperone Sarah and Violet to Cinema Village for an early-afternoon matinee (a documentary about some modern painter he's never heard of). The theater, upon arrival, is mostly empty, and they easily find seats center-screen and settle in for the film. As the lights dim, Tyson sinks back, lets his mind wander.

After the movie, they'd all grab a quick lunch, maybe stop by the Strand Book Store, where he always fixated on what Tyson Parks titles they had in stock (and made sure to harass whoever was on desk duty to order more if necessary). He'd also sign whatever was there (assuming something was there), which he still got a thrill from, even after all these years. Before the food and books, however, he'll have to make it through the next couple hours of low-budget documentary filmmaking. He sighs heavily, ignores a sidelong glare from Sarah, and does his very best to give a shit.

As trailers for other documentaries he'll never watch play out on the screen, he stares fixedly down at the fabric Band-Aid strapped to the end of his damaged finger. He taps it against his leg, hoping the sting will help him remember what the hell he'd written the day before—just a snippet, a scene, a character... but nothing comes to him. He presses the bandage between two fingers of his alternate hand, gives the tip a little squeeze, hard enough to make him grimace with pain.

A trickle of blood slides from under the bandage and down his finger to the knuckle. Irritated, he sticks the bloody finger into his mouth and sucks, dirty Band-Aid and all.

From the seat behind him, a man starts laughing. A bit hysterically, Tyson thinks, since absolutely nothing funny is happening on the screen. *Unless a subtitled trailer about Indonesian genocide tickles your funny bone, that is.* He turns, curious what anyone could possibly be laughing about during such a tedious, artsy-fartsy screening as this one...

...and sees nothing but empty seats.

No laughing man. No *nobody*. The theater is practically empty, and the dozen or so rows between him and the back wall—where the single projection window glows like the eye of an electric cyclops—are unoccupied.

Frowning, he turns around and nearly screams when he sees a leering, white-haired old man staring back at him from the seat directly in front of his own.

*There was no one there,* he thinks frantically. *I remember... that seat was empty. Come on you guys, it was EMPTY.*

Tyson sits, hunched and tensed, waiting for the old guy to spring at him like a ghastly Jack-in-the-Box, or at least say something, *anything*—complain about them talking, or whine about Tyson bumping his seat—something to confirm his normality. His *reality*. But the bastard just sits there, head turned like a demon-possessed little girl, *staring* at Tyson, as if in anticipation of something, the likes of which Tyson cannot fathom.

Because the screen shines brightly from behind the man's head (which Tyson thinks looks sort of like a shriveled walnut with a halo of luminescent bleach-white hair), he can't clearly make out the details of the stranger's face. Mouth, eyes, and nose are trenched in deep shadow, backlit by the large projection of an old woman in a pink wig painting dots on a canvas the size of a house. Tyson slowly turns his head to see what Sarah's reaction to the strange man might be, but her eyes are forward as she carelessly plunks popcorn into her mouth, hypnotically chewing, eyes glazed silver by the glow of the film.

"Bedwetter!" the old guy snaps, his voice a gravelly, roughened whisper.

"Excuse me?" Tyson says, and is surprised—and more than slightly annoyed—to hear Sarah *shush* him quietly.

The silhouette of the man's oddly shaped head turns back around. He says nothing further, and sinks low into his seat, effectively disappearing from Tyson's view. A few minutes later, Tyson hears him laughing again—again, for no discernable reason at all—and he wonders if he'd previously misheard the laugh as coming from *behind* him.

*Because it's the same laugh, I'm sure of it.*

Tyson gnaws a knuckle on his right hand, fighting the urge to confront the man, to wring his bony neck until he shuts the hell up. Instead, he grimaces and focuses on the film.

*No sense ruining the afternoon,* he thinks. He makes the executive decision to forego the remainder of the documentary, and closes his eyes.

---

WHEN THE movie ends (and he's elbowed awake by Sarah), Tyson quickly stands up, only half-pretending to stretch the stiffened muscles of his lower back, arching forward to study the row of seats in front of him.

The old man is not there and, for reasons Tyson can't put his finger on, he isn't the least bit surprised.

# TWENTY-FOUR

OUTSIDE THE theater, Tyson spends ten minutes trying to hail a cab. Sarah offers to walk to the corner and try her luck on 5th Avenue.

"No, no, I mean, it can't be this hard, not in this area. Here!"

A taxi with a lit sign slings itself recklessly across two lanes and rubs the curb in front of the theater. Tyson turns to Sarah and Violet, a smile on his face. "Still have a bit of the old hunter-gatherer in me!"

Violet rolls her eyes and Sarah starts to reply when her face flips from amused to annoyed. "Hey!" she yells, eyes focused on something behind Tyson.

Tyson spins around in time to see a young, heavily-bearded hipster popping open the back door of their taxi.

*MY taxi.*

"Hey, bud!" Tyson barks, but the man ignores him as he climbs into the backseat. Tyson steps briskly toward the car. "I said hey, man! What the fuck!"

The hipster offers Tyson a smirk and a brief, dismissive glance from behind round, green-tinted glasses, then shuts the door, already mouthing instructions to the driver, who seems none-too-worried about the apparent heist of his services. At the car, Tyson slams a fist on the taxi's roof, lowers his face to stare into the window.

"Look at me, COCKSUCKER!" he roars, and punches the window with a fist.

The hipster looks less amused now. He shifts in the seat to move away from the window. The driver yells something indecipherable. Tyson doesn't give a shit. "This is my cab, asshole!" he yells, stabbing a finger at the man. "I'll rip your fucking face off! I'll stab out your fucking eyes, you hear me?" He jerks at the door handle, ready to make good on his threat. The doors have been locked, but that only infuriates Tyson even further. "I'll fucking find you, and I'll fucking KILL YOU!"

Tyson's voice is thundering, his eyes wide and wild. He presses his face flat to the window, eyeballing the slack-jawed passenger who is now yelling frantically at the driver to *Get out of here!* The driver accommodates, shoving the ancient gearstick into DRIVE and goosing the gas pedal.

The cab tears away with a squeal and a cough of smoke, knocking Tyson back a step from the curb. He unleashes a final, swift kick-in-the-ass to the fender as the car shoots forward. Tyson takes three steps into the street, as if he has every intention of following the cab into traffic. Instead, he shakes a fist in the air, his face bright red. "If I ever see you again, I'll murder you! I'll murder your fucking wife! I'll kill your fucking children! Rip out your goddamn throats! You hear me? You'll all DIE!"A hand pinches his elbow and he spins, spittle flying from his chin. "What!"

Sarah stands at his side, her hand pulling back from his arm as if shocked, her expression a mask of fear and confusion. Violet stands on the sidewalk, mouth hanging open.

"Jesus, Tyson! Honey... relax. It's just a taxi. There are others. We can..."

"Fuck others," he grumbles, but allows her to pull him out of the street. He ignores the honk of a passing car, the small cluster of people watching the show from outside the theater. He wipes his mouth with the back of a hand, takes a deep breath. "Okay, yeah... sorry about that. Fucking thief."

"Why don't we walk, huh? Ribalta is good for lunch, and it's just a few blocks. Then we can go to the Strand, okay?"

Tyson nods, gives her a weak smile. "Yeah, sure. That sounds aces, hon."

He wants to say something comforting to his daughter, but Violet has already begun walking ahead, moving fast, as if wanting to put distance between herself and her madman of a father. He settles with taking Sarah's hand in his, suddenly calm, almost happy.

As they walk, he tries to forget the images that had come into his mind only moments ago—the vivid, colorful ones that showed him all the different ways he could have torn that fucking thief apart, limb-from-limb. Beat him to death in the street until he was nothing more than a pile of hot bloody meat.

He breathes in deeply and gives Sarah's hand a reassuring squeeze, feeling hungrier by the second.

---

**BACK AT** home from their lunch and an all-too-brief visit to the Strand by 4 P.M., Tyson is able to sneak a few hours in his office, ostensibly to get some more writing done.

He's caught off guard, however, when Sarah knocks on the door and announces dinner. He is about to complain that he'd *just sat down, for Christ's sake* when he notices the darkened windows. The vintage Black Forest cuckoo clock on the wall, a gift from Billy for Tyson's 40th birthday, which features carvings of two black ravens in mid-scream, shows it to be nearly nine o'clock at night.

*Five hours...* he thinks, feeling a chill so strong he shivers. Not only had he not written anything...

He hadn't even made it to the chair.

Tyson is on the opposite side of the desk, facing those words—DO THIS IN REMEMBRANCE OF ME—and he's *kneeling*. His hands are spread out wide, like the arms of a revivalist preacher calling forth the power of the Holy Spirit. His body is slick with sweat, his shirt and boxers soaked through. The muscles in his arms tremble violently from the strain of keeping them aloft, and his knees are so viciously cramped that he nearly cries out trying to straighten them as he stands, leaning on the desk for support.

"Be right out!" he says cheerfully, staring wildly at his hands, which shake so badly he has to squeeze them into fists just to get his damn nerves under control.

After a moment to collect himself (and get the feeling back into his legs), he sneaks out of the office and to the upstairs bathroom, where he takes three Advil, swallowing them with a palmful of tap water from the sink. He stops at his dresser and changes into a dry T-shirt, figuring the sodden boxers can wait.

When he finally makes it to the dinner table, where the women are not-so-patiently waiting, he slugs two glasses of cabernet in quick succession before taking a bite. Luckily, Sarah and Violet are also drinking their share, too busy chatting and eating to observe the speed of his intake. It's only about ten minutes into the meal before Sarah comments, with mild surprise, that the first bottle is long gone, and the second is crying for mercy. She looks at him curiously, then down at his glass. Tyson thinks she is about to say something when Violet breaks in, saving him the need to make more excuses for his behavior.

"Heading back to Providence in a couple days," she announces casually, ripping a roll in half and slathering it with enough butter to clog Tyson's arteries by proximity alone.

"Oh?" Tyson says casually, trying (and failing) to hide his disappointment.

"Tuesday, actually. A few of my friends who stayed in town during break are getting together. Probably be gone two nights, three at the most."

Tyson glances at Sarah, who's having an even harder time masking her unhappiness at the news than he is. "But honey, you just got here. And who are these friends? Do I know them?"

Violet rolls her eyes, stands abruptly, and begins clearing dishes to the sink. "I don't think so, Dad. I'm sorry you guys,

I don't mean to bum you out. But look, I'll be back for the entire rest of break, okay?"

"I'll get that, Violet," Sarah says, but having had a few glasses of wine herself, makes no move to stand. "Do any of these friends happen to be a boyfriend? Or is this more of a, you know, platonic gathering?" Sarah gives Tyson a sly, if unsteady, wink. He smiles back, albeit weakly, his stomach clenching at the thought. *Oh please, not yet, Lord. Not yet. Let me keep my baby girl a little while longer...*

Violet doesn't bother replying to Sarah's question, a rare rudeness for which, in this case, Tyson is grateful. When Sarah finally stands to help Violet with the cleanup, he sits back, content, and studies the two women in a state of peaceful repose, standing hip-to-hip at the sink, whispering like schoolgirls. He knows he should help as well, but he's tired through-and-through. Besides, he enjoys seeing them together like this—at home, within reach—happy and tipsy and content. So, instead, he plays it lazy and stays seated at the table with his glass of wine, watching the two most important people in his life engage in light conversation as they sip from their own freshened glasses at the counter, letting hot water run into a sink full of soapy foam and plates covered with the remains of penne arrabbiata and Caesar salad.

As he sits there, smiling and sipping cabernet sauvignon, watching the women work, he's surprised to find himself wondering what it would be like to see their insides.

# TWENTY-FIVE

THE MEDITERRANEAN stretches vast and blue outside Diana's window. The new day exhaling cool morning air through the open doors of her terrace, the sea's breath licking her bare skin—kissing eyelids, cheeks, lips; gently tousling her hair. She smiles and moans with pleasure, as if being wakened by a lover. Despite the chill breeze, she pulls the soft silk sheet off her body, exposing herself fully to the salty air, relishing the way it whispers through the sheer white fabric of the door's curtains to discover her bed, and linger.

She stretches her long body, loosening taut muscles, olive-toned skin contrasting warmly with the cream-colored sheets. She doesn't want to open her eyes, to spoil the glorious effects of a new morning. Her spill of black hair is thrown carelessly across the down pillow, tickling her face, her shoulders. Her muscles this morning are wonderfully sore, from both her long swim in the sea at Mala beach the previous afternoon and the passionate night of sex with the woman she'd picked up at the Saphir bar in Monaco late last night. She recalls how they had laughed and kissed and stumbled their way back to her villa via the coastal path, remembers them both stopping to take off their heels, yelling sweet curses as they threw them into the bay, walking barefoot the rest of the way, the ancient cobblestones cool and smooth beneath their feet.

Diana rolls over, putting her back to the terrace facing the sea, and finally opens her eyes to the new day. The sun-drenched sheets, ignited with a peach glow, lay like a rumpled mountain ridge between her and the slender, dark brown back of the stranger in her bed, the rest of her hidden away beneath the fabric.

*So beautiful,* she thinks… then finds herself pushing away the small spark of irritation that the woman is still there, invading her morning. That was the downside to bringing home strays for a much-needed night of sex, you had to put them out when you were done—back into the streets of Cote d'Azur, leave them to wander into other homes, other beds.

Despite her annoyance, Diana replays the previous night's lovemaking in her head, wondering if the girl might be worth keeping around for breakfast, if only for another hour of having her mouth between her legs. Her lips curl into a languid smile, the one that can capture a man or woman from across a room, pull them to her as if tied by a string (and if that didn't work, there were other means).

*Yes,* she thinks, her lust waking with her body, reaching for that lovely shoulder, *another hour will do just fine.*

A brazen melody breaks the spell. Brow furrowed, Diana pulls back her hand, raises her head from the pillow, eyes searching the room. *Where is the damned thing?*

Her black dress is spilled over an antique, pink-cushioned Eleanor chair on the far side of the room, still resting where it had been tossed and forgotten the night before. Somewhere among its folds her cell phone sings for her attention. The sleeping girl groans and shifts her body, spurring Diana into action. The last thing she needs is the dreaded, and forced, "good morning" smirk from a meaningless lover.

She swings her legs out of bed and walks briskly across the room, ignoring the brilliant blue of the open sea beckoning from the open doors, no longer as tantalized by that chill breeze that now raises goosebumps on her exposed and unwashed skin.

"Fait chier..." she says, hands yanking at the folds of her dress to reach the source of the repeating melody. Finally, her fingers feel the tremble of the phone's vibration and she snatches it up, staring at the screen. "Ah..." she says, the rising anger quenched by possibility. The phone number is unlisted, but stamped with the country code for America.

She answers eagerly. "Oui, allo?"

"Madamoiselle Monstresor." The man's voice is deep and direct, her name a statement. She knows immediately who it is, and the thrill rushing through her body causes a shiver.

"Un instant, s'il vous plait," she says quietly.

*Please God, tell me the hunt is finally over...*

Shooting a quick glance toward the sleeping girl, Diana strides onto the balcony, closing the doors behind her. The sun is warmer now, and the reflection of countless sapphire gems winks at her from the surface of the Mediterranean. She knows her nude body is fully exposed to an entire coastline of tightly bunched villas and curling pathways, even the Russian-inspired spires of St. Nicholas, but modesty is not something she concerns herself with, especially not now, not with this man's voice in her ear.

*Tell me,* she thinks, but says only, softly, in a perfect American accent: "Yes."

"Diana," the man says, the satisfaction in his voice evident, even from a continent away. "I've found it."

---

AN HOUR later, Diana Montresor is showered, dressed, and packed. The girl has been sent away, her flare of hurt and shame at the curt dismissal unnoticed by Diana amidst her quickly made plans. *Finally...*

A car is on the way to drive her to Nice, where she will catch a flight to JFK. She's already called ahead to the building manager who will see that her New York City apartment is cleaned and freshly stocked prior to her arrival. The private detective will be meeting her for a debrief and supply her with the other item she'd requested.

Per her instructions, he'd stopped short of confronting the artifact's current owner with any information, it's enough for now that he knows the exact location, and further details that will assist her brokering of a deal with this supposed "famous" writer she's never heard of. Regardless, the American detective has done enough for now.

She wants to do the rest herself.

As the black SUV pulls up to her villa—windows tinted, body polished to a high-gloss—she gives a silent prayer of thanks her search will soon come to an end. Her dying grandfather will know that she has succeeded, and her ancestors can finally rest in peace.

*There can be no mistakes now. It's time to end things. Once and for all.*

Diana watches from the window of her second-floor office as the dark-suited driver steps from the car, and smiles. It is a very different smile than the one she uses to lasso lovers from a bar. If the girl from last night were here now, she would see no welcome or warmth in it, and the eyes she would have recalled as being deep-brown, sensuous, and lustful would be replaced by ones that are wide, hungry, and not brown at all, but black as a starless night.

# Part Five

# VIOLENT BEGINNINGS

# TWENTY-SIX

TYSON SLAMS the door to his office, paces back and forth, back and forth, clenching and unclenching his fists as he digs a tread into the large oriental rug. He goes to the floor lamp—the stand a cheap Pottery Barn iron turnbuckle design, the beige drum shade dingy from age and a thin coat of dust—and clicks it on.

He doesn't notice or care about the tired-looking old man—the very same laughing hyena from the movie theater, the one who called him a *bedwetter!*—now sits in his brown leather club chair, better known within Chateau Parks as Tyson's personal reading chair.

"Don't need this shit don't need it don't need it don't NEED IT!" he says as he paces, eyes wide and wet, face contorted into an ugly, anxious frown that tics occasionally into an angry sneer. Spittle flies from his lips and his heart hammers inside his chest as adrenaline rides like a runaway train through his veins. Dark thoughts tumble and toss like an angry sea, his mind caught within a savage storm in full gale. A deep, dangerous thunder rumbles ominously, deep in his brain, reverberating inside his head as if it were an echo chamber.

The right side of his face is stamped by three blood-red streaks that run from the corner of his eye to the top of his lip. Where she'd *hurt* him. Where that bitch had *attacked* him.

He stops pacing, one of his stormy thoughts igniting like a beacon. "I should SUE her!" he yells, his voice so loud in the enclosed room that he winces at the sudden break of silence, the harsh violence of his own enraged voice causing him to recoil.

*It's assault,* the man in the chair says, his blind, milky eyes bulbous with excitement beneath his bald, misshapen head.

Tyson nods, as if hearing the man's words. *But he didn't actually speak, did he? No no no... that wrinkled old mouth didn't move, it stayed tight and stretched, those bloodless lips dull gray against pale white, like two fat worms at rest.*

"Either that, or have her arrested," Tyson says, lowering his voice. "It's assault, goddammit!" He touches the fresh wounds and winces. He inspects his battered fingertips, sees the traces of drying blood. *Damn her. Damn her to HELL.*

*Perhaps you should do worse than sue her, friend. I think she needs to be punished, don't you? An eye for an eye and all that. The Bible says it, friend.*

"Punish her, yeah. Okay, yeah, I see that..." Tyson mumbles, tasting the words on his tongue, unsure how they arrived there. "God DAMN her, though!" he roars suddenly, and he could have sworn the old buzzard in the chair flinched a little. Just a little.

"Okay, okay, let's relax here," he says, his breath coming in deep gulps. He needs to calm down enough to think straight, remember back on it, recreate what led to her violence. For the life of him, he simply cannot understand what—what exactly—even happened...

How did everything go so terribly, terribly *wrong?*

"First, we ate dinner..." he begins stoically, as if recounting the facts to a box of dull-eyed jurors in a courtroom.

Then he'd opened another bottle of wine and watched some television with Violet. When his daughter went up to her room, he and Sarah decided to retire early. They were both wiped out from the past couple days' events.

While they undressed, Sarah told him the story about the warehouse worker whose leg had been broken by the desk. She said the guy who sold it to her—*Anthony* or *Anton* or some other shit—called her to see how the desk had gone over. She asked about the injured worker's well-being, and when she asked, then *insisted*, on hearing about the poor man, this *Anton—I think that's what it was, yes, that's the bastard's name all right*—reluctantly told her that the worker had died; the trauma and blood loss apparently too much for his body to handle.

*Why the hell is she telling me this?* he thought as he brushed his teeth, watching her carefully in the mirror's reflection as she leaned in the doorframe, wearing a silk robe and not much else. *And who the hell is this* Anton *anyway?* His eyes narrowed, and he watched her more closely as she talked and talked and talked...

*Oh my, aren't you SAD?* he thought. *Aren't you just ALL broken up into tiny little itty-bitty pieces?* Yes, yes... he watched her *closely*. Looked for tells, for some sort of give-away in her tone, in her expressions.

*That desk must have cost a fortune. I'm sure this Anton prick likely gave her a great deal. The old friends and family discount, uh-huh. I'm sure they worked something out, all right. Hell, they were probably* still *finalizing the details on that transaction. Oh yeah, that was a big ten-four good buddy. That was a DIRECT HIT. He could tell now, now that he* knew. *He could look at her and SEE she'd slept with this prick, this young, handsome devil of a salesman. The slut.*

"Well, that's about the worst thing I've ever heard," he said, then spit a mouthful of water, saliva, and toothpaste into the sink. "So, if I'm getting this right, you're telling me my birthday gift is a murderer."

"Oh, come on, you know that's not..." Sarah said, and gave him a severe look. "I'm not trying to tarnish anything. I don't know. I mean, I *saw* it happen, Ty. It was awful. And to know that poor man's dead. Just awful."

"Yeah, it's pretty bad all right," he said, rubbing his face with a hand towel. "But hey, nice of Anton to call and give you the update, huh? I guess I should be grateful he didn't knock on the door during the party to let us know the horrible news. I mean, that would have been equally appropriate, don't you think?"

Sarah glared at him icily, and in the far reaches of his mind he felt the burn of shame.

He ignored it.

"I *asked* him about it, Tyson. He had called to make sure you liked the desk, and I asked about the man who'd been injured. He didn't even want to tell me! I forced it out of him."

*I bet you did. I bet you're real good at making him do* EXACTLY *what you want. Ho boy, I just bottom-dollar betcha.*

"Okay, okay," he said, and gave her a wan smile as he walked out of the bathroom and turned off the light. "I don't mean to be insensitive."

He sensed her soften. When you'd been with someone as long as they'd been, emotions became palpable things that existed in the ether, physical energy that could hurt, anger, or comfort. He'd countered her *anger* energy with a puff of *comfort*, and the two feelings had meshed gracefully together to form *inconsequential*. Soon, it would dissipate altogether into *forgotten*, like everything else.

If emotions were a religion, the Bible would be alcohol and Jesus would be a good night's sleep—that which forgives all. And Sleep Jesus was exactly what he needed right now. *Badly*.

After the lights were out and she'd climbed into bed with him, he tried to let go of the events of the last few days: the amnesia-filled marathon session at the desk, the humiliation of pissing his pants, the strangeness of finding himself kneeling on the office floor, the laughing old timer at the theater...

Unbidden, he suddenly envisioned the desk dropping like a black-death school bus from the sky and crushing that idiot warehouse worker's leg. He could almost *see* the blood spraying across the concrete, hear the throat-tearing screams.

He smiled in the dark as he thought about the scene. After a moment, he realized that smiling was probably not an appropriate response. Neither, for that matter, was the giggle bubbling at the back of his throat.

*Just what in the hell is wrong with me?*

He brushed away the images and the thick cobwebs of confused emotions, the garbled thought patterns. He tried instead to focus on his work, to try and remember the novel he'd spent so much time writing. One of his favorite things to do when working on a book was to think about the next parts while falling asleep, and again when waking up, those lucid-dream states where the mind was untethered by reality, letting the imagination project wonderful scenes in bright, full color and crystal-clear sound. But he couldn't think about what was coming next because he couldn't remember what he'd *already* written… and it was frustrating the bejesus out of him.

What was the story? Where had the idea—the *words*—even come from? Was it based on the novel he'd already done? Had he simply modernized it, like Harry had requested?

He recalled something about witches and men in black robes; blood sacrifices under the moonlight. Gothic crap. It sure didn't sound very modern. Cliché, perhaps. But not modern.

Frustrated at the cage of thoughts he found himself trapped within, his mind snarling and pacing like a tiger, he decided to try and simply turn his brain off altogether, hit the big ON/OFF light switch inside his head, slow the spinning wheels cranking away in his thick skull, and get some much-needed sleep.

Ready to do just that, he'd rolled over and lain an arm across Sarah's warm body. He slid his hand gently high, then low. *Naked,* he realized, and felt his pulse quicken as a rush of blood flowed to his cock, which stiffened to sledgehammer strength so fast it was as like he'd thrown the wrong damn switch.

*Coulda sworn I'd hit the one that said* OFF, *boss. Musta flipped* HORNY *by mistake!*

Tyson pulled off his boxers and rolled on top of her. At first, she groaned ambivalently, pushed him away, mumbled some bullshit about being tired.

*Pretend I'm Anton, honey,* he thought, and the idea of her cheating, the *image* of her with another man, made him even harder, his need more urgent.

He kissed her hungrily and, without much preamble, pushed himself roughly into her.

"Oh," she said, sounding suddenly very awake, surprised, and—*possibly, I guess, yeah okay, just possibly*—like he may have even hurt her a little.

*And then what?* he thinks now. Because, truth be told, the rest is a bit of a blur.

He remembers feeling more randy than he'd felt in *years,* and her body felt so warm, so soft. He could almost FEEL the blood rushing like a wild river beneath her skin. Then... okay, right... then he'd risen to his knees, thrown aside the bedcovers, lifted her bottom from the mattress, and moved faster, *faster.*

She'd said... *what?* Something like: "Slow down..."

But it was as if he couldn't hear her, as if she was speaking to someone else completely. Someone in a different place, a different world, a different time.

"Okay... okay... HEY!" she'd said... well, *yelled*, really, now that he thought about it.

In response to her telling him to back off he'd flipped her over with a grunt, then thrust himself into her from behind and she'd... oh God... she'd *screamed*.

Or...

Yeah, SCREAMED something at him.

Was that right? *Could* that be right?

The rest is so damned hard to piece together! He remembers that he'd gripped her very hard. And... yeah, that's right, he'd put his hand over her face. Covering her mouth. But that was to stop her from screaming, which makes sense, right? He didn't want her to wake Violet, that's all. It would have been embarrassing.

But she kept at it. Kept screaming.

So he'd grabbed her by the back of the neck, and pushed her face down into the pillow...

"STOP! FUCKING STOP!" Her muffled cries.

She was crying... sobbing... *and he didn't care.*

But then she'd kicked out with her heel, caught him square in the stomach. He bent like a tin can and fell backward toward the foot of the bed. She'd spun, gasping for air, crying and cursing and she began to punch him, hit him, slap him.

*She was out of control. I had to stop her. I...*

He can't recall the details...

*Had he hit her?*

NO.

*Impossible!*

But... maybe.

*Yes, okay, maybe I gave her a light slap.*

Then she'd clawed at his face, nails scratching three neat trenches into the flesh of his cheek, and *he'd* screamed—no, he'd HOWLED—and leapt from the bed, grabbing his boxers from the floor and all but running out the door, down the stairs, like a monster driven away into the night, a vampire who'd been shown a crucifix. A dark spirit cast out.

"Fuck you fuck you FUCK YOU!" Her screams followed him into the hall, down the stairs. Continued to batter him as he ran away, moaning, grunting obscenities...

Tyson stops pacing. Unclenches his fists. His breathing steadies, his eyes go wide.

*Had* he hit her?

Had he struck a woman? His partner? The love of his life?

"Oh, dear God..." he says, and his knees weaken, his stomach flips over, his spine turns ice-cold. "Oh, sweet Jesus, what have I done? Oh no, oh my God, Sarah..."

"Relax, relax," says the decrepit geezer in the chair, and this time he *is* speaking. The abrasive, ancient voice scraping the air like sandpaper on skin.

The part of Tyson's brain—the fairly small, mostly unused part hiding deep in the middle, beneath all those useful tactile and visual lobes, the sliver of gray matter reserved for a human being's rare need to skew reality, to find a way to logically interpret the supernatural—sparks to life, a minor neural awakening that allows him to start *believing* what's happening to him. To finally accept what's been sitting in front of him this entire time.

In other words, he can finally *see* the fucker.

He notes, for example, that the geezer is wearing an antediluvian, loosely-tied cravat the color of mud over a shriveled, stained collar. A sack-coat jacket, frayed and rumpled, sags over the angles of his bony frame. If Tyson had seen him on the street, he would have pegged him as a steampunk survivor, sprung from the dusty pages of an H.G. Wells novel.

"You're the guy from the theater. How are you..." Tyson mumbles absently, his brain fuzzy, a buzzing white static crowding his clear-headedness.

"If you ask me, she deserved it. Deserved ALL of it, if you ask me."

Suddenly the hoary sack of bones is blabbering like a gossipy housewife, chatting up Tyson like they're a couple old-timers rocking on a wooden porch, as if they're the very best of friends...

And they are. Aren't they? The very *best* of pals?

Tyson takes a step toward the reading chair, staring dull-eyed, as if hypnotized... then turns toward the office door. "I should apologize. Make sure she's okay. I..."

He no longer wants to look at, or acknowledge, the shriveled, pupilless creature in the chair. The filthy old man that simply *could not* be there. He doesn't want to hear what the nasty old buzzard is saying, doesn't like the way the words catch and scratch like a worn-out vinyl record.

Besides, there *is* no man. He isn't there. Of course not.

That would be impossible.

"Maybe, instead of all this drama with the woman, we focus, okay?" the not-there-man says reasonably, almost pleadingly. "Besides, she's sinful, that one. Sin-sin-sinful. I suggest, Mr. Parks, that we focus on our story."

Tyson nods. Yeah, that feels right. That feels *good.* Sure, he'll get some writing done. Forget about all this nonsense. Sarah and her feelings. Sarah and her stories of murder and accidents.

He walks across the office and clicks on the desk lamp, then lays a hand atop the desk, pressing his palm against the dark stone surface. His skin prickles with an excitement so sharp he might have described it as touching a live wire, one that pulses with a mild, but powerful, electric current.

In the deep shadows of the office, lit warmly by the varied pools of light, the desk looks haunted and beautiful. It looks... *vast.* Black and heavy and gnarled, and yet it glistens like a new car, a shiny black car painted the color of outer space. It looks like it has its own *inner light*, its own internal source of radiance. As if it sheltered a beating heart born from a distant, gaseous star.

As Tyson stares in dumb wonder, the ivy tendrils clinging to the sides of the desk slither along its surface, then lift free, wave gently in the air, beckoning him closer. Beckoning him to sit.

"Yeah? You sure?" There's a dry smile on his face—a mischievous, but knowing, smile—as if he's getting permission from his high school sweetheart to unsnap her bra, feel the rush of happiness, of *belonging*, from cupping a warm, bare breast for the very first time.

He feels the same sensuous thrill fondling the waving, wood-carved vines.

As the sprung twines of ivy brush against him playfully, he runs a hand along the desk's surface, caressing it as he would Sarah's bare back when she lay next to him, moaning softly from the pleasure of his touch.

He giggles like the village idiot as tips of the sharp stems reach up and entangle his palm, his fingers, his forearm. The whole desk seems to swell, as if taking a deep breath in, then letting it out. Tyson can almost hear its heartbeat—that great, black star of a heart hidden deep beneath the symbols and engravings pulses ever stronger, ever louder, a distant planet sending sonic waves through space that's just now reaching his puny, human brain.

Tyson gently pulls his arm free of the branches, walks around to his chair and sits down. Dreamily, he opens the laptop.

Sensing motion, he lifts his eyes and—like a boy wakened from a sweet dream to find a madman staring down at him in his bed—he jerks backward, sucking in a fearful, disgusted breath.

The old man is hunched at the edge of the desk. He'd moved impossibly fast, deadly silent. This close, Tyson notices those wide, white eyes are smeared with inky black wisps that drift across his eyeballs like thin, gray clouds across a pale sky. His face is puckered and coarse with brittle hairs, his head bald and misshapen. Cratered. As if his skull had been broken inward at some point. At Tyson's fright the old man chuckles, coughs, then hocks something suspiciously brown onto the floor.

"What comes next?" Tyson rasps, forcing himself to look away from the ghost, the figment of his imagination, and back to the laptop, to the climbing word count in the lower corner of the screen. He moves the blinking cursor to the bottom of the last block of text, focuses on the white page, on a reality he still understands.

In response, a steady chorus of whispers rise from the desk. The leaves from the hovering strands of ivy rustle words and ideas, as if blown by a hard breeze only they can feel.

The gruesome faces carved into the wood begin to mumble prose. Tyson fights against the feeling of being in a strange and powerful temple, listening to chants and prayers of the mad congregants.

In his mind the temple is black, the altar covered in blood, the worshippers leprous.

"Yes, I see it now."

Strange and horrible visions flood Tyson's splintering mind. He nods, momentarily pausing to let this new train of ideas assemble in his head. Then he brings his hands to the computer, surprised he isn't bothered by the sticky keys, or distracted by the messy patches of dried brown stains stamped across the screen where, when closed, it had pressed against bloody letters.

It doesn't matter because he doesn't need to see the words. He isn't worried about phrasing, or plot, or dialogue. All those usual hang-ups are flushed away as he listens, and listens, and listens. The entire plot of the story is injected into him like a drug, a hot needle stabbed directly into his imagination, the words and sentences in his head building like skyscrapers of prose. Phrases become cities. Paragraphs become continents. Entire chapters flood his mind with a speed and clarity he would have never thought possible.

It's so simple.

He just has to listen.

Listen, and write exactly what he's told.

After a few moments, he closes his eyes and exhales slowly. It's all there, and he's giddy with it. He's *high* with it.

And when he's ready, when he has listened to it all, he opens his eyes, rests his fingers on the keyboard...

...and begins to write.

# TWENTY-SEVEN

SARAH STEPS into the kitchen a little after 8 A.M., thankful she doesn't work Mondays. If she did, she'd be calling in sick, because that's exactly how she feels.

*Sick. Damaged. Broken.*

Grateful once more that Violet is an early riser and a coffee drinker to boot, Sarah fills a large mug with the black elixir—no cream or sugar on this bright, shiny morning. No thanks. Black and strong. Something to clear the cobwebs. *And take away the memories…*

*Dear God, what HAPPENED last night?*

Sarah falls into a chair at the kitchen table, buries her face in her hands. *I won't cry, damn it. Not again.* There are footsteps on the stairs. Violet. Sarah sniffs and wipes invisible tears from her face, takes a sip of hot coffee—relishing the friendly burn in her throat, the spark of caffeine rushing to her head—then takes another. When Violet steps into the kitchen wearing a white hoodie and jeans, her dark hair pulled back in a loose ponytail, Sarah does her best to force a smile.

Regardless, Violet gives her an odd look, as if noticing something is *different* about Sarah, but not able to figure out what it is: A new haircut? Different shade of lipstick? Lost a few pounds, perhaps?

*Or maybe she looks abused?* Sarah thinks shakily. *Oh, and frightened. Sure, now I see it. She looks like someone whose partner of over a decade, a man who has never so much as raised his voice at her in anger...* raped *her last night. How's that for a diary entry? Uh-huh, yup, and when she tried to fight him off? He punched the side of her head with a closed fist! She'd never even been slapped before! So, that was interesting. Yes, last night was a most enlightening experience. A real eye-opener. Barriers were broken, ladies and gentlemen. Taboos tossed out. Think some real progress was made in the whole "physical play" arena. Whips and chains are on order, and we're deeply engrossed in the* Fifty Shades *trilogy, although it's still tricky not to see the main characters as those vampires from* Twilight*—that dimwit girl and the glittering asshole. But that's fan fiction for ya!*

"Are you okay?"

Sarah looks up sharply, unaware she'd been zoning out, lost in a tumultuous sea of black thoughts, the tiny boat of her sanity tossed amongst waves jagged as broken glass. She takes another drink of coffee, nods and smiles.

*Just nod and smile, nod and smile. That's how all the battered girls do it. Didn't you know? No? Oh, well, Tip #1, I guess. So much to learn...*

"I'm fine, thanks. How are... how did you sleep?"

Violet pours coffee into her own mug and turns, dark eyes suspicious, and leans against the counter. "Did you and Dad have a fight? I heard yelling last night. Woke me up from a pretty sweet dream, in fact."

Sarah smiles so brightly she can almost feel the sunbeams shooting out her asshole. *Most likely I look like a crazy person. Better work on that whole "masking the pain" thing.* She starts to reply, then feels her lips twitch, her bullshit smile falter. A tear falls down her cheek, but she's nodding, still nodding. "Oh, I..."

And then Violet, her coffee cup left behind, forgotten on the counter, is moving quickly toward her, bending down to embrace Sarah where she sits. "Oh my God, Mom, what happened?"

It's the *Mom* that finally does it, Sarah thinks. The straw that snapped the camel's back, as they say. Because it's at the word "mom" Sarah stops trying to mask the pain and instead wraps her arms around her daughter's neck, buries her face into the soft fabric of her sweatshirt, and sobs so hard it takes all her effort not to simply start screaming instead.

# TWENTY-EIGHT

TYSON STANDS in the dark. He feels nothing. Sees nothing.

All around him, endless darkness. A boundless void that he's trapped within.

"Hello?" he yells. The word drifts into the stale air then dissipates, devoured by the vacuous dark.

But as he listens more closely, perhaps hoping for a response, for some sign of life... there *is* a sound. A repeating *TROMP TROMP TROMP*... the volume steadily increasing as if an army were marching closer, closer.

*Like the monkeys in the* Wizard of Oz. *But they didn't march, they FLEW, didn't march at all, they flew...*

But he recognizes that sound. Something about it is intimately *familiar.*

Frightened, Tyson runs. First in one direction, but when the sound grows louder, he turns and runs off a different way, terrified of what's coming, of *who* is coming.

He hears music. Singing. Out of breath, he stops running, puts his hands on his knees, panting... and listens. *It's a song,* he thinks. *And it's one I know. Sure, I know this! I was a child, and my brother and I would put on the record and listen to it over and over and over and we'd laugh and laugh...*

...to a man's voice. A haunted man. A *trapped* man.

*Remember when you ran away and I got on my knees and begged you not to leave?*

*WELL!*

In the dark, Tyson smiles. He *does* know this. A song by... *Napoleon* something... the singer wore a paper hat. The chorus is so familiar, and the tune floods him with memories from his childhood: his poor dead brother, his broken parents who always fought, who always struggled...

*They're coming to take me away Ha-Ha, they're coming to take me away, Ho-Ho, Hee-Hee, Ha-Ha, to the FUNNY FARM...*

"Yes, I remember," he says, his voice musty and lifeless in the ebon void. He feels a hand on his elbow and turns, looks down to see the old blind man, face tilted up toward his own, shriveled and bitter and poisoned. "To the funny farm," he tells the old man.

"Not for you, no, not for you," he mumbles, his breath rank, his blackened tongue rolling between stubbed, broken brown teeth. "Other plans. Big plans for you. For *us*."

The music swells louder, and Tyson winces because it's echoing around in his head and now there's a dull, throbbing pain in his right temple, which he rubs at until the skin feels raw. "Who are you?" he asks listlessly, as if rhetorical.

"Nothing. No one. A dream, a dream. Or a nightmare, perhaps," the old man says. "Ideas!" he shouts suddenly. "A muse!" He pokes Tyson hard in the chest, again and again. "A muse for *you*." He wraps bony arms around Tyson's neck and pulls himself up, *crawls* up Tyson's torso like a diseased white monkey and puts his mouth next to his ear, so close that sour breath settles hot and moist against his skin.

"Now… *LISTEN!*"

Tyson jerks awake with a cry, head rising from where it rested on the stone desktop, the movement so violent he nearly falls out of the chair when the wheels push backward over the thin rug. He grips a plastic armrest with one hand, steadies the other against the edge of the desk. Taking deep breaths, he looks around the office in a panic, sees yellow late-morning sunshine pouring in through the windows. The daylight fells like less of a promise and more of an accusation. Bright, creeping guilt.

*Jesus Christ, it's* morning?

Confused, he starts to stand, but a sharp pain in his lower back stops him, sends him back crumpling back into the seat. "Ow, ow, ow…" he whimpers, clutching at the hard knot. "Damn it…"

In all his years of writing, in the decades of deadlines and late nights pushing word counts higher and higher, not once has he ever fallen asleep at his desk. Never. He wipes cool saliva from his chin and cheek with a shaky hand, rubs his tired eyes. He feels *terrible*. Drained. Exhausted.

*I need a break, I need to…*

Then he remembers the strange dream, and the horror of the previous night with his beloved Sarah... *My God, what's happening to me?*

He feels a depthless hollow open inside him, a cold space that pulses in his guts, opening ever so slowly, an all-consuming aperture. As he sits there, waiting for the knot in his back to unknot, he's good and truly frightened. Scared because he knows the answer to his own question. He's a horror writer after all, and if this was his story, and he was the character being put through the ringer by some omniscient writer, there would be only one answer that makes sense.

"I'm going mad," he says aloud. "Someone's punched a hole in the bag, and now I'm losing my fucking marbles."

*It's the pressure! I'm under too much pressure. It's confusing me. Splintering my mind...*

*Screwing with the inside of my head. Tearing it apart. Please... please God, no...*

Feeling the cramp in his back loosening, Tyson cautiously stands, shoves the chair away with the back of his legs, turns away from the desk. He doesn't want to look at it. Not right now. Maybe not ever again.

*I need to pull myself together. Get things right with Sarah. I need to fix things. I need to get CONTROL.*

The *chirpchirpchirpchirp* of a digital ring comes from outside his office door.

Tyson doesn't have a cell phone. Has no interest. No desire to be "always connected" to the world. He has only a house phone and an automated message service, and even though the number is unlisted, fans or crazies eventually find it out somehow, fill up his voicemail with bizarre bullshit, forcing him to change the number every few years. No big whoop. But the idea of having all those calls coming to him *real-time?* That would be a true nightmare. Calls while working, while at the movies or the park, while having dinner with Sarah or sitting on the crapper. Thanks, but no thanks.

But now the sacred house phone is ringing, which means someone has made it through the gauntlet of knowing the *newest* phone number for the automated message service and are *also* on the approved list of persons who know the correct code to punch in, the final gateway to pass to reach Tyson directly.

It's a short list.

And since two members of this Sacred Order of Approved Contacts are (likely, hopefully) sitting in this very house—*most likely plotting ideas for my painful demise*—that leaves an even shorter number of possibilities.

He hears a muffled *Hello?* from the kitchen. Violet has picked up. Is Sarah even here? Has she left? Has she left *him?* Tyson listens closely, hoping to hear who his daughter is talking to.

After a moment, she laughs. *And hey, that's good, isn't it?*

He hopes so.

Footsteps. He can almost track her path through the wall as she approaches... a knock at the office door. He sits back down, rests both hands on the desk to steady himself. The knot in his back throbs, his body not pleased with his decision to resume this position. He winces, tries to work up a smile. He dares not move.

"Come in," he says, going for carefree, for a tone that says *everything's fucking-A dandy.*

Violet enters holding the wireless extension. She does *not* look happy to see him.

*Oh shit.*

"Hi, hon."

Violet reaches him in three long, brisk strides. She extends her arm over the desk, the phone resting in her palm, turned upward.

*She doesn't even want to get close to me.*

He tries to get that smile revved up again but is less successful this time.

"It's Harry," she says icily, her arm rigid, her fingers splayed flat, a clear indication he should take the phone while avoiding any and all physical contact.

"Okay," he says, and despite his daughter's scorn, he's finds that he's curious. "Thanks, baby." He plucks the phone neatly from her open palm.

"Did she do that?" Violet asks, with what Tyson hopes is a note of concern, and indicates the three dark scratches along his cheek by brushing her own youthful, unspoiled face.

"Yeah. Just a misunderstanding." He doesn't meet her eyes. "You know."

"Uh-huh," she says, any trace of a conciliatory or concerned tone tossed away. She turns on her heel and makes for the door like a thrown dart. "By the way, you stink," she says without turning around, then slams the door closed behind her.

Tyson stares at the closed door a moment, lets out a heavy sigh, the rotting stink of his own breath evident even to him. "Well, that's just great..."

"What's that?" Harry's voice filters out from the phone.

Tyson stands once more—oh so carefully—and walks to a sun-drenched window. He stares numbly at the rear yard, absently studying the tidy square of browning grass the size of a giant's postage stamp, the rain-streaked wooden deck adorned with a rusted grill, two dirty wicker chairs and a spattering of browned maple leaves. The sight depresses him.

"Hiya, Harry. What's cooking?"

"Well, geez, Ty… I dunno, what's cooking with you?"

Tyson frowns, holding the phone away from his ear to study it, as if it might grow teeth and bite a chunk from his earlobe. "Uh… nothing?"

"Bull. Shit." Harry says, and then, inexplicably, begins to laugh. "Bull *shit* I say! I mean, come on man! What's up with you, anyway? You are the ultimate enigma, I swear to God. You know someone for more than twenty years only to find out you don't know them at all, am I right? Now look at you, using email and everything. Like a big boy in the new world. I love it!"

Tyson would be concerned, nay, worried, at what Harry is saying were he not saying it with such utter jocularity. *It's how he sounds when he calls to talk about an offer,* he thinks, but knows that can't be right, because there's nothing out there *to* offer. "Hey, Harry? I'm sorry, I'm not following this thread. What are we talking about?"

"Oh, you're gonna play that game, huh? Okay, fine, let's play it your way." Harry clears his throat, takes on an inquisitive tone. "Hi there, Tyson. It's your agent, Harry Sled? I was curious if you might happen to know why someone emailed me—from *your* email account, no less—what appears to be a complete, totally never-before-seen, and unbelievably polished manuscript for a brand-new novel? Can you explain that one, Mister Man?"

"What..." Tyson starts to say, then stops, his jaw hung dumbly ajar.

His eyes shift to the laptop.

To the desk.

"I sent you that? Are you... uh... I mean, are you sure?"

"Are you kidding me right now?" Harry says loudly, and Tyson senses movement on the other end of the line. He hears pages flipping. "I'm staring at a 312-page manuscript that pinged my lovely assistant's email inbox around 2 A.M. last night. She saw your name and the attachment and totally freaked out. Man, she was up half the night proofreading it for me so I'd have it first thing this morning when I got to the office... Oh, by the way, she *hates* it! Ha! Said she had to stop a couple times because she started feeling queasy. Can you believe that? I had to give the poor kid the day off! She looked *terrible*. I honestly felt bad for her."

"Harry, I..." Tyson tries to interject, but Harry is on a roll and nothing will stop him. *He sounds hysterical,* Tyson thinks, then walks back to the desk, sits down, and wiggles the mouse.

The laptop screen lights up.

"Anyway, she's a pro," Harry continues. "So, she prints it out—oh, just a few typos, by the way—and it was sitting on my desk when I walk in the door. Tyson, I read the damn thing in three hours! I didn't even stop to shit, man! I couldn't turn the pages fast enough."

Tyson opens the email program, clicks the icon for the **Sent** folder.

And there it is.

He *had* sent it. 1:58 A.M. He has no recollection… why would he do that? He hadn't even reread the damn thing! He bends over, squinting to see the Subject line.

Subject: My New Novel

And, below the attachment field, in that big white box reserved for correspondence, is nothing but four short words:

Don't fuck it up.

"I mean, sure, it's hardcore horror, don't get me wrong," Harry's saying, and Tyson wonders if the man has taken a breath the entire phone call. His voice is rising like an oncoming train. "And it's certainly a lot *darker* than anything else you've done, and yeah, okaaay, William Morrow *might* want us to soften a few of the more, uh, graphic moments… but let's stick with the positives, shall we? Jesus, Tyson! You did it!"

"Harry…"

"You're back, baby! This thing is gonna shoot you and me right to the top, man!"

"Harry, I…"

"You hear me? Tyson? You there? Tyson… buddy? Holy shit, Tyson… I honestly can't believe it. We're gonna kill them with this thing. I mean, really slay 'em! You're back baby, you feelin' me? You're BACK!"

# TWENTY-NINE

A FEW MINUTES after hanging up with Harry, Tyson enters the living room, moving slowly, eyes darting side-to-side, as if expectant of a sneak attack from a blind spot. Violet is curled up in a padded chair with a Joy Williams paperback, and Sarah is lying down on the couch, face turned toward the cushions, her back to the room. Tyson stands there a moment, knowing darn well that his daughter has seen him and is ignoring him, and that Sarah is most likely in a state of half-sleep, willing away his actions from the previous night.

Willing away *him*, most likely.

"Guys?" His voice cracks, and he clears his throat. "Sarah?"

Violet lowers her book but doesn't close it. Sarah doesn't move.

"Sarah. Can we talk?"

Abruptly, without warning, Sarah turns over and sits up. Her eyes are blue fire, aimed at him like target-locked weapons, and they do not miss their mark. She stares through him, and he feels every iota of her hate hit his chest like the blast of a shotgun. *If looks could kill, I'd be a pile of ash right about now.*

He puts his hands up. "Please."

She stands without a word and walks straight for the hallway toward, he assumes, the bedroom. *Likely to pack a suitcase.* "Sarah, Sarah, I'm sorry. Can we... please, I've been out of my mind, please."

She tries to push past him but he reaches for her. *Gently.* She spins on him and there's a brief moment when he expects her to take another swing at his face, to batter his chest with screams and rebuke and tears, to tell him how much she hates him, how she will hate him forever.

But here's the reality: when you are joined with someone for over a decade of life, and when that decade has been a *good* decade—a litany of loving moments, shared compassion and consistent, unflagging support—you build a level of trust, a balustrade of understanding, of love.

Of forgiveness.

And so, despite her eyes flashing a warning that causes him to physically wince, the blow does not come.

"*Fuck* you," she hisses, her muscles tense as iron beneath his hands.

Tyson hears Violet's sharp intake of breath from behind him. He feels sick.

"Take your hands off me."

Tyson does. He lifts them away, holds them, palms-open, at his sides.

"Please, I'm begging your forgiveness here."

---

AS HATE bubbles beneath her skin, and Tyson waits for an answer, Sarah thinks—in a flash of memory—about her parents. Of her father, who would regularly come home drunk and loud, yelling at her mother, who, for better or worse, was strong enough to defy him, to yell right back. To give as good as she got. Things would inevitably smash and shatter as he drunkenly screamed and cursed, said horrible things about his wife and, even worse, his only child. Sarah would hide in her bedroom, beneath her covers, door locked, to wait out the storm. Always knowing that the next morning, like clockwork, her father would be waiting for her at the breakfast table. Smiling, loving.

*I'm sorry if I scared you,* he'd say. *You know how much I love you and your mother.*

In those instances, she would look to her mother for reassurance, to know if forgiveness was the right thing to do. The correct answer to his cruelty.

Her mother had always nodded and shrugged. Smile weakly, as if saying: *What are you gonna do?*

Once, when Sarah was a teenager, her mother came to her room after a particularly savage encounter with Father, the dark shadow of a swelling bruise on her cheekbone. That night they'd cried together for a while. At the time, Sarah had wanted to confront him, to do her best impression of her mother and throw his hate and disgust right back into his rapidly-aging face.

Instead, she stayed with her mother, locked away in her room, both of them craving a reminder of what familial love could feel like.

That night, before her mother had drifted off to sleep, Sarah suggested they leave him. Run away.

Her mother had laughed.

"We have such a history, Sarah, he and I. It feels like the future is already written, the story already told, from beginning to end." She'd sighed wearily. "You can't run from that."

To the best of Sarah's knowledge, he never struck her mother again. And things *did* improve, slowly, over time. Almost to the point of forgetting.

But she wonders now, in her own moment, if that's what her mother had meant: that forgiveness led to forgetting. She'd never asked for further explanation.

Part of her hadn't wanted to know.

And, so it was, that forgiveness became the norm. The answer to male violence. A flawed solution engrained into her since childhood, her past filled with a history of backing down, of enabling bad behavior.

"Sarah, please," Tyson says. Begging.

Sarah looks across the room to Violet. Dear, sweet Violet. She sees the fear in her youthful eyes, as well as the curiosity. Sarah sees a childhood version of herself sitting there, looking on to see what decision will be made.

Defiance, or supplication? Together... or apart?

Was Violet staring at her own future? Or the end of the past?

It was up to Sarah to decide now. Was their story over, or had the future already been written?

Sarah lets out a held breath, her shoulders slump and she leans forward, her forehead to his chest. She allows him to give himself back to her, and she to him.

This was a storm, she knows, that had passed through the home of their relationship. They had not escaped unscathed—the roof may need work, a few windows are broken, and some shit had fallen off shelves in a couple of the rooms—but it's nothing that can't be repaired with time, and care, and many, many days and weeks—perhaps months—of apologies.

*Always the fucking apologies,* she thinks, hiding the sour grimace that creases her face.

TYSON EMBRACES her, knowing deep-down the work which lays ahead. The things he will need to do to reestablish their previous, hard-won trust.

"I'm so, so sorry," he whispers into her ear, and lifts his eyes to see Violet watching them. She's crying, silently but without shame. Tyson is glad she's there to see this, glad he's laying himself down before the women he relies on to keep him sane and respectable. Alive. "It will never happen again. I swear to God."

"I know," she mumbles into his shoulder, and he's nervous because she isn't crying, which is somehow worse. Like she knows her lot and has accepted it. The idea makes him sick to his stomach, and he swears to himself that he will spend the rest of his life making it up to her. Making it right.

But now, as awkward a transition as it might be, he *must* tell them. *Who knows?* he thinks. *It'll give us something else to think about. Hell, to celebrate.*

"Listen, guys..." he clears his throat, starts again. "I know the timing stinks, but I want to tell you both... well, that was Harry on the phone."

Violet rolls her eyes. "Dad, really?"

But Sarah steps back, stares at him oddly. He senses she's caught somewhere between great interest—a habit born from that decade of being his partner in all things, including his career—and disbelief that he would mention something so trivial during this moment. Unless...

Unless it isn't trivial. Not even close.

Regardless, he pushes on, hoping he is right to do so.

"I know, Vie, just... bear with me here. Look, I sent him the new book, and he *loved* it. I mean, he went crazy for it. He's... well, he likes it enough that he's going to try and renegotiate the deal with William Morrow. He thinks we've got a bestseller."

Tyson says all this timidly, awkwardly. Normally, he would have been shouting the news, laughing and celebrating with Sarah, giddy at the relief of it all. But instead, he waits in silence, lets the quiet room remain quiet. Quiet... and fragile. The air feels brittle as an eggshell.

"Sorry..." Sarah says, rubbing at her eyes. She takes a step away from him. "What do you mean... you finished the book? When?"

Tyson does his best to explain that he's been inspired, that it came to him in a mad rush, that he'd never felt anything like it before. And, once he'd finished it, he sent it off to Harry, late last night, in a moment of mad elation.

And now, after a breakneck few days and the creative explosion, he is very tired, very happy, and very, very sorry.

But the book *is* done.

"Tyson, I'm happy for you, but..." she pauses, as if doing the math in her head. "I mean, that's not possible. What about proofing it? Rewrites? Edits? I mean, my God... are you telling me you wrote, what..."

"Just over eighty thousand words." He shrugs. "Probably the shortest novel I've ever written, but I think it packs a punch. And besides, the editors will do their edit, and I'll do my final polish, so, you know, it'll be fine. Bottom line is I've fulfilled my contract, and Harry sees no issues with them accepting it. Anyway, I'm having lunch with Harry later this week to go over some details."

Sarah's eyebrows go up. "Harry's taking you to lunch?"

"Yeah, just like old times," Tyson says, all of them knowing full-well that Harry hasn't bothered wining-and-dining Tyson for many years, that even getting a face-to-face with his agent has become more and more of a process, one that normally ended in frustration, and an email.

Sarah puts a gentle hand to his wounded cheek. And for now, that will have to do.

"I can't say I'm not a bit shocked here, but... Congratulations, Ty."

"Thanks," he says, and takes a step back, addresses both women. "Look, I've been an ass. We all know it, so let's get that out there. But this could be a big moment for *all* of us. I want to take you guys to dinner tonight. I want to take the two most important people in my life to a nice, celebratory dinner. What do you say?"

Sarah and Violet exchange glances, and Tyson feels his heart thumping in his ears. Nervous sweat breaks out on his forehead and cheeks.

Violet shrugs, and Sarah turns to face him, expressionless. "Where?"

"Harry called in a favor," he says, rushing forward before he somehow loses them again, or says something that will ruin the momentum of his impossible luck. "We have seven o'clock reservations at *Gabriel Kreuther.* All three of us. Luckily, they're a bit slow on Monday nights, so..."

Violet squeals and leaps up, runs to her dad and hugs him. Tyson hugs her back hard, relishing it. He looks for Sarah over his daughter's head and their eyes meet—hers kind and forgiving, his thrilled at suddenly, in the space of a few minutes, having everything back he almost lost, all he ever wanted.

Or so he imagines, anyway.

Still, if he could stop time, live in this same moment the rest of his days, it would have been a good one to hold onto.

Part Six

# THE BREAK

# THIRTY

RAIN BEATS steadily against the taxi's roof and smears the surrounding windows, temporarily transforming the reality of the outside world into a dull impressionist painting. Tyson pays the driver, feeling only a remote hint of anxiety at the double-digit fare. Things are looking up, and at the *very* least he doesn't have to worry so much about money in the short-term. If he hasn't already, Harry will soon deliver the book to Morrow, and although it may not be *completely* in-line with his original pitch, Tyson prays it's close enough to keep them from demanding he repay the advance.

*So why the lunch?* He frowns as he lifts the umbrella, avoiding the running water along the curb and stepping hurriedly to the entrance of Café Luxembourg. Tyson knows Harry isn't the "celebration" type unless a deal has closed and a handsome check has been cut, so the timing is suspect, although not wholly unwelcome. Tyson could do with a little affirmation. A little cheering up. In the last week things in his life have gone sideways, and a little straightening was in order.

*No more booze, for one thing.*

Tyson had discussed his behavior with Sarah, and they both agreed that given the anxiety of deadlines, a birthday, and the stress of his money concerns, it's probably not the best time to be chugging whisky like a man drowning in a sea of Bushmills.

Sarah also wanted him to regulate his time in the office.

This had been a much tougher point for Tyson to comply with.

The last several days he'd pretended to sleep through the night while catching intermittent naps. Actual *sleeping* was difficult, if not impossible, despite him doing his very best to ignore the *voices*. Every night he'd lie in bed, in the dark, praying for sleep, only to be tugged to consciousness by urgent whispers, instructions that would seep into his brain like spilled ink through a ball of cotton. The words a black spell that crept up the stairwell, originating from the other side of the office door.

From the *desk*.

In the morning, he'd finally have his writing session and oh what a *relief* it was to sit there typing, getting it all down. Getting it all *out of his head*. After the frantic session which had produced *Black Altar,* he found a rhythm to the work that was less frenetic. Less... *suspicious*. Oh, he still typed like a madman, of course. Hard and fast.

But this time, he wasn't typing a story.

The desk hasn't spun any new yarns since the first book. Now it's mostly nonsense. Gibberish. *ALL WORK AND NO PLAY MAKES JACK A DULL BOY* sorta bullshit. Horrible things, insane things. Evil things. He writes for hours, often in languages he doesn't recognize, then deletes the whole file—dumps the worthless pile of words into the digital wastebasket and flushes it into cyberspace. It's madness, really, if he ever dared stop and think about it.

Two more of his fingertips have split open, and he's lost the nails on both those fingers. He keeps a box of cloth Band-Aids in his desk drawer now, swaps out the bandages while he works, once they become too sodden with blood.

There's also the matter of the desk itself. It *enjoys* Tyson being there, and he thinks that sometimes it gets a little... *excited*. Maybe even *too* excited, like a puppy left home all day who wants to jump up and lick your face when you walk through the door.

The desk isn't a puppy, of course. And it isn't interested in face-kisses.

Instead, it reaches for him with those eerie ivy tendrils as he works, poking at his fingers, stabbing playfully at his heavily whiskered chin, pierces the skin of his arms and neck with needle-sharp barbs.

When this happens, there's a distant, shadowed part of him that thinks he should be screaming. Should be running for his fucking life. After all, desks weren't *alive*, were they? No, no. Of course not. But whenever that small, nearly forgotten voice starts to wail and reason, the newer part of him—the *successful* part of him—simply wills it away. Shrinks it down to the size of a cricket and shoves it into a tiny black closet, where it can scream all day, all night, and no one will hear a goddamned thing.

Overall, though? Things aren't so bad. In fact, Tyson feels his life might be getting slowly under control. Things have finally settled down between him and Sarah, and if he's spending more time in the office, well damn it, that's just *paying the bills, baby.*

*And if Miss Moneybags isn't gonna contribute to the cause, then she'd better keep her damned mouth shut about how many hours he works. So what if he spends all day in the office working? Tries to keep his head above water financially, keep his career progressing? That's his RIGHT. His and his alone! And if Sarah doesn't like it, she can get the hell out of his house. Go marry one of those wealthy bankers her mother always tried to set her up with, until she realized her only daughter was a lost cause—falling for a writer, of all things. Can you get lower than that? Hell, Sarah is probably on the phone to that old hag right now, bawling her eyes out, getting ready to leave him for some stockbroker son-of-a-cunt! Sure, yeah, that's exactly what's going on here. That crafty slut is probably locking in a blind date right now. Well, GOOD LUCK TO YA! YOU LYING, CHEATING, STUCK-UP RICH LITTLE...*

"Enough!" he yells. The word spits out of him like a command, ordering the manic voice in his head to silence, a voice he no longer recognizes, because it's certainly not *his.*

He glances around the wet street to see if anyone is staring, but his self-rebuke was barely audible in the persistent sound of falling rain, smothered by the noise of the city. And besides, New Yorkers are used to folks talking to themselves.

"Mr. Parks!"

Tyson catches himself locked in a stationary position, one hand resting on the cool, wet silver handle of the restaurant, the other curled around the handle of his umbrella. *How long have I been standing like this?* he thinks, a queasy sensation running through his gut. The rain patters against the umbrella like tapping fingers while the city traffic growls and sloshes its way through the rain-drenched street behind him.

The voice he heard was faint. Probably imagined.

He shrugs, pulls on the door handle.

"Hey, Mr. Parks! It's me." The voice is directly behind him now.

Tyson turns and sees a lithe figure in a black raincoat, a man's face shadowed by a wide-brimmed fisherman's hat. He carries no umbrella, and the haze of gray rain creates a veil between them that forces Tyson to squint for a clear view of the stranger's face.

"You don't remember me, huh? This is pretty strange, right? To have never met you at all and now twice just like that—bam bam? Long odds," the man is saying, talking fast, his voice muddled by the white noise of raindrops sky-bombing into the dirty pavement. "What's that word again? Oh yeah, *serendipity*. Ha! Of course, you'd know better than me, being the writer."

*The kid from the subway,* Tyson realizes, his sluggish brain making the connections as the guy yammers on like an idiot. The one he signed the book for. Ben something...

"Howard," the young man says quickly, as if he's read Tyson's mind. "Ben Howard."

Tyson doesn't have much in the way of intuition himself, but even he notices the strange look in Ben's eye, that despite the handsome boy's bright smile, there's a hint of fear, as well.

*Yes... afraid. But of what?*

"No more research?" Ben asks, still holding out for a response.

Tyson, momentarily flummoxed by the comment, finally gets the synapses firing well enough to recall their conversation on the train. "Oh," he says, building steam now that his muddled thoughts have cleared. "No, I won't be riding the subway for a while. Taxis will do fine, I think. What about you? No book to sign?"

Ben tilts his naked palms to the air, rain pelting off his long fingers like dancing sprites. "No sir. I just saw you walking and, well, wanted to say hello."

Tyson nods. He's growing increasingly cold and wet despite the umbrella. He wants a steak and a drink... *well, coffee will have to do*. "Okay, then. Nice to see you, Ben. Take care now."

As Tyson begins to turn away, Ben reaches out and lays a hand on his shoulder. Not aggressively, and with no implied hostility. He simply places a hand there, as if reassuring him. Or praying with him.

Tyson jerks away, startled, and sees the young man was no longer smiling. Ben is frowning now, his eyes troubled and dark. "Mr. Parks, you seem like a good man, and I really am a fan of your work, believe it or not. But I think you're in trouble, sir. Very bad trouble. You..." Ben hesitates, searching for the words. "To be honest, I'm not even supposed to be talking to you."

"Sounds like a plan," Tyson says, grabbing for the door handle once more.

"Wait, please." Tyson pauses despite himself, despite his growing unease with the direction of this conversation. "I'm sorry to sound ominous. I'm trying to... Okay, look, here's the deal. The thing? The thing that's with you? That's sitting in your house right now?"

Tyson feels a chill that has nothing to do with the weather. His muscles clench. He stares at the chrome door handle, his hand upon it. The bandaged fingers.

"Mr. Parks. You know what I'm talking about, don't you?"

Tyson turns his head, stares at the man. Sees the fear in those eyes.

Wonders if that same fear is in his eyes as well.

"You need to get rid of it, Mr. Parks," Ben continues. "Give it away, sell it, but get it out of your life." He once again places a hand on Tyson, this time on his forearm, like a beggar. His skinny six-two puts him nearly eye-to-eye with the older man. "Please..."

"Fuck off me!" Tyson yells in a voice he does not recognize. He swats the hand away from his shoulder. Riding a surge of hate, he dips the umbrella, ignoring the eager rain that washes over him unblocked, and jabs the point of it at the young man's chest. "What the fuck's wrong with you? Get back! Get out of here!"

Ben jumps backward to avoid the umbrella's stab, but does not run. The two men stare at each other a moment, rain drenching them both. Tyson feels enraged, and confused. He doesn't mean to be so angry, but...

*The man attacked him! Grabbed him! He's obviously a rabid fan. A nut!*

"Get lost! Beat it, you fucker!" Tyson roars, and now Ben does take a few steps away, his face a complex mix of hurt, fear, and compassion.

"I'm sorry, sir," he says quietly, sounding almost embarrassed. His eyes dart everywhere, anywhere but back at Tyson's face, at what he's seen there. "I have to go now. Please, remember what I said."

Shaken, Tyson watches as the kid walks away, disappears into the chess pieces of other New Yorkers, evaporates into a memory, albeit one that nagged. He wipes a sheen of sweat and rainwater from his face, takes a deep breath and turns once more to enter the restaurant.

And freezes.

A spark of self-awareness fizzles like a sunken sparkler in the dark of his mind, stopping him in his tracks, forcing him—*begging him*— to think. To *consider.* Standing in the rain, heart pounding, he focuses for a long moment on that dull, distant spark...

*You're in trouble, sir. Very bad trouble.*

Tyson, quite suddenly, feels very *tired*. Very... *sick*.

"Something's wrong with me," he mumbles, yet still he does not move.

The wind whistles in his ears, passersby mumble into their phones, cars honk and splash like unruly children... all of it singing a slurred melody, the sad song of New York City in the rain.

There is a weakened, dying part of Tyson that wants to pull his fingers away from the door, stuff his hands into the pockets of his raincoat, turn around, and walk away. Let himself be swallowed by the other New Yorkers with their black umbrellas, disappear behind the curtain of ash-tinted rain that drowns the city, washes away color and transforms its bustling inhabitants into blurry ghosts.

*Oh, to be a ghost!* he thinks wildly. *Wouldn't that be something? To be done with all this pressure? This world? Money and relationships and old age and deadlines and criticism... all GONE. Washed away by the rain, into the gutters. I'd be FREE.*

Tyson looks up to study his reflection in the glass door of the restaurant. His distorted image offers a small, sad smile; one filled with regret, and apologies.

"Shall I long for thee until I become a flower?" he says under his breath, and the reflection, trapped in the glass, only smiles more broadly. "Shall I wither away?"

*No, old friend,* the reflection says coldly, its eyes white as snow. *I'm afraid that won't do. Besides, Narcissus you are not. So, if you're done caterwauling, do us a favor, will you? And GET THE FUCK INSIDE!*

Scowling, he lets out a breath, yanks open the door, and walks into the restaurant, leaving the laughing visage of his ghostly reflection behind.

# THIRTY-ONE

HARRY LOOKS awful.

Normally, Harry's a neat-as-a-pin, not-a-hair-out-of-place sorta fella. He wears expensive suits and accessories, keeps his hair perfectly shaped with some sort of undetectable gel that Tyson always wonders about. He smells faintly of rich cologne, his teeth are denture-white, and he always appears fit, sharp, and reservedly energetic, as if he could host a party, negotiate a million-dollar contract, or scale the side of a mountain at the drop of a hat.

To see Harry like *this* is almost unthinkable. His hair is gelled back, per usual, but he's missed a spot where it sticks out on one side, a kind of sideways Alfalfa. He wears a dark suit that's badly wrinkled and his navy-blue tie is loosely knotted and off-center, as if he was a traveler recently woken after falling asleep on a train. Standing opposite him, Tyson is shocked to smell alcohol on Harry's breath, but he's even more shocked to see the man's face heavily stubbled, his eyes baggy with exhaustion.

*Maybe he's dying. Maybe the poor bastard has cancer, and he's letting all his clients know one-by-one. Why not? It happens to the best of us, after all.* Tyson tries to smile at his agent, his old friend, but finds it hard to keep the thing in place.

"Hiya Harry," he says, as he always does when greeting the younger man, but this time he says it more reservedly, as if the old joke isn't totally appropriate. "You, uh, okay?"

Harry responds with the rictus grin of a sun-bleached corpse and stands to shake Tyson's hand. "Never better, Ty. Sit down, sit down... you want a drink?"

Tyson notices the last hurrah of an Old Fashioned on the white cloth near Harry's wrist, the single square ice cube taking up half the glass, glistening like a talisman. He takes a cursory glance around, checking to see if anyone he knows is seated at the nearby tables, but the only folks that stand out are a cluster of three men in business suits, most likely bankers. Adjacent to them is a table of two women eating salads while ignoring a pink-faced baby in a highchair, the chubby infant currently doing its best to pound green peas into green mush using tiny, tight fists. Tyson shakes his head and sits down. "I'm okay, thanks. Just a coffee."

Harry flags down the waiter, orders another Old Fashioned for himself, a coffee for Tyson, and skillet steak specials for both of them. When the waiter leaves, Harry leans in close, and Tyson realizes, with the tiniest bit of alarm, that Harry doesn't just smell of booze... Harry's *drunk*. Maybe not totally shit-faced, but he's three or four hops past tipsy, without a doubt.

"Tyson, my man. I have treated you poorly," Harry says, still grinning that horrible, stretched grin, his eyes bloodshot but bright, be that due to excitement or alcohol Tyson can't guess. "And you came through, buddy. You came through and you put me in my place. I had you pegged... look, I'll admit it, okay? I thought you were a goner. You know? I've seen it before; many, many times. Writers—well, the good ones, anyway—they rise up..." Harry illustrates this rise with the flat of his hand pointing at an upward angle, "...they *peak*... and then they decline." Harry's hand slices downward through the air to slam against the table. Silverware rattles. "Sure, there are comebacks. Peaks and valleys, et cetera. But, man, I thought after the last few books... well, as I said, I was wrong. Bygones and water under the bridge, okay?"

At the table beside them, the baby is battering his, or her, dinner plate. "WAH!" it bellows. Tyson hears one of the women soothe it before continuing to chat with their friend. "WAH! WAAAH!"

The drinks come and Tyson sips his black coffee, which is too hot, and studies Harry warily. "I think I'm missing the point, if there is one." Tyson's voice is even, but tinged with annoyance. "Why don't you clarify?"

Harry puts up a palm, belches, and cocks his grin to one side. "Fair enough. No more bullshit. Well, here's the point. I challenged you to a boxing match, and you KO'd my ass in Round One, comprende? This book... man, it's the real deal. It's like... shit, man, it's revolutionary. It's gonna be HUGE."

Tyson nods patiently, waits for Harry to come all the way around to whatever point has dragged him out on a rainy day when he would have preferred to be home, in his office, *working*.

"Anyway, the reason I've got you here. Sorry if I'm... I gotta tell you bud, I haven't slept much since we spoke Monday morning. That's what? Four days? I've just been... *jacked* up, you know? Hyper. Regardless, here's what I wanted to tell you." Harry looks around, sips his drink, and leans in so close Tyson can smell the ripe stink of sweat under his rumpled suit, count the red veins in the whites of his eyes. "I pulled the deal, brother."

Tyson feels as if he's been slapped. He can't move. His body goes numb.

"That's right. Yanked that motherfucker right off the table." Harry sits back wearing a cocky grin and waving his half-empty glass around like a baton. "And man, I gotta tell ya... they were *pissed*." He chuckles at this last part, and Tyson thinks it's the laugh of a man sitting in the electric chair, just before that black hood is pulled down over his eyes.

Madness. Broken madness.

Tyson, however, could give a shit. He shows Harry his teeth. "You did what?"

The agent takes a big swig of his drink, wipes his mouth with the back of his hand, and rolls out that shit-eating grin again. "That's right big fella. *Fuck them*. You think I'm gonna give William Morrow this monster of a novel for... what? A hundred-thousand-dollar advance and a twenty-percent royalty off retail? No way. No how. Not happening. You and me? We're taking it out. I'm gonna shop it around, get some other editors to read this thing, and boy—ho boy—is it gonna get heated out there. Gonna be a regular feeding frenzy, my friend." He sticks one manicured finger into Tyson's face. "You are a hot property once again, Mr. Parks. The *hottest*."

The steak platters arrive but neither of them reach for cutlery. Harry eyeballs it with a measure of disgust, as if he wants to push it away. Tyson does everything he can to keep calm. Nearby, the baby is screaming.

"Harry," he says, "we *have* a deal. It's a good deal. I'm happy with the deal."

Harry waves his hand. "Nah, no good. We're gonna shop it. That's why I wanted to meet, to let you know. To get you excited! Big money coming our way, Ty. Big money!"

Tyson shakes his head. "No. Harry... you don't..." He pauses, glances around furtively, and lowers his voice. "Harry, that money is gone. *Spent*. I couldn't give it back if I wanted to."

"WAAAAAH! WAH! WAAAAAH!" the baby screams, and Tyson turns instinctively toward the damnable thing with every intention of throwing the mother his best *what the fuck* glare.

When he does, he notices the women aren't paying attention to the child, nor, it seems, did anyone else in the restaurant appear bothered by the loud cries. "Hey," Tyson says to the women, but they ignore him.

The baby, however, turns its head.

Its eyes are chalk-white. Its head misshapen. Long, scraggly white hair sticks out from the side of its pinkish skull. Its face is not round and smooth, but heavily lined. Pruned. And red as the inside of a rare steak. When it opens its mouth to wail once more, a black tongue springs from between its fat, cherubic lips like the head of an eel. "WAAAAAAH! I'M POOR!" the infant shrieks, and Tyson feels his stomach drop as it *smiles* at him, showing jagged brown teeth. "WAAAAAAH! I'M A SCARED SHIT-FOR-BRAINS! WAAAAAAH! WAAAAAA! WAAAAAAAAAH!!!"

The baby thrusts a green-stained hand toward Tyson, mushed peas dripping from its clenched fist of slick fingers. Its voice, when it speaks, is rough and deep. "DON'T BE A PUSSY, PARKS! DON'T BLOW THIS FOR US!!!" it screams, white eyes bulbous, mouth opened wide to expose an endless black maw. "WAAAAAAAH!" It points a pudgy finger at him. "THAT'S YOU! WAAAAAAH! FUCKING CRYBABY! WAAAAAAH! MAN UP, YOU LITTLE BITCH!"

"Tyson? You okay, man?"

Tyson gasps, realizes he'd been holding his breath. He lets it out, his tight chest loosening. "Jesus Christ," he says, wiping his forehead with the cloth napkin, mumbling to himself. "No no no no no..." He drops the napkin atop his untouched plate, closes his eyes and rubs them hard, runs his hands through his hair.

"Tyson? Tyson, good God, what's wrong?" Harry stands, reaches a hand across the table.

Tyson pulls his hands away from his head, takes a deep breath and slowly turns his head back to the infant's table.

The baby is, once more, just a baby. A normal baby eating quietly, its face docile, intent, innocent. A small smear of pea mush colors its adorable chin. Its eyes are blue as sky.

"I'm fine," Tyson says, and swallows the bile stuck in his throat. He picks up the napkin, sees it spotted with grease, drops it and wipes more sweat from his forehead with the sleeve of his coat.

"Hey man, if this is upsetting you that much, I'll call them back," Harry says, looking worried. "I'll have to grovel, but it's not a big deal, Tyson. I mean... but I think..."

"No," Tyson says quickly, and raises a hand for the waiter. "No, let's do it. I trust you, Harry."

Harry holds his eyes on Tyson a moment more, then nods, looking relieved, and settles back into his chair as the waiter approaches.

Tyson shoves the plate of napkin-covered food to the middle of the table. "That said, I think I'll have that drink now."

# THIRTY-TWO

"SEND HIM up, please. Thank you."

Diana hangs up the phone that connects her apartment to the doorman out front, pours herself a mineral water and waits for the detective to arrive.

When the knock comes a few short minutes later, she's quickly reviewing the information he'd sent via email—looking for angles, for a way to infiltrate this family smoothly, without incident, and convince them to do what's right.

To give back what is rightly hers.

She jumps up as the steady knocking escalates to the redundant action of chiming her doorbell, as if the man has been waiting ten minutes instead of ten seconds. She walks across the room and pulls open the door, not sure what she's expecting to see... but it's certainly not who's standing in her hallway.

She's never actually met the private detective in person, but through their phone conversations and the bluntness of his emails she assumed him to be an older man; a grizzled-veteran, ex-cop type. Instead, she finds herself staring at a stranger, one carrying a thick envelope under one arm and the other raised, knuckles out, prepared to repeat the inane banging on her door. He smiles, and when he does Diana almost laughs at herself, realizing she's made a mistake, that instead of the private investigator coming to meet her, he'd simply sent his assistant instead. Or perhaps a younger brother, or a son.

Because this man *is* young—much younger than she'd ever imagined—and not grizzled at all. If anything, he's, well... *nerdy.* He wears khakis and white sneakers, a blue oxford shirt buttoned to the neck (no tie) beneath a loose-fitting black raincoat. On his head is a tacky, bucket-style fishing hat, beige with a red-and-blue ribbon band. He's Black and skinny, but tall. Handsome. *But young*, she thinks again, as if he should be on a college campus instead of skulking the streets for young runaways and bail-skipping criminals.

*And horror writers with stolen property, of course.*

"Diana?" he says, and she recognizes the voice immediately.

*I'll be damned,* she thinks. *It's him.*

"Yes, hello," she says, realizing she must be looking at him with all the uncertainty she's feeling, because his polite smile becomes a knowing grin, as if he can read her thoughts, if not her expression. She catches herself, realizing she's being rude about the whole thing. "I'm sorry, it's just that you're not what I was expecting."

"Black?" he says, the grin creeping into his charming eyes.

"Young," she admits. "For a private detective, I mean. I suppose everyone assumes black suits and fedoras and whisky-guzzling middle-aged men. I blame Hammett," she says, hoping levity will counter her rude behavior. "But please, come in. I'm so grateful you've come."

Ben Howard steps inside (after carefully wiping his shoes on the mat outside), removes his hat and nods toward the spacious—especially by New York City standards—apartment. "I'm a Mosley man myself," he says, moving into the living room as she closes the door behind him. "Nice place."

"Thank you. Would you like something to drink?"

"Nah, I'm good." He holds up the thick envelope. "This is everything I sent you digitally, plus a few new details. Nothing earth-shattering. Thought you'd like hard copies."

She takes the envelope and sets it down on the white marble coffee table which neatly centers the only other furniture in the room—a plush red Porter sectional couch and two adjacent Chinese sandalwood armchairs. "Coffee? Tea? Are you sure?"

"Yes, thank you," Ben says, taking one of the chairs. "So... should we debrief? Go over any questions you might have?"

Diana picks up her soda water and sits on the couch, curls a leg beneath her, letting the other dangle off the edge in a strategic pose of nonchalance. "That would be lovely. There are one or two pieces of information I'd like to tidy up... but I'd also like to make sure, before we talk, that you brought the other thing we discussed."

Ben smiles and scratches his chin, studies an Ed Ruscha hanging on a nearby wall, the modern painting contrasting elegantly with the more traditional décor of the apartment.

The image is a deep, blue-hued mountainscape, the word **S I N** stenciled across it in bold white letters. "The gun? Yes, I have it."

Their eyes meet, and she's surprised at his lack of reaction to her pupilless condition. It's as if he isn't seeing her at all. Seeing, rather, *about* her.

She finds the idea unsettling and pushes it away. "Good. May I see it?"

Ben nonchalantly pulls a small black handgun from the pocket of his raincoat, sets it atop the manila folder resting on the coffee table. "It's loaded. Six shots. If you need more bullets, I can give you a list of nearby gun stores who will sell them to you, and the type, of course."

Diana leans forward and picks up the weapon. If Ben is alarmed at all about this, he doesn't show it. His attention, in fact, has floated back to the Ruscha painting. "It's okay," she says, popping open the cylinder, checking the bullets, and clicking it back into place. "It's really a precaution. You know, protection."

"Well," Ben says carelessly, "they're a nice family. I don't think you'll have any problems there."

"Of course." Diana sets the gun on the table, reaches for the envelope. "Now, onto other things. As I said, I feel like there are a few loose ends in regard to the sale, and the provenance of the desk as it pertains to the dealer's acquisition."

Ben nods solemnly, as if taking it personally that he'd failed in checking all the boxes Diana had asked for. "Yeah, that's right. That information is in only one place, and there's only one man who has access. I tried following the ship manifest, but that was a dead end. Whatever port they'd loaded the thing from, there was no record of it. And the other stuff you wanted, same deal. Other than that, though, you have everything you asked for."

"I do, and I don't want you to worry. I think I can acquire the last few bits myself before moving forward."

Ben raises an eyebrow, then sits back in the stiff wooden chair, hands dangling over the polished arms. "Oh?"

Diana gives him her best smile, gratified (and slightly relieved) to see Ben finally break his cool, licking his lips unconsciously and shifting in his seat. *Haven't completely lost it,* she thinks. "Don't worry, Mr. Howard. No guns will be involved. I have other means at my disposal."

Ben offers his own winning smile. "Lanky brunettes with wicked jaws," he quotes, shaking his head, and Diana is so surprised that she does something she hardly ever does in front of company, and certainly not with a stranger: she laughs out loud.

# THIRTY-THREE

SARAH WALKS with Violet as far as the subway entrance, then hugs her tight and kisses her goodbye. Their week together is up, and she'll be back to school in a few hours. Sarah feels she's losing an ally, and tries to hold back tears when they embrace, but when Violet starts to cry into the scarf at Sarah's neck, she can't help but follow suit.

As horrible as the week has been, their bond has strengthened to that of Mother and Daughter, albeit via a pathway of heartache.

*Now, if I can somehow repair my other relationship, life can go on,* she thinks as she watches Violet go down the stairwell, turn a corner and disappear.

Back at the house, Sarah does her best to busy herself. She debates calling one of her friends for lunch but knows it will inevitably lead to talking about Tyson and she prefers to avoid the subject of *him,* at least for a while. She considers grocery shopping, but they're still fully stocked from the party.

The gym? No, too wiped out. A book? A movie? No, no, no.

She considers calling Anton, ask him to come get the desk, to take it away, ship it back to whatever foul port it had been taken from. She'll get Tyson another desk. A nice one that doesn't scare the shit out of her, or turn him into a madman.

*You're kidding, right? The desk? Really?* The voice inside her head says, taunting, disbelieving, disappointed. *Why don't you blame the coffee maker? Or, wait, I know—the new chair! That ergonomic, overpriced, multi-levered monstrosity is sure to turn any well-mannered man into a drooling, maniacal rapist. Now you're definitely thinking clearly. Oh hey, let's throw the television out while we're at it. Can't be too safe, ha-ha!*

While her inner-voice mocks her, Sarah walks, dream-like, into the hallway and down the stairs. She finds herself standing in front of the office door.

She didn't *mean* to go to the office, has no real reason to be there... and yet.

She puts her hand on the brass knob, turns it slowly, and opens the door.

It's bright inside. Sunlight pours in from the garden windows. There's no sense of evil, or darkness. It even smells nice. Like wood polish and old books.

*And Tyson,* she thinks, and feels a pang of guilt. Like an intruder. Like a mistrustful, snoopy housewife. *Don't you mean house-partner?* The constant word-fixer springs to action in her head, the one that continually translated "wife" to "partner" or "girlfriend" and seems to never take an hour off. *Maybe one day we'll make it official, and if nothing else I can use the goddamned word WIFE every now and then.*

She strolls toward the desk, sneakers silent as she crosses the dark wood, the large oriental rugs. The monstrosity looms before her like a demonic church altar, its black wood glistening in the sunlight, the intricate carvings mysterious and disquieting, its size intimidating. As she studies it, she gets the peculiar feeling that the desk both fills the room and, in a way she can't put her finger on, *empties* it as well. As if it was somehow pulling the surroundings into itself, like a black hole, or a gateway to another world. A portal.

Sarah tries to laugh off the thought, but the closer she gets to the thing, the more she can almost feel the *pull* of it; a strange vibrating energy surrounding it she hasn't felt before. Her skin prickles and the hairs on the back of her neck rise. She stares at the message carved deep into its face—DO THIS IN REMEMBRANCE OF ME.

*And just who the hell is* me*? And what exactly is being* done *in here?*

She has the sudden idea—the realization—that it's not the Bible being quoted. At least, not without a sense of irony, or mischief. These carved words have little to do with the Christian God.

*Devilry.*

Leaving the carved message for the moment, Sarah walks around the desk, one steadying hand on the back of Tyson's chair, to face it from the front. Staring at the giant hunk of wood, she suddenly wonders if, perhaps, there's a totally different reason for Tyson's binge writing sessions, his out-of-the-blue-sky creative output, his aggressive, out-of-character behavior. A reason that has little to do with desks and strange carvings, and much more to do with a different kind of evil.

Drugs, for instance.

*Could it be?* She tries to imagine Tyson sitting here, snorting cocaine or popping pills. *Was it so very strange?* she wonders, and, quite suddenly, feels like a total fool. Of course it isn't strange! He's under a tremendous amount of pressure, has been given an impossible deadline… yes, yes! The insane work hours, the not-sleeping, the irritability. It all makes perfect sense.

*He probably bought some pills off someone. This is New York City, after all. How hard could it be to find drugs on the street? Hell, maybe he got them from…* Harry. *Of course, the guy who would be SO eager to keep his prized racehorse running.* Oh yeah, she could easily see the bastard floating Tyson a few uppers, or a vial of cocaine, something to get the "old creative juices flowing." *Son-of-a-bitch!*

Feeling both sickened and oddly relieved, Sarah slides the chair smoothly out of the way and studies the desk's drawers. She allows herself a moment to admire the delicate veins of twisted ivy carved around the edges, the bizarre faces etched as drawer handles, the strange symbols and other figures—naked men and women in copulation, varying religious and occult symbols she both recognizes and has never seen before, visages of creatures (likely mythological) staring out from the desk's corners and along its edges.

*It is quite beautiful*, she thinks, able to consider it with less animosity now that her concern had switched away from the desk and toward her new—and far less insane—theory that Tyson is simply on drugs.

She steps closer to it, gently rests a hand on one of the smooth veins of carved ivy. Without warning, Sarah's mind is flooded with the sudden—and quite powerful—image of her body lying upon the stone desktop. *Like the dream,* she thinks, and shudders, but not with revulsion, or fear.

With pleasure.

With *lust.*

She has the overwhelming impulse to push Tyson's notes, his computer, and his stupid lamp off the cool stone slab, let it all crash to the floor. The mad urge to strip off her clothes and sprawl naked across its surface is so intense that she gasps, her fingers already reaching for the button at the waist of her jeans. She takes a moment to consider whether she'll undress here or in the bedroom. Does it matter? She's alone, after all.

*Maybe I should wait until Ty comes home, and then we can fuck on it,* she reasons. *He can take me right here. Hell, it's certainly big enough.* Sarah's hand moves over her body, caressing, feeling the heat from her skin and her head pound luxuriously with an overwhelming sexual desire. She unbuttons her pants, and is about to kick off a sneaker, when a deeper part of her mind springs forward. Alarm bells ring and red flags wave madly inside the part of her neurological makeup that fights psychotic impulses, that seeks restraint, that keeps her *sane.*

"Whoa!" she says in a breathless gasp, moving away from the desk so fast that her back smacks the hard bookshelves lining the wall. She pants heavily and sweat drips down the back of her neck, tracing her spine like a cold finger. "What the hell was that?" she asks the empty room.

After taking a moment to catch her breath, she steps forward again. Slowly this time, cautiously. She gently presses a fingertip to the desktop, as if testing whether a stove is still hot to the touch.

This time, a new image pulses through her mind.

Once again, she sees herself splayed atop the desk, naked, her pale skin slick from head-to-toe. But this time, the image isn't sensual. There's no sensation of pleasure, no erotic tingling below her belly. In this vision, she's tied down, bound at ankles and wrists. And it isn't sweat making her skin glisten, it's blood. *Her* blood. She'd been cut badly—on her arms, legs, chest, face.

She's been flayed.

There are hundreds of small punctures and slices, as if she's been tortured over a period of time, her blood running off the edges of the surface into eager, waiting hands...

*Like the dream,* she realizes, and pure terror chills her skin. She jerks her finger back and the vision drains away, leaving her feeling oddly empty.

Almost... disappointed.

"Okay, enough of this bullshit," she says aloud, and takes a deep, shaky breath. "It's just a stupid desk, Sarah. Now let's get this over with."

Before she can think any further or question her actions—*or the visions*—she reaches for the top left-hand drawer. Grimacing, she pinches the face that serves as a knob, and yanks it open.

Nervously, she looks down into the open drawer and sees... nothing.

No papers. No notepads. No battered Moleskine filled with old ideas. No tray filled with pens and paperclips. *No drugs.*

*Okay, next.*

As she starts to shove the drawer closed, however, something shifts inside of it. Something out of her sight. Something heavy, like a large paperweight that's somehow trapped in the back of the drawer.

Curious, she tries to pull the drawer further out, but she's either reached the extent of its depth or something is jamming it, hindering it from sliding its full length. "Huh," she says.

She reaches her hand into the drawer, past the wrist, patting her fingers and palms against the back of the aged wood in search of... *something.*

"Snoop snoop," a voice says.

Sarah's head snaps up. She scans the empty office but sees no one. The voice... it sounded close, but oddly distant as well. As if she'd heard it through the thin walls of an old house, the kind you might find in a John Saul novel, where whispered secrets are carried to prying ears through antiquated ventilation shafts.

*Who...* and then her thought is cut off.

Inside the drawer, something hard and thin is wrapping itself around her forearm.

Sarah looks back down, puzzled. Her logical mind can't make sense of what's happening. The information being relayed to her brain—that something inside the desk has coiled itself around her thin wrist, and is now *squeezing*—isn't registering as possible.

"I don't..." she says quietly, almost apologetically.

More thin shoots lift lazily from the side of the desk and slide inside the drawer, like snakes being drawn to a fresh meal. One vein snakes around her thumb. Another grips her pinky. The coil holding her wrist *pulls hard* and she stumbles forward, half-bent, into the desk, hip pressed against the wood, her hand held firmly from inside the open drawer. Whimpering, she tries to tug her arm back, to pull it *out*, but it won't come. She realizes with an odd, almost numb, feeling of despair, that the tendrils wrapped around her arm are dense with prickly thorns that bite painfully into her flesh. Combined with the feeling of tiny wooden leaves brushing lightly against her punctured skin, she suddenly feels as if she's unwittingly stuck her hand deep into a rose bush (a bush that has somehow come *alive*) and cannot pull it free.

From the wall of shelves behind her, Tyson's stereo clicks on.

She screams in surprise as white noise erupts from the speakers, any remaining calm or reason slipping cleanly away between one heartbeat and the next, her nerves filling instead with a hot, all-consuming terror. She twists her head in time to see the receiver light up, the radio dial needle wiggle jaggedly left-to-right, as if searching for a station. *What to play, what to play,* she thinks for no reason at all. Or has someone else thought it? Can this really be happening?

Before she can answer herself, there's another vicious *yank* on her arm, as if the desk is snapping at her to *PAY ATTENTION TO ME!* She spins around as more ivy lifts free to wrap around her forearm so tightly that the flesh between the black coils bulges bright red with the pressure of blood beneath her skin.

She groans as a melody begins to play over the speakers, the volume gradually increasing until the music distorts, the bass vibrating the very shelves the speakers rest upon.

*Don't leave me in all this pain, don't leave me out in the rain...*

*Come back and bring back my smile...*

Laughter. Sarah cries out, eyes wide enough to show whites as the sensuous voice of Toni Braxton blares from behind her head. She wraps her free hand around her forearm and tries desperately to pull it from the constricting grip of the entwined branches inside the drawer, but they hold her fast and, to her chilling horror, she sees *more* movement along the surface of the desk now.

The carved faces are all *looking* at her, their wooden visages grinning and laughing. The engraved animals snap and snarl and bark, the naked figures of men and women furiously dance and fuck and writhe.

The goddamned thing has *come alive!*

And still the music keeps playing, the song so loud that her head is filled with it, overriding her thoughts, drowning out her grunts of exertion. Her struggle. Her fear.

*Bring back those nights when I held you beside me!*

*UN-BREEEAAAK MY HEAAARRT!*

*SAY YOU'LL LOVE ME AGAAAAIN!*

The drawer slides open and the vines which hold her arm force her hand outward, then, with a jerk, *twist* it so her palm is flipped over, the pad of her thumb pressed firmly against the edge of the desk, the back of her hand facing the lip of the open drawer.

Half-in, half-out.

As her arm is unnaturally wrenched, she shrieks in pain, forced to turn her entire body to keep the bones in her wrist from snapping. Frantic now, she pulls madly, crying for release, but the coils of wood only squeeze more tightly, the thorns digging deeper into her flesh, cutting her badly enough that blood runs freely down her wrist, drips from her fingers into the open mouth of the drawer. She bends awkwardly across the surface of the desk, trying to find balance, some new leverage. Desperate, she kicks at the wooden legs, pounds the stone top with her free hand. Screams for help, for mercy.

*That damned music! I can't think I can't THINK!*

Sarah sobs and begs, tugs and jerks and fights with all her might to get free, to get AWAY!

Meanwhile, the drawer slowly slides open, further and further.

She has only a moment to think:

*It's winding up. The son-of-a-bitch is cocking its damned fist.*

Then the drawer—as if pulled taut by an invisible rubber band—releases.

It *slams* into the desk, ramming full force into the back of Sarah's knuckles. There's a loud *crunch* as two of the metacarpal bones in her hand shatter.

She lifts her head and screams her throat raw as Toni Braxton's voice blares through the office, as if eager to match her desperation.

*UN-CRY THESE TEAAARS!*

*I CRIED SO MAAANY, MANY NIGHTS...*

*UN-BREAK MY HEEAAR-AAART!!*

The drawer slides slowly, methodically, open once more.

"Stop!" she screams. "Please STOP!"

And, inexplicably, "I'm SORRY!"

A dry voice whispers into her ear and she dares not turn to look at it, dares not see who—or *what*—is standing beside her, jabbering into her ear, its breath hot and foul.

"Snoop!" it says, its voice a serpent's hiss. "You hit us? We hit you *back*."

Sarah arches her head and shrieks as the drawer slams shut again, snapping bones in three of her fingers against the hard edge. All the faces trapped in the black wood howl with delight, mocking her own screams, her cries of pain, relishing it. *Feeding* on it.

Entering shock, she slumps across the desktop, arm bent awkwardly, and tries one last time to pull her bloody, broken hand free of the wooden vines clutching it. Sobbing, her face smeared with snot and sweat and tears, she stares through blurred vision to where the ropes of strange wooden ivy have lifted away from the desk. Through her shock and pain and terror one word shoots across her mind like a crackle of lightning splitting the sky:

*Impossible!*

But the thought is soon lost in another white-hot blast of agony as the drawer whips shut with a *CRACK* against her broken bones, her split, bleeding flesh...

Again, and again, and again...

# THIRTY-FOUR

THE BRAKES of the train screech as the car slows. Violet hoped to find a seat where she could sit and read, but the car is full. Instead, she slips on her headphones and tries to ignore the guy reaching over her for the handrail. He smells of body odor with a lovely aromatic undercurrent of spoiled cabbage.

She isn't thrilled about leaving and is already wondering if she's made a mistake. Things at home are definitely... *off.* Her father, never a mountain of stability to begin with, seems downright neurotic and, apparently, borderline violent. What he'd done to Sarah is something Violet will never be able to forget, or truly forgive. Yes, she loves her father, but these last few days she's seen a side of him she'd never known. How long, she wonders, has he been acting like this? Has Sarah been putting up with this bullshit all this time and Violet has simply been too narcissistic, too wrapped up in her own little world of college and parties, to notice?

She hates the idea of Sarah having to cope alone, but also prays it isn't as bad as it seems. Or, at least, it's a temporary thing the two of them will eventually work through. Her dad *is* a great guy, and he's always been there for her—was there when her mother died and, if she's honest with herself, is there for her now as she drains the coffers dry to get an education from one of the best universities in the country.

It's this train of thought that gives Violet pause, a sick feeling growing in her stomach.

*My God, am* I *the cause of all this? The money? My tuition... it must be stretching things for him financially. I knew things were bad but are they worse than I thought? Is all this—the way he's acting, the strain of their relationship—* MY *fault?*

Before Violet can ponder the question (or her encroaching sense of guilt) further, the music pulsing through her headphones is interrupted by the *beep-beep* of her phone's alert tone.

She has a voice message.

Brow furrowed, she wonders why the call didn't come through, but assumes the subway train must have been too far underground at the time. She pulls the phone from her jacket pocket, sees the message had been left by SARAH.

The sick feeling in her guts grows tenfold for reasons Violet doesn't understand. But as the train slows to a stop at 110th Street, she listens to Sarah's breathless, horrible, terrifying message.

Violet feels the blood rush from her face. Without further thought, she pushes through the dense pocket of people entering the train and flees from the car a moment before the doors slide shut. Her backpack—crammed with dirty clothes, books, and toiletries—bounces against her back as she sprints for the stairs.

As she takes them two at a time, she thinks about calling a taxi, but realizes it might be faster to run the half-mile to the Mount Sinai Emergency Room.

It takes her only seconds to make the decision.

She runs.

---

TYSON FINISHES lunch with Harry and walks to Westsider Rare Books, the midday stroll to his favorite bookshop more an effort to clear his head than a desire to actually purchase anything (especially given Harry's disconcerting power-play, and Tyson's newfound questionable finances).

After he spends some time browsing the densely packed shelves, and another chunk of time autographing the small stack of Tyson Parks first editions brought out by the proprietor (a pock-faced old hippy named Chet who is always happy to turn a profit on Tyson's occasional visit), Tyson makes the unusual-for-him decision to walk home rather than take the subway. He's enjoying the exercise, revitalized by the chilled, sweet post-rain breath the city rarely offers during the sacred days that mark the transition from fall into winter.

It's late afternoon approaching dusk when he finally arrives home, feeling refreshed and invigorated, feeling *himself* for the first time in what feels like a long while. He's still worried about Harry, sure, but his mind is clear, and the city's air settles like thin armor on his weather-reddened skin.

In his elated state, he doesn't notice the unusual cold of the house's interior, the slight breeze passing through the air. The broken window in the adjacent room.

Humming a showtune, he pours himself a drink and sits down at the kitchen table to playback his messages.

There is only one.

He listens, wide-eyed, to the frantic, tear-strewn message Violet left with his service. As the automated voice relays the time of her call, he checks his watch, a soft moan escaping his mouth.

If Violet's message was correct, Sarah's already in surgery.

Panicked, Tyson stands abruptly—eager to hail a cab and get himself to the emergency room—and by doing so knocks his drink off the table.

"Damn it."

Surrounded by early evening shadow, he flicks on the lights in order to retrieve the dropped glass before leaving.

It's only then that he sees all the blood.

---

**TWENTY MINUTES** later, Tyson is running through the automated doors of Mount Sinai's emergency waiting room. The rain has started again and he's soaked through, his glasses fogged to the point where he's forced to remove them in order to find his daughter, who he locates hugging her knees on a blue chair in the corner of the room, rocking like a frightened child.

Violet embraces him and recounts her knowledge of events, which was slim as she could only relay what she'd heard in Sarah's brief message.

Some sort of freak accident. Sarah had fallen and broken her hand—*badly.*

"It's really weird, Dad, because the policeman who was here earlier told me no one answered the door, and he could see through a window that she was passed out on the kitchen floor. They had to break the window just to get inside," Violet says with quick, gulping breaths. "There's no way she just... *fell*, or whatever. Something *happened* to her."

"What do you mean? What happened?" Tyson asks, shaking and nauseous, part of him knowing he doesn't want to hear the answer to his question. Not really.

"No idea. But Dad, I talked to the surgeon before they put her under. She told me the hand isn't just broken... it's *mangled*. Something like twelve different bones are shattered, and she'll probably have permanent nerve damage. It's really bad," Violet says weakly, her voice thick with emotion. "What the hell happened to her?"

Tyson hugs his daughter close, rubs her back as she cries quietly against his thin raincoat. "I don't know," he says.

But deep down, with a bizarre sense of something akin to pride, he *does* know.

And while consoling his daughter and waiting for the doctors to desperately try and put his lover's hand back together, Tyson fights the incredible—undeniably horrible—urge to smile.

# THIRTY-FIVE

"MY DEAR, you must understand that I can't give out that information." Anton stares at the woman sitting on the other side of his desk with open suspicion. "Frankly, I'm surprised you'd even ask. I have a feeling you know it's impossible."

Anton noticed the woman as unique the moment she walked into the showroom. She's tall and well-dressed (in a slightly European fashion), olive-skinned with striking black hair. He immediately pegged her as old aristocratic money, a vibe that contrasted only slightly with her obvious youth. He figures she's not a day over thirty, and strikes him as someone who knows what she wants. And how to get it.

And what she wants, it turns out, after the usual dance of greetings, small talk, and banal inquiries about some of his showroom pieces, is to know who, precisely, had acquired that Victorian gothic desk, and—if it isn't too much trouble—how much they paid for it.

At first, he played coy, mentioning the great many antique desks he'd sold that month alone, but of course always knowing *exactly* the desk she meant. In fact, he's been thinking about that very item more and more in the past week; even fantasizing—*those carvings, the slick black oak, the flawless stone slab that serves as its top*—about it. Truly, it is one-of-a-kind, and he'd let it go for a song. Of course, twenty-five thousand dollars is a sweet song to listen to, a tune that always brings a smile to his face with its steady beat and gay chorus. But he also knows he could have commanded nearly six figures for it, assuming he felt like putting in the time and energy to market the item, versus simply making a lone phone call to a certain writer's wealthy girlfriend who once mentioned she was in the market for something similar.

Yes, he had let go of it easily. Almost *eagerly.*

*And why do you think that was?* he asks himself, for well past the hundredth time.

He doesn't know the answer. It just *felt* like the proper thing to do. Frankly, part of him was glad to be rid of it. He would never even hint such feelings to a client, but that desk had given him the creeps. And that was *before* the accident, and the subsequent death of Marco, whose fifty-three-year-old heart had called it quits while on the operating table. Regardless, he'd made the sale, delivered it—along with seven strong men, heavy-duty dollies, and a pulley-rig. He still isn't completely sure how they fit it into the office, despite his studious pre-measurements.

Regardless, that was that.

But now there's this woman. This mysterious Mademoiselle Diana Montresor, like a femme fatale from an old mystery novel, with her many questions.

In addition to her preposterous demands, she also *very* much wants to know when, exactly, the desk arrived in his possession, and from whom Anton himself had acquired it.

She attempts to make all these inquiries logical by making the case that the desk is somehow her property—or, more specifically, the property of someone she represents. Someone from afar. A mysterious grandfather, a Count, or some such romantic nonsense.

Anton laughed at first, but found her interesting (and, truthfully, very attractive), and so offered to speak more about her concern, which is how they had ended up in his office, chatting like old university mates; he with an eye on asking her to dinner, and she with the questions and those brilliant black eyes, that cunning smile.

Attractive or not, he can't help but see her as a predator—perhaps a Lycan in human form, a skin-walker, a Therianthrope whose other shape is most likely a puma, or a jaguar.

"Of course," she replies smoothly. "I admire your ethics, Anton. However, I just want to speak to the owner for a few minutes. I want to make them an offer to buy the merchandise back. A substantial offer, I should add."

Anton puts his feet on his desk, amused. "Then why not let me broker the deal? It's what I do after all. If they bite, you get your desk, they get wealthier, and I get, shall we say, twenty percent?"

But Diana is already shaking her head. "I'm afraid not. I must see this person directly. If they've become too attached to the piece, I'll want to know before conducting my business."

Anton tries to place her accent. At first, based solely on appearance, he thinks she might be Greek. Then figures her for Italian. Hearing her speak, he ends up at French, but with an accent he's never heard before. "If you don't mind me asking," he says, "and please accept my apologies if this is horribly rude, but... your eyes..."

Diana tilts her head, then brushes her hair back from her face in a startling gesture. "It's called aniridia. Or a form of it anyway," she says apathetically, as if describing the provenance of a particularly rare objet d'art. "It's a genetic condition. Simply put, I was born without an iris in either eye, at least visibly. I inherited it from my grandmother, who also had it, and eventually went completely blind." She shrugs. "That may be my lot as well, but there's nothing to be done about it, I'm afraid. So, now that you know such a personal secret, how about you share one with me? Where did you get the desk?"

Anton laughs lightly, not wanting to hurt her feelings but beyond impressed with her manner of dealing with both her condition, and her powers of negotiation. "Fascinating," he says under his breath, then drops his feet and leans forward, switching his posture back to business. "Well, as I've said, that's all classified. There's nothing more I can tell you. I'm sorry you wasted a trip." He gives her his best salesman smile, the one that closed a thousand deals with thousands of wealthy men, wealthier women, widowers and widows, desperate husbands and bored housewives. "However, may I suggest we continue the conversation over dinner?"

Diana returns his smile with one of her own, and Anton finds himself smitten. *By God, she's beautiful,* he thinks. *The most beautiful woman I've ever seen.*

As she peers deeply into his eyes, he feels himself falling in love. Her eyes are glistening like pools of ink, and he finds himself staring into them. It's almost as if he's *drifting* closer, straight for those beautiful dark windows into the soul; they're so large... so perfectly spherical, and... *expanding.* Growing like black holes that he floats toward and falls into, as if he were a naked astronaut floating through space, pulled in by her gravity, slipping delightfully through cosmic clouds of luscious daydreams where their future together flashes in his mind as memories—long trips and handsome children, mad adventures, and peaceful old age. He badly wants to sleep with her, to feel every inch of her skin, kiss every part of her body.

He barely registers her speaking.

*I'm afraid I haven't been completely honest, Anton. I already know who has the desk, but confirmation from your own lips would have been helpful. Sadly, I still need to know who you acquired the desk from. I'll have to make sure those accounts are settled, you see. I suppose you could say it's personal. Quite personal.*

And still he falls, and falls, and falls into his strange, romantic thoughts. It is a feeling not unlike sinking, but wholly pleasant.

*I'll also need you to confirm the price, please. My detective, though thorough, was not able to acquire that bit of information, and it would be most helpful for my own negotiation.*

Part of Anton—a distant, uncaring part—knows that he's answering, divulging information he has no right to share...

but it's as if he's left his body and is now somewhere far away, embraced in the warm, pink ether of true love.

She asks her questions, and he answers them gladly, his body pulsing with lust, overflowing with a deep love he's never felt for anyone. Soon, he is swallowed whole by his own thoughts, his bizarre fantasies, and everything melts into a blissful, nurturing darkness that he hopes to never return from.

---

**LATER, WHEN** he comes back to himself, he assumes he'd simply dozed off.

There is no sign of his mysterious visitor.

He laughs about it. It's quite unlike him to lose his reason in flights of romantic fancy, and even more strange to fall asleep in the middle of the day—in his own office, no less.

*I must be getting narcoleptic in my old age.*

His cheer fades somewhat when he looks at his watch to find the day nearly over; to realize he'd so badly lost track of time.

Nearly four hours have passed since he and Diana first sat down in his office, and while he should be alarmed, the only emotion he feels is disappointment.

He'd forgotten to ask for her number.

# THIRTY-SIX

WORRIED ABOUT Sarah and, to a large (albeit unspoken) degree, her father, Violet decides to extend her stay in the city for an additional week. She notifies the school of a family emergency and lets her professors know she will be missing the first few classes of the new semester. Her decision pleases Tyson immensely (despite his weak protestations to the contrary), both because it means he can spend more time with her and, less selfishly, because it will help keep Sarah's spirits up.

After an initial eight-hour delay in the hospital waiting room, they'd finally been able to see Sarah, who, after what was being deemed a successful surgery, was admitted for overnight observation.

Tyson recoiled at the sight of her.

She was pale as a ghost, drawn and skeletal in appearance. Black bags sagged beneath sleeping eyes and her left arm was covered in a blue cast, fingertips to elbow, and two large steel pins jutted out of the plaster covering the hand. The arm was attached to a bedside pulley that kept it elevated and away from her body while she slept.

He and Violet had stayed until midnight, during which time Sarah became alert only once. Groggy and bleary-eyed, she had looked at Tyson, frowned, and turned her head away.

The doctor told them to come back in the morning.

Now home, Violet helps Tyson tape heavy plastic over the window the police smashed for entry, then vacuum the glass off the carpet and nearby furniture. They clean the smeared blood off the tiles of the kitchen floor, the stains on the countertop and on the cell phone, from which she'd managed to call for help. They consider scrubbing out the drips of blood dried into the hallway carpet like red-spattered breadcrumbs, the staggered path of which led from the edge of the tiled kitchen floor to the closed door of Tyson's office.

"Why would she go to your office?" Violet asks.

Tyson shrugs. "No idea. Anyway, we'll deal with it tomorrow, or I'll have a service come," he says, and Violet, exhausted, doesn't argue. That final decision of the evening made, she wearily kisses her father on the cheek and goes straight to bed.

---

AS 2 A.M. approaches, Tyson feels neither fatigued nor complacent. He makes a drink and paces the living room. He wishes he had remodeled the roof when he'd had the means; sitting in the cool night and watching the stars on a sleepless night would have suited him fine.

After his second drink, he pours a third and, after a momentary hesitation, finally musters the courage to follow the pattern of dripping blood to the office, deathly afraid of what he will find there.

Once inside, he flips the switch by the door, which turns on a rarely used overhead light. The blood is less obvious in here, blending with the dark hardwood and deep reds of the rugs. He follows the spotted trail to the desk.

And finds... nothing.

It's as if she'd walked to the desk and vanished. There's no blood on the desktop, nothing on the floor. He wipes a thumb across a few red specks on his laptop and sees a fine mist of scarlet on the top page of his manuscript, but those things are easily taken care of. He sticks his thumb in his mouth, sucks the flesh clean, the tang of blood on his tongue quickly swallowed away. He crumples the top page from the stack of papers, the only one that appears to have been soiled, into a scrunched ball and throws it into the waste basket.

After checking it for blood, he settles into his chair, runs his fingers along the wood lip of the desk. He inspects everything closely and pauses only when he comes to the top-left drawer, which is not fully closed.

Frowning, he pulls it open, not surprised that it slides out smoothly and easily, as if it were greased. Along the edges of the rectangular cutout where the drawer meets the desk, he notices filaments of pale pink skin; tiny pieces stuck along the edge of the wood, a few no bigger than a flake of dandruff, and none bigger than a fingernail.

*Speaking of fingernails,* he thinks, and gently removes one (slightly mangled) rose-colored fingernail from the bottom of the open drawer. He thinks it looks like a pinky nail, but it's hard to tell. All her fingers are fairly small.

Humming an old Ramones tune he can't recall the name of, Tyson cleans away the skin fragments with a tissue and tosses it into the lined trashcan, where it falls alongside the crumpled, blood-sprayed page.

"What happened to the blood?" he says, and waits, as if the desk might reply. Then he lies his head flat against the cool surface of the stone desktop. The voices whisper again, except this time he has no problem understanding exactly what they are saying.

"Uh-huh," he says, and chuckles like a schoolboy whose feet are being gently tickled. "That makes sense, all right. And yes, I like it. I really do."

As he listens, a thin and exceptionally sharp tendril of wood uncoils near the bottom of one of the desk's legs. It slips up his pant cuff and gently pierces the skin, inserting itself into the meat of his calf with the expertise of a well-tuned junkie tapping a vein.

Tyson doesn't notice or, at least, doesn't mind. What is writing if not the metaphorical giving of one's blood, after all? Isn't this just more of the same?

Meanwhile, the voices continue to whisper, frantically telling Tyson everything he needs to know, everything he wants to hear, and he can't be more thrilled.

And oh, by God!

It's fascinating stuff...

They're telling him a new story.

Part Seven

# NEGOTIATIONS

# THIRTY-SEVEN

SARAH RETURNS home the next day.

Tyson and Violet went to the hospital early and were pleasantly surprised to find her sitting up in bed, eating a full breakfast, and watching the news on a television mounted high on the wall between herself and the patient she shared the room with, a towheaded teenager with a busted leg.

Sarah assures them she's feeling okay, that the doctor said she could leave when she wanted. She has a prescription for painkillers and a follow-up appointment with the surgeon at his office in mid-town the following week.

What she doesn't tell them is about the terror she'd felt at nighttime. The horrible dreams, the recurrence of the visions she'd had when attacked. Her inability to quantify what had actually happened. Her fear of having had a psychotic episode, of being broken—that she's begun the long walk down that dirty, pit-filled road toward mental illness.

"The doctor says I'll be fairly pain-free in a couple weeks and can get off the harder meds, but until then I need to take it easy. Not do any heavy lifting, obviously."

Tyson is overwhelmed with joy at seeing her lucid and, seemingly, her old self again. "I think we'll just have to bring you breakfast, lunch, and dinner in bed for a while. Maybe load up your Kindle with a bunch of those John Connolly books you like so much." He beams at her, practically bursting with happiness and relief, and is only the slightest bit disappointed that her general mood is less than thrilled, distantly unhappy, and certainly not loving. Her smiles toward him are empty, and when she meets his eyes they're emotionless. Almost vacant.

*It's like she's putting on some sort of act,* he thinks, but dismisses the negative vibes as best he can. The important thing is that she's alright, and that she's coming *home*.

They're all going home, together, and right away. Immediately, in fact.

After all, he has a lot of work to do.

---

**SARAH DOESN'T** speak to him during the drive, choosing to sit in the rear of the Mercedes with Violet while Tyson drives them through the city like a chauffeur. He catches her eye once or twice in the rearview mirror, but she looks away each time, as if caught.

*Or disgusted.*

Despite her refusal to discuss what happened, sticking with her story of "falling awkwardly," a see-through fable so blatant it had more than one nurse giving Tyson the wife-beater stink-eye, he can't think of what he might have done—at least as it pertained to her injury—that she would hold him in such obvious contempt.

After all, he isn't the goddamned *snoop,* is he?

No, he most certainly is not. *She's* the one that went into his office, and *she* was the one who decided to dig through his drawers, through his PRIVATE stuff. Oh, yes, he'd been *well-informed* of the situation. And yet he's the one getting the sidelong glances, the distasteful looks, the *silent treatment.*

*As a matter of fact, I'm pretty sure they're BOTH giving me the business,* he thinks, eyeballing the rearview mirror when he isn't avoiding taxicabs or asshole jaywalkers. *Look at them. Conspirators. Whispering secrets, making up lies about me, about my* WORK.

"You two okay back there?" he calls, trying to sound cheerful, like part of the group. Only Violet offers a half-hearted response, staring out the window as if bored, or upset. *You two don't fool me,* he thinks sourly, and wallows in brooding silence for the remainder of the drive.

As they enter the townhouse, the shrill ring of the phone shatters the stillness.

Tyson ignores it, continues holding Sarah's (good) elbow lightly as they walk down the hall toward the stairwell. "Violet, would you?"

He walks Sarah up the stairs to their bedroom, gets her settled, fluffs her pillows and makes sure she has a glass of water for her pain medicine. He gets her a book and the remote control for the small flatscreen TV they'd recently added to watch late-night shows while snuggled together in bed or have the news on in the mornings when getting dressed. Tyson feels a pang of remorse at the thought, disturbed by how far they've drifted from those comfortable days in such a short time.

"Anything else you need?"

She attempts a wan smile and shakes her head. "Just gonna sleep. Still pretty wiped out from everything."

"Of course." He takes a few steps toward the door, then stops. He turns back, takes a moment to look at her—to *really* look at her—his Sarah, his great love, his soulmate. He sees the pain she's in, a pain made even worse by the distance between them. The emotional partition is almost palpable, a living thing that had snuck into their home in the night and settled into their private, personal spaces, building its nest from strips of pain, broken shards of grief. To Tyson it seems the two of them now live in a bleak house on a distant moor, surrounded by fog, their calls to one another growing more distant every passing day, and as the fog thickens, they drift further and further apart.

"Sarah, honey..." he says, and she looks not at him but the small remote control, as if studying it for defects. "I know... I..."

He takes a quick step toward her, the suddenness of the movement causing her to look at him sharply, and he prays that isn't fear in her eyes. The words come in a rush then, a whispered, hurried, insistent stream of forbidden truths. It's as if, for a moment, he has found the will—the *freedom*—to be himself once more.

"Baby, it's not me, please understand. This isn't me."

She watches him steadily, her eyes slightly lidded, but not with malice. "No?"

He points toward the door, finger trembling with accusation.

Neither of them think it insane when he lowers his voice, as if not wanting to be overheard. "It's... this sounds crazy, I know, it does, but Sarah... it's that *desk*. I think, my God how do I start? It's making me do things... *think* things... it's, I don't know, affecting me somehow." He points the accusatory finger at his own chest, stabs himself with it to emphasize his words, his defense. "This isn't *me*, Sarah. It's..."

"The desk." She speaks the words with such indifference that he wonders for a beat whether the drugs are making her stupid, or if she's just that fucking cold.

He nods sheepishly, and opens his mouth to continue, but she shakes her head, looks down to her shattered hand. When she speaks, it's with such softness, such delicacy, that if they'd carried any other conjunction of vowels and consonants than the ones she actually uses, they might have been words of love, or forgiveness.

"It's not the desk, Tyson," she says, then raises her heavy eyes, bruised with exhaustion, to look at him directly. "It's you, Tyson. It's you, honey. It's always been you."

Tyson straightens in affronted surprised, and closes his open mouth. They stare at each other a moment, her words settling down on them both, covering their feelings like an early frost on summer flowers, killing them.

He sees, with a souring stomach and a weakening of his knees, that there is no love in her eyes. Not for him.

Not anymore.

"Dad!" Violet yells from the bottom of the stairs. "It's Harry. He says it's mucho important. His words, not mine," she adds.

Tyson gives Sarah a wide-eyed, questioning look, the mask of a reaction he might have once used when sharing a moment with her. He clears his throat, puts on a weak smile. Deciding, for now, to pretend she hadn't said those words at all. That the look in her eyes was a lie.

"Well," he says, his tone light, "it seems I'm needed." He doubles-down on his parody, making a funny face he knows Sarah loves, the one where he crosses his eyes and pushes out his bottom lip. For a split-second she smiles, as if also wanting to play the game, join him in pretending things are okay. And the moment is enough—enough for him—and he thinks, perhaps, that it isn't as bad as he thinks. That the wounds to their relationship aren't fatal, that maybe she's just tired, and in pain, and...

But then the smile is gone, and her eyes drift away.

A cold rush of loneliness floods his chest and chills him. "Well," he says awkwardly, "I guess I better go see what old Harry wants. Guy doesn't answer my calls for months, and now I can't get rid of him. Agents, right?"

"Mmm." She turns toward the windows, as if willing him to be gone. To disappear.

"Just... let me know if you need something," he says emptily.

"Tyson?"

He turns, and perhaps it was the last threads of a summer's dying love, or perhaps nothing more than pity, but she's at least looking at him once more, with something in her eyes he can't quite place. A strange amalgam of hope and hate, love and pain. "It's okay," she starts, then, hesitantly, "you know, if you take it in here. I'm kind of curious, to be honest. Use the extension."

"You sure?"

She nods, and for a moment it's Sarah again, the woman he loves. The woman who loved him. The icy emptiness in his heart melts a little, and he walks to the phone on the nightstand, picks it up, and presses TALK.

"I got it, Violet," he says into the receiver, and hears the *click* as she disconnects.

"Hiya, Harry. What's cooking?"

# THIRTY-EIGHT

SARAH STARES at the light coming through the windows as Tyson mumbles the occasional "uh-huh" or "okay" into the phone.

*Fucking Harry. Pulling Tyson like taffy at a county fair. Stretching him to a breaking point. And look who suffers for it. There's plenty of blame to go around, of course. I was the dope who brought that* thing *into our home, after all.*

She sighs and rolls onto her side to watch Tyson talk, wincing at the pain in her arm as it brushes the bed, lighter than a falling fly's wing but painful as a hundred bee stings.

*That, however, is a situation I plan on resolving,* she thinks, trying not to feel disgusted at Tyson's lumpy body, his drawn, haggard face, his dumbass expression. Feeling sick with herself, at what her life has become, she closes her eyes, focuses on her breathing, on ignoring the pain licking up her arm like fire...

"You're shitting me!"

Sarah's eyes fly open and she turns her head. Tyson has turned to look at her as well, his eyes wide and vibrant. Young.

He shakes his head slightly as he stares down at her, his expression a mix of disbelief and surprise. *He looks like a man who's been told he just won the lottery, or that a distant uncle just died and left him a massive estate, most likely in some drab foreign country, atop a steep cliff overlooking a gray, stormy ocean.*

Despite her pain, despite their distance, and despite the inexplicable horror of what happened in his office (something she will not think about right now, no no... that's something she'll save for later, when she's strong, when she's *ready),* she hopes it's good news for a change. She *does* still love him. At least she thinks she does. Hopes she does.

But...

"I understand," Tyson says, holding her eyes with such intensity it cuts her from her thoughts. "Okay, thank you Harry. Uh-huh, yes, that's right. Sure, email it over and I'll... uh-huh, well, send a messenger then. I'm here all day. We've... okay. Okay. Bye, Harry. Yes. Goodbye."

Tyson presses the button to end the call, then walks to the foot of the bed and sits down, his back to her.

"Ty?"

He turns to her and smiles—as big and dopey a smile as she's seen on his face in years. She wants to hold him and kiss that dumb face, kiss away the last couple of weeks, love away all the pain and strangeness and *evil,* the bizarre occurrences. She wants her life back, wants it back desperately.

"Tell me, dummy," she says, not unkindly. It's their old banter, their easy back-and-forth, their old, comfortable love and concern for one another. God, but it feels wonderful.

"Well, first off, I never got the chance to tell you," he says, "but at lunch Harry revealed that he'd loved the novel so much that he pulled the deal from Morrow, said he was going to shop it."

"My God, can he do that? It seems like a bad idea to upset..."

But Tyson waves his hand at her, indicating none of it matters, that it's somehow irrelevant. "Yeah, I know, I know, but... he did it anyway. But he also let them read the thing, just in case they want to increase their offer. You know, before he shopped it." He pauses and stares at the floor, as if he's lost his train of thought. Like he's been turned off and now needs to recharge.

"And?"

Tyson continues to gaze at the floor. His words, when they come, are slow and methodical, as if he doesn't want to mess them up, to twist them so that, once they enter the world, their very definition changes, and whatever news he has will end up being something completely different.

"They were pissed about the deal, of course. But they read the book anyway. Well, Harry says they went crazy for it." Sounding more confused than excited, he continues slowly, as if in a daze, or describing a particularly strange dream. "They think it'll be the biggest thing I've ever done."

He turns his gaze away from the floor, looks into her eyes.

*My God,* she thinks, *he's trembling.*

"They raised the advance to half-a-million," he says quietly. "Harry thinks we can get twice that in foreign sales, and he... well, he said he's already fielding calls from studios for the movie rights. Apparently, word spreads fast."

Sarah sits up, feels a hot twinge of pain in her wrist, but ignores it. "Tyson..."

"The best part?" he says, wearing the dopey smile again, and sounding more like himself. Like the *old* Tyson. "They say the half-a-million is on top of the advance they've already given me. Harry worked it out, you know, with the old advance. The money I already spent."

"Already spent..."

But Tyson waves her off again, and it's a credit to her curiosity that his repeated usage of that little maneuver doesn't bug the shit out of her. "Okay, so..."

"So... they told him, and this is Harry's exact quote: 'Consider it a bonus.'"

Tyson begins to laugh, and then he stands up and laughs even harder. "A BONUS!" he roars, and his face reddens with apoplectic glee. "Baby, oh baby!" he half-yells, half-sings. He lifts his arms and begins to dance like he's trying to pull water from the sky, and Sarah thinks she's never seen him look so *free*.

"Tyson," she says loudly, unable to contain her own stupid grin as he stops his ridiculous rain dance and begins hopping from foot-to-foot, swinging his elbows side-to-side like a guy with ants in his pants. "Honey... what the hell are you doing?"

"The Twist, I think!" he yells, giddy as a Baptist preacher in a revival tent.

He reaches out to pull her off the bed, momentarily forgetting the fact that her hand has been shattered into pieces, that only a day ago she'd been bleeding out on the kitchen floor, staring numbly at a splinter of bone poking through her skin like she was in a horror movie.

She waves him away with her good hand, laughing despite it all, despite everything. Tyson's moods were always infectious, and this is no different. Every time she wants to loathe the bastard, every time she wants to *hate* him, all she can pull from that deep old well of emotion is love. Love and more love.

*And ain't that a bitch?* she thinks, and watches her lover, her best friend, as he dances.

By the time Violet comes running into the bedroom to see what the ruckus is all about, Sarah and Tyson are both laughing uproariously, and Violet wonders, for a split-second, whether the two of them have gone completely mad.

# THIRTY-NINE

TYSON DOESN'T feel comfortable working while the men repair the living room window, so he sits in the kitchen sipping coffee while trying to read an advance review copy of a new story collection he'd been asked to blurb.

He considers leaving the house altogether, but Violet is away for the afternoon and Sarah can't be left alone. She is, for all intents and purposes, bedridden. She suffers from waves of terrible pain and weakness, the latter brought on mainly by the pills, so much so that Tyson has to help her to the bathroom when necessary, then back to the bed. He brings her food and water, books or magazines. He doesn't mind. In a few days she'll be up and around once more, arm in sling, and eventually she'll be able to go back to work, although the small antiquities shop where she works part-time certainly doesn't need her rushing things. Tyson called the shop earlier that day and Mr. Flagg, the owner, was more than happy to fill in while Sarah recovered.

Temporarily giving up on the book of stories, Tyson strolls to the window, does a cursory glance at the work being done. The contractor, standing on the sidewalk outside and yapping into a cellphone, gives a thumbs-up, which Tyson reciprocates with a small wave. He considers checking in on Sarah but decides to go to his office instead.

As always (and especially since his latest publishing windfall), he feels an immense relief when he sees the desk waiting for him. *Don't worry, Daddy's home,* he thinks cheerily as he strides to his chair. He runs his fingers along the desk's edge as he always does, enjoying the gentle tickles of the ivy reaching out to stroke and playfully stab at his fingers. Every now and then they prick him too hard, drawing blood, but that's okay. He's grown used to the feel of fabric band-aids on his fingertips (an assorted six out of ten currently sport the flesh-tone bandages), and it does little to slow his typing speed.

And, for better or worse, that's really all he's doing. *Typing.* The words are simply dictated to him. Not out loud, of course, but quietly, into his ear, into his *brain.*

He opens the laptop and brings up the new novel. He's only about twenty thousand words in and is itching to get back to it. It's such an amazing *rush* to know—to absolutely KNOW—the *exact* words he's going to type next. No absent-minded musing, no beating his fists against his head to find the right phrase, no pacing around the office to come up with the perfect plot twist, no notebooks filled with ideas and snippets of dialogue or character traits... just the *words.* It's... pure. Yes, that's the word for it.

*Pure.*

He aches to feel the keys beneath his fingers, and the desk feels similarly. The ivy stretches upward, waving like weeds at the bottom of a cold sea, soothing him... coaxing him to work. The faces in the woodwork all chatter—incessantly, but oh so quietly—in rushed, eager whispers.

Admittedly, Tyson doesn't care much for those faces. If he were being *completely* honest with himself, they sort of scare the shit out of him. He often feels himself being *watched,* seeing strange, subtle movements out of the corner of his eye, like someone just out of his vision is taunting him with malicious expressions, sticking out their tongue and wiggling their ears. But he doesn't think they're doing that, no... he thinks that, perhaps, the looks they give him—when he is distracted or looking a different direction—are *cruel* faces. Snarling, teeth-gritting, *hateful* faces. Other times, of course, they seem perfectly happy. When he's writing, for instance, they talk excitedly, or laugh, or—every now and again—*sing.*

Still.

There's a distant part of his brain, the part that remains of the *old* Tyson, that finds the animated qualities of the desk exceptionally disturbing.

Finds the whole thing... *wrong.*

But he'd never voice such a thing, not again. It was a mistake, what he'd said to Sarah. It was a mistake to question things. After all, he's a success again. He is, as Harry loves to say, *back.*

"I know, I know," he says, running his fingers lightly through the strands of wooden stems and paper-thin leaves. "Soon, I promise."

Across the room, the old man sits hunched in the chair like always, bone-white eyes staring straight ahead, mouth working as he gums his blackened tongue.

But he stays quiet.

For now.

Tyson figured the creepy bastard will continue to stay that way as long as he gets back to work sooner rather than later. He also knows that if the old man gets impatient, he'll be sure to let Tyson know. In spades. Lately, the old bag of bones had begun turning up in some extremely odd places, like a real-life Cryptkeeper leaping out of a web-strewn coffin just to scare the bejesus out of somebody.

Just yesterday, after Tyson took the morning off to care for Sarah, the old man popped up in the shower, jabbing at Tyson's naked ass with his bony finger and hissing at him to "GET TO IT! TO IT! TO IT!" It scared him so badly his foot slipped in surprise and he almost took a spill. *Lucky I didn't crack my head open on the side of the tub.* He was still shaking when he reached for the towel to dry off.

Tyson shudders at the memory. *At least the old fart had been clothed. Still wearing that damned parlor suit, thank God. I wouldn't want to see that guy's prick...*

"Ow!"

Tyson's thoughts break off and he grabs his right hand, hissing at a sharp pain. He lifts his palm to see a three-inch gash running from the base of his thumb to the knuckle of his forefinger. "What the hell was that for?"

Having broken from his thoughtful reverie, he notices, with a stab of sick fear, that the tips of all those floating ivy strands are now *facing* him—hovering ominously in mid-air.

They're pointed right at him. Like snakes emerged from the basket by a charmer's flute, ready to strike when the secret, high-pitched note is blown.

*There must be thirty of them,* he thinks, swallowing a baseball-sized lump of fear. He knows, of course, that those wooden points are razor-sharp, and it quickens his pulse to see them, to see the desk, acting... *aggressively.*

Quickens his pulse, hell. It scares him shitless.

He shifts his gaze to the old man. "I'm going to get back to work as soon as these assholes are done with the window," he says, trying for hostility, but thinks he probably sounds more petulant. "I can't work with them here. It's distracting."

The old man waves him off with disgust, stares with blind eyes out the window. The bland sunlight does nothing to help his features, only bleaches his dead, pale skin even further, makes him almost translucent.

Some of the floating strands move closer, a few now only inches from his face and arms, a couple flicker close enough to his eyeball to click against the lens of his glasses.

*Tap tap scratch. Tap tap scratch...*

For now, the rest only watch. Waiting, he supposes.

*Yeah, but waiting for what? A sign? A green light from the old man?*

*Jesus,* Tyson thinks. *That guy could fill me full of holes with a thought. Slice me apart like a damned melon.*

"You worry too much," the old man grumbles from across the room, picking at his dusty cravat as he stares into the sunlight. "I like it here," he adds. "Good light."

Tyson's about to reply that he couldn't give a rat's ass about the light when a single thread of vine coils around his finger and tugs. *Hard.*

"Hey!"

Another vine grabs the thumb of his opposite hand and pulls. Three more dart at him, enjoying the game, each one grabbing a finger, pulling them forward and side-to-side.

"Okay, okay. Ha ha! Okay, now... Ow... Jesus, stop it. That hurts, damn it!"

The old man chuckles as blood from Tyson's fresh scratches drips onto the surface of the desk and disappears. He watches, mortified, as it's *sucked* into the stone.

Meanwhile, the vines are tugging harder, *jerking* his fingers nearly out of their sockets. "Stop!" he yells, but now more reach for him...

There's a hard knock at the door. "Mr. Parks? It's Jimmy."

*The contractor.* Tyson panics a moment, wondering how he'll explain...

But, in the next instant, they're gone. Hidden away once more.

His fingers are free and the old man has disappeared. The chair sits empty. Tyson is sweating profusely from fear, from his bizarre struggle with the desk. Shakily, he wipes his face with a sleeve, sticks his bleeding hand behind his back, out of sight.

"Come in," he says, attempting calm.

Jimmy opens the door, looks around as if expecting... something.

*He looks spooked. Well, he must have heard me yelling. The fucking* SNOOP.

"How's it going?" Tyson does his best to sound normal. To sound *sane*.

"Oh, ah! Yeah, sorry. We're done, Mr. Parks," he says in the thick accent of a native New Yorker. "I just need you to come give it a lookover and make sure you're good, then we can get outta your hair."

"Excellent," Tyson says, and means it. Not because the window replacement is done, but because he'd never been more relieved to get the hell out of his office.

And away from the goddamned desk.

# FORTY

"I'M GLAD to see you up and about," Billy says, picking at his penne while consistently reaching the bottom of his wine glass.

Sarah *does* look better, Tyson thinks, and the fact she's able to come to the table after only a few days back at home, to sit and have dinner with them, is a good sign. A step in the right direction.

Tyson usually revels in such moments—all his favorite people in one place, sharing a meal, some good conversation, a few laughs. But tonight, his heart isn't into it, his mind occupied with worry, with conflicting thoughts, a fear of something he can't put his finger on. It's like knowing there's someone hiding behind your bedroom door, and that you have no choice but to walk through the doorway, into the dark, and feel their grasping, lunatic fingers.

Violet is especially chatty, and Tyson knows she's excited about returning to school the next day. It's been a stressful week for all of them, and he figures Violet needs to be back with her friends, back to her routine.

"So," Billy says, now well into his cups. "Should I address the elephant in the room?"

Tyson's fork freezes halfway to his mouth, and he notices Sarah pale and look away, as if hoping to find some way to distract their friend to avoid what's coming. Even Violet frowns at her dinner plate.

"I guess not," he mumbles, reading the room. "Regardless, I'm not one for subtlety or sanctity of family secrets, so I'll just ask. How the *hell* did it happen? And don't tell me you fell, love, because I won't believe you."

Sarah shrugs, sticks some pasta into her mouth. "It's what happened. I tripped coming down the stairs, my hand caught under me funny and… snap."

"More like snap, snap, snap, snap…" Billy says, but with a light touch. "I don't see how a fall breaks so many bones, personally. But what do I know? Like I said, I'm just happy to see you back on your feet. Will there be… and I hate to ask… permanent damage?"

Tyson could strangle the man. *Why the hell is he grilling her? Good lord, can't we have one meal where it's not layered with all this fucking drama?*

"You know," Tyson says loudly, sucking at his own wine and smiling too broadly at the rest of them. "This *is* a celebration. My book sale?"

"Ah, that," Billy says. "I'd forgotten all about it, I'm afraid."

Tyson frowns but Billy laughs and raises his glass. "Of course, mate, apologies. To your fabulous sale. Good to see you back on top."

They all clink glasses and the mood lightens. The conversation turns to talk of a trip abroad for the family, perhaps using some of the advance money for a cottage rental on a Greek island somewhere.

Tyson is just starting to have fun again when a loud buzzer squawks from the front door. They all stop talking at the same time.

Someone is at the gate.

---

***SHE LOOKS** like the damned Exorcist.*

That is Tyson's first thought when he sees the tall, well-dressed woman waiting on the sidewalk. She wears a wide-brimmed hat (despite it being well into evening) that shadows her face from the glow of the 1920's-era lights dotting the street. A heavy bag hangs from one clenched hand, dangles at her thigh.

"Mr. Parks?"

"How did you get this address?" he says curtly, assuming it's another nutcase fan that can't differentiate between reality and fiction. The crazy bitch probably figured she'd put on her Halloween outfit and head over to the old horror writer's house for a late-night séance or some bullshit.

"As strange as this may sound," she says, sounding saner than he expected, "I'm here to talk about your recent birthday gift. I'm sorry if it's intrusive, but we must speak immediately. You see, that desk is the property of my grandfather and was sold illegally. It belongs to him. You might call it a family heirloom, one that was stolen from us."

"The desk," he says flatly, frowning.

She takes a step toward him, and now her face does catch the light, igniting the shadows there. *By God, she's a knock-out,* he thinks, ensnared by the dark pools of her eyes, now brushed with gold stars, reflections of the porchlight's glow.

Tyson finds himself torn between shutting the door in her face and, intrigued, letting the woman into his home. *How does she know about the desk? Why would she lie?*

*Because people are liars, THAT'S why!* The voice inside his head is loud, determined, and wholly not his own.

"I'm sorry, I have guests. You can talk to my agent if you need something..."

"Do this in remembrance of me," she says softly. "Does that ring a bell, Mr. Parks?"

Frozen, he stares at her, open-mouthed.

"Like I said, it belongs to my grandfather."

She steps through the front gate, her shining black eyes never leaving his.

*She is so very beautiful, and those eyes...*

"And I'm afraid he'd like it back."

# FORTY-ONE

"THIS IS the most ridiculous thing I've ever heard," Billy says delightedly. "And I love every word of it!"

In the end, Tyson invited the woman inside for reasons he can't piece together. He even poured her a glass of wine, although he could barely recollect having done so. Once seated at the table, wine in hand, she proceeded to introduce herself as Diana Montresor, granddaughter to a Count Jean Montresor (admitting the title has less to do with wealth than his family line, which stems from nobility), who currently resides in an estate in the old-town section of Boulogne-sur-Mer, along the northern coast of France.

"That... *desk*, as you know it, has been in my family for generations," she told them, eyes blazing with age-old fury, her voice almost musical with the rise and lilt of an untrace-able accent. "It was stolen at the turn of the 18th century during a particularly bad time for heretics—the inquisition was spreading across Europe like a plague, and many of the people in the count's serfdom were frightened by him. Thought him evil, a brother of the devil. They literally called him *Fra Diavalo*. Combine that with Naples and France heatedly engaged in a constant state of conflict, and it was only a matter of time before personal vendettas were calculated as military strategy. Easy enough to sell to the peasants, anyway. The attack by peasantry—paid as mercenaries—and the theft itself were calculated by the same person. A vicious, conniving *le salaud*... Signor Federico Croce."

Tyson listened patiently as she went on to explain that when her ancestral family was attacked, sometime between dinosaurs and Twitter, a fuckhead wizard and a group of peasants-playing-soldiers had apparently, and quite savagely, murdered anyone living there at the time—including women and children—before stealing certain artifacts that had been in possession of the Montresor line for nearly three hundred years.

*Since the dark ages,* she'd said.

Preposterous.

Now, it takes all his willpower to stay focused on her continuing stream of nonsense, but his head has begun pounding, and the way the woman speaks—the languid accent playing like a melody beneath her words—clouds his mind, confuses his thoughts. As far as he can follow the woman's bizarre lineage, it appears this mysterious grandfather, this Count Jean, was the great-great-grandson of a woman named Julianne Montresor, who was the daughter of an 18th century count named Etienne Montresor, who, as this strange woman tells it, is the poor bastard whose family was murdered, his entire world ripped apart...

*Most likely on a cold, stormy night, his French McMansion surrounded by armored men with torches,* Tyson muses, wanting to laugh at the bizarre tale but finding himself unable to find the humor in it.

"It was my ancestor, Julianne, who was taken captive by Croce when she was only twelve years old. A little girl forced to watch her family murdered with a knife on her throat, her brother cut to pieces, her mother raped and stabbed to death. After they murdered Etienne, she became Croce's concubine, and yes, it's as disgusting as it sounds. She was repeatedly assaulted and beaten at will by him and his men, made to do unspeakable things which she, much later, painfully recounted. For years she survived this abuse, finally escaping his clutches and fleeing to distant cousins living in the north of France, where she told her tale to anyone who would listen. The French government, at that time, was less concerned about punishment for the murders and far more concerned about an artifact which Etienne had been harboring, now in the possession of Federico Croce."

"As were the Italians," Billy adds gleefully. "Good thing Hitler wasn't around, he was a sucker for those occult artifacts. You could have had a world war on your hands."

"Yes, but no one really knew, or fully understood, its power. They knew there was dark magic involved, necromancy of the highest order, but as far as using it against an army? I don't think that was ever truly tested. And though you jest, there were rumors about Hitler and his men searching for it during World War II, but it was never found."

"I'm sorry. What's this artifact exactly? Sounds like we're talking about something on the level of an Ark of the Covenant, or the Holy Grail," Sarah says. Tyson gives her a darting glance, surprised Sarah is so engaged with the woman's story.

"Not quite," Diana says, taking a sip of wine, grimacing slightly at its apparent subpar quality. She sets it down, folds her hands on her lap. "In any case, there is nothing holy about this item, you might even say it's the opposite. A thing of pure evil. It was this object that Croce truly came for, all those years ago. A sacrificial altar that had been used for occult purposes for hundreds of years, and yes, including my ancestor, who was a warlock, if you'll pardon the term. Trust me, it's pretty damn sinister. Etienne was essentially an herbalist with a fascination for nature and old—mostly quite useless—spells. He was known more as a healer than any sort of magician. Regardless, he was lord of the castle and the surrounding environs during the 1700s.

"After Croce's death, the altar was hidden away, no one knows where, or by whom. It was taken away from mankind and from anyone who could use it for misguided, or potentially evil, purposes. Over the years, it resurfaced here and there, more as legend than fact. Rumors swirled about a powerful object—sometimes called an altar, sometimes a table, often even a desk." She gives Tyson a sidelong glance at this, but he chooses to ignore it. "Call it oral tradition or heretical gossip, but there are horror stories about men and women killing all manner of things upon it, from pigs, to virgins, to infants stolen in the night." Violet winces and squirms in her seat, but Diana continues, undeterred. "When it finally resurfaced in the late 18th century—nearly a hundred years later—a blasphemous cult, one said to worship Satan, had an addition to the altar constructed using black magic of the worst order, to enchant it, bring it to *life*. Only this time, for the modern world."

Tyson scoffs, but says nothing.

"Regardless, whether or not you believe the supernatural elements of what I'm telling you, please do believe me when I say that it's an evil thing, a powerful thing, and, to my knowledge, practically indestructible."

Violet interrupts. "If it's so evil, why would you want it back?"

Diana shrugs one shoulder. "To bury it. Seal it away somewhere safe, the way you'd cage the Devil were he roaming the earth."

"Wait a minute," Tyson says, more to stall than anything. He laughs awkwardly, surveys the other faces at the table. Besides a small upward curl of Billy's lips, no one else seems to find the woman's story as amusing, as downright *ridiculous*, as he does. "Are you suggesting..."

His eyes shift, his gaze lingering on the darkened corridor which leads to the office. He imagines those long black tendrils slipping beneath the office door, clinging to the walls of the hallway like dead ivy, unseen, but aware—oh yes, very much *aware*—of what is currently being discussed in the kitchen over a bottle of wine and some absolutely batshit family history. Diana takes notice of where Tyson's attention had been drawn, and she nods.

"Exactly right," she says, breaking into Tyson's thoughts. "That thing is in your home, Mr. Parks. Human beings were sacrificed, their blood drained, in the same place where your computer sits now. Babies were torn apart inches from where you keep your pencils."

"Okay, that's enough..."

"Because now it's been transformed for a more *practical* purpose," she continues, undaunted. "All the better to keep it circulating, finding new owners... new servants... to spread whatever evil it wishes to spread. In some ways, men like my great ancestor and Signor Croce are nothing more than tools for that creature's bidding. Understand this, Mr. Parks, it's not just the stone, it's what lives *beyond* the stone. That is from where the true evil, the true *power*, pulls its strings. The strings attached to my ancestor, and to Signor Croce, and to you, Mr. Parks." She glances above each of his shoulders, a small smile on her lips. "I can almost see them *pulling.*"

Tyson barks out a loud, harsh laugh. In the quiet of the kitchen, it's an unsteady, worrying sound. The kind of sound a man in a madhouse might make upon seeing a demon hunched on his toilet, its giant red pecker leaking blood into the basin.

"What else?" Sarah asks, ignoring Tyson's glare. "What else has it been? You know, before..."

"Its current form?" Diana says, eyes lifting in thought. "There are many rumors, of course, but I've heard of it being used in a variety of ways. Most recently, but still many years ago, it served as a rich man's buffet table, if you can conceive of eating off such a thing. Fifty years prior to that it was in a church. Can you imagine? They served communion from it." Diana sighs, as if the topic brings a weight with it, an emotional burden she has grown tired of shouldering. "Wherever it was, though, however it was utilized, rest assured it has always had one true owner. A man I've told you about already."

"I don't understand," Sarah says, looking paler by the minute.

Diana lifts her wine glass with long, manicured fingers. She stares into the red liquid, then brings her black eyes up to meet Sarah's. "This man is an extension of the great evil which lives beyond. Whether that place is hell, or something we can't conceive of, I can't say. The easiest way to put it, I suppose, is to say the desk is possessed... controlled by a raging spirit who refuses to relinquish its power, even in death."

"Signor Croce..." Billy muses, his coy smile not so certain anymore. Then he brightens, patting his friend on the shoulder. "Can you believe it, Tyson? It's like Christine... but wood!"

"That's right, Mr. Tuck," Diana says, and Tyson realizes he'd never mentioned Billy's last name. *Maybe she* is *just a crazy fan. Like that guy who chained himself to the fence a few years ago, stayed there until I agreed to write a sequel to* Deep in the Night. *Police had to use bolt cutters to get the bastard out of here.*

"Mr. Parks, you and your loved ones have been forced into the throes of an epic battle between two very old, very powerful families." She pauses, looks Tyson in the eye. "Both of them deadly, I assure you. You harbor something beyond your understanding, a gateway to something so evil you could not begin to imagine."

"Hey," Tyson says with a smirk, "don't forget, lady. I'm a horror writer."

Billy snorts at this, but Diana is not amused.

"Jest all you want, Mr. Parks." She scrutinizes him a moment, lips pursed. "Perhaps you've discovered the power already?"

Tyson's smile fades. He feels Sarah's eyes boring into him from across the table.

"Yes, I think you have," Diana says. "So, in that case, I will share something with you, and I hope you will take it to heart."

"I'm all ears," he says, sucking down the last of his wine.

Diana nods, leans toward him. "Then know this. Very soon that thing is going to stop feeding you," she says, as if relaying a secret. "And you will begin feeding *it*."

She leans back, frowning at her wine glass. "And when that happens, Tyson, you will be lost, body and soul. Forever."

For a moment, no one speaks, each lost in their own thoughts.

"Okay, so why now?" Violet says finally, breaking the spell that had settled over the parlay at the dining room table. "Why are you here? Why didn't you pick it up before, when it surfaced... wherever you said. How hard could it be to find a piece of furniture with the resources you obviously have?"

Diana smiles a little—a careworn thing that ages her beyond her 30-something years. "When Croce fled the inquisition, the Pope's men colluded with the army to track down and kill men such as him and my ancestors. When he finally was hunted down—burned to death in an Italian chapel like a trapped rat—it was Julianne, her fortune and title fully restored, who had a hundred men sweep the Croce estate, searching for where the blind old bastard might have hidden the altar. She found nothing, of course. The altar was long gone."

*Blind...* Tyson thinks, looking forlornly at his empty wine glass, wishing like hell it was full of scotch.

"Most believe it had been with Croce at the church where he burned, then taken away by a servant or a friend, sold to another master with the financial means and corrupt spirit to bargain for such a thing. To continue what Croce, what my own ancestor, in fact, had started. Regardless of how, the artifact vanished from the earth, constructed into some other form, another skin in which to hide.

"Across generations, the Montresor family searched for it, as I've said. Followed rumors, and rumors of rumors, to no avail. My grandfather once told me it was like chasing a ghost, or a phantom. Something you see out of the corner of your eye, melting into a wall just as you try to reach out and touch it.

"Since adulthood, my grandfather searched relentlessly, spending a fortune on detectives around the world to find clues of the mystical stone's whereabouts. In the process, he procured many other fascinating, and useful, artifacts, some of them even more dangerous than the one I assume sits in your father's office. When my parents died, he took me in, and I became an assistant of sorts in the hunt, in the harboring and study of the artifacts he'd found. We are keepers of what the world considers forbidden knowledge. You would not believe how much power lies buried beneath ignorance, young lady, beneath the fallacy of religion or the idiotic blindness of cultural prejudice."

"You're crazy," Tyson says, his patience waning.

"Am I?" Diana examines Tyson carefully. "So, tell me Tyson, you haven't noticed anything... strange? No bizarre occurrences? No..." she glares pointedly to Sarah, to the cast enwrapping her arm. "Accidents?"

"Why don't you just tell us what you want," Sarah says.

Tyson wants to kiss her. He doesn't know, of course, that beneath the table she's stroking the cast encasing her hand, thinking of the warehouse worker whose leg had been crushed, who later died. He doesn't know she's thinking of the way he'd screamed...

Diana, however, is unperturbed. "Simple. I want to buy it. After all this hocus pocus and tall tales of demonic powers and ancient families, it sounds almost trite, doesn't it? Well, that's the modern world for you." She turns her attention to Tyson. "I'll give you ten times what you paid for it. If my information is correct, that comes to approximately two-hundred-fifty-thousand dollars, am I right?"

Violet's eyes go wide, and even Tyson feels a greedy jolt hearing the number. *That would get me close to a million-dollar day,* he thinks. *Talk about one for the diary.*

"I will wire the money to an account of your choosing, direct from my overseas bank. The transaction will take a few minutes, and I can have men here to take the desk away in the next hour," Diana's voice rises, sharpened by the confidence of her impending victory. "Just think, Mr. Parks, you can all go to bed tonight knowing you have a handsome amount of tax-free money in the bank and, more importantly, that evil thing removed from your house, out of your lives forever. Can you honestly tell me that doesn't sound attractive?"

"I think we've heard enough of this," Tyson mumbles. "Get out of my house."

For the first time, Diana seems thrown off. Her confidence shaken. "Mr. Parks, I don't think you understand..."

"I said *enough!*" Tyson roars, slamming a hand on the table and standing so abruptly he bangs the edge with his hip, knocking over the empty wine bottle, which Billy expertly catches and rights. "It's been super-wild, honey, and insanely entertaining, but now it's time for you to go."

"Dad..." Violet stands as well, her face pleading. "Dad, we should think about this."

Tyson glares at his daughter, incredulous. "What? No. NO."

Billy looks from face-to-face, as if trying to figure out which one is making the most sense. Sarah hasn't moved. She just sits, staring blankly at the table.

"Let's go, lady," Tyson says roughly. "Out! Now!"

Diana rises gracefully, unhurried. She nods to Tyson and picks up her bag from the floor. She takes a step toward the living room, then stops and tilts her head downward, eyes on the floor rather than the people behind her, as if she knows the futility of her words. "Perhaps... if I came back, gave you time to discuss it..."

"If I see you at my door again, I'll call the police," Tyson says, breathing heavily. "I'll tell them you're just another shit-bird fanatic who won't stop harassing me. And know this, lady. The cops around here? They know me. They *like* me. I've contributed handsomely to their causes, and they've taken care of screwballs like you before, and I'm sure they'll gladly do it again. Now, let's go, baby. Crazy called and they want you home."

Diana walks another few steps toward the door, and this time when she stops, she turns all the way around, her face serene, head slightly bowed, servile. "I promise I won't bother you again, Mr. Parks. I did not mean to offend or upset you or your lovely family. What's yours is yours. You are not thieves. You had no idea what you were getting into. If anything, I feel sorry for you." She glances back to the table, where Billy and Sarah still sit, and beyond which Violet stands, arms wrapped around herself protectively. "For *all* of you."

She takes a step toward Tyson, rests a hand on his forearm, gazes into his eyes.

"Could I ask one small favor before I leave? I've come a long way, after all."

Tyson rolls his eyes, clenches his hands into fists. "What?"

"May I please, just… see it?" she asks, focusing her penetrating black eyes on his.

*Like the eyes of Argus,* he thinks, and feels himself weakening.

"Fine," he says, and is the most surprised person in the room to hear the word leave his mouth. "I guess. If it will get you out of here, then what the hell." He shakes his head, frustrated, confused. "Come on, then," he says, and starts toward the hall. "Let's make this quick."

## Part Eight

# VIOLENT ENDS

# FORTY-TWO

TYSON LEADS Diana to his office. He opens the door and steps inside.

"Hang on a second," he says, and walks through the rectangle of light slanting across the floor, disappears into the dark.

Diana stands in the light of the hallway and waits, murmured voices like the whispers of ghosts filter into the hallway from the kitchen.

After a moment, the standing lamp at the far side of the room clicks on and a pool of amber light coats a leather club chair, a burgundy rug bleeding out from beneath.

Tyson hears Diana give a small gasp but pays her no mind. He walks across the office and turns on the desk lamp, the light from which fills the area well enough to see the details of the desk's design.

"There it is. Terrifying, isn't it?" His tone is teasing, but part of him secretly prays the damned thing will behave itself. That the old man—*Signor Croce, I presume*—will not appear, all bulging white eyes and that raspy, broken record voice. He feels the slightest tickle against the bottom of his wrist, one of the small vines giving him a secret greeting. He smiles, thinking about the moment when the bitch will be gone, when they'll *all* be gone, and it will just be him and the desk again, alone, doing the glorious work.

Diana takes two hesitant steps into the office and drops her large bag onto the reading chair, startling Tyson. He removes his hand from the desk, swatting away the loose tendril, all his focus now on her.

"That's it, all right," she says. She has her back to him.

He waits as she rummages for something inside her bag.

"It's obvious you've become quite attached," she says. "I'm so very sorry."

Tyson opens his mouth to protest, to explain there's nothing to be sorry *about*. That she's had her peek and now it's time to go and sell her insane stories to the tourists and street bums.

Then she turns, and he sees the gun.

His initial response is confusion. "What..."

There's a flash and a *crack*, like the sound of a heavy book dropped onto a wooden floor, and Tyson is punched hard in the hip, as if clipped by a speeding car. The blow spins him around, knocks him off his feet and sends him, arms spiraling, into the bookcase behind him. He grasps for a shelf, a handhold, but finds none. He slumps, breathless, to the floor.

Diana watches him a moment, a vile expression of pity on her face.

Then she turns and strides briskly out the door.

He tries to move. He badly *wants* to move, to run after her, tackle her, stop her from... *where is she going? Oh God, where is she GOING?*

Tyson hears Sarah yell something indecipherable, then Violet screams—a loud, shrill, terrified scream. She has time to call out for him. "Dad!"

Billy's voice, strangled and terrified. "NO!"

The *CRACK* of another gunshot, this time from the kitchen. Violet shrieks. Something breaks. Crashes. A plate, perhaps. Or a wine bottle.

There's a second shot, followed immediately by a third.

Billy screams, "Violet, RUN!"

Loud footsteps. Something heavy—a body, perhaps—thumps into the wall outside his office, slamming hard enough to shake the books on the shelves.

Tyson lifts the hand he had pressed to his wound. It drips blood. "OH GOD, PLEASE STOP!"

The gun fires twice more in quick succession—*CRACK CRACK*—and the sound is horribly loud in the tight corridor.

More footsteps, lighter footsteps, moving fast—*running*—for the stairway that leads to the upper floors. They pound up—higher, higher—and then there is one final shot, this one close to the open office door. Near the bottom of the stairs.

The running footsteps stop.

All the screaming stops.

"NO!" Tyson roars, and slides an arm beneath him, tries to leverage himself to his knees so he can... *What? Save them? Save WHO? That fucking madwoman just killed your best friend. Your family!*

*NOW GET THE FUCK UP!*

Tyson rolls over and pushes his suddenly very heavy body onto one elbow. His hip burns in agony, and the broken bones in there *crunch* and *crackle* as he tries to swivel onto his ass, to confront her, to do *something.*

Instead, he watches, helplessly, as she walks slowly, casually, back into the office, her movements controlled and smooth, her face stoic, as if bored. The gun is held at her side, and Tyson can almost imagine a stream of death slipping from the tip of its barrel like smoke. She walks toward him, past the desk, stopping a few feet away. Just out of his reach.

She stares down, her face still expressionless.

"You miserable, psychotic bitch," he says, tears flowing down his cheeks.

"Not really. Not quite. If you'd only taken the money, this could have been avoided. But it's obvious you're in too deep, Mr. Parks. It's using you, and the damage needs to be controlled. You need to be stopped before you can do more harm. I was hoping for a different outcome, and I'm sorry I found you so late, but to be frank, you shouldn't have been so accepting. I blame your naked greed, your imbecilic manhood." She says this bitterly, as if scolding him for having bet on the wrong horse in the sixth race. "All this death," she continues, looking around at figurative bodies and blood, as if wondering how it had all come about, as if she were simply a bystander who stumbled unawares into a scene rife with violence and gore.

She raises the gun and points it steadily at his chest. He wants to speak, to offer a counterargument… but is momentarily distracted by movement from behind her.

The desk.

It's *reaching* for her.

At the last second, a moment before she pulled the trigger and finalized her business, Tyson thinks maybe she sensed what was happening.

Too late, of course.

*Much* too late.

The first black tendril shoots out with blinding speed, like an arrow sprung from a longbow, and winds itself through the trigger of the gun, coiling around the fingers she holds it with. Tyson can see her trying to pull the trigger once, twice, again and again, her teeth bared in frustration and, he'd guess, a lot of surprise. The coil of wood squeezes, and he hears the *snap* of her fingers as they break.

"No!" she screams.

A second strand—a long sliver of dark ivy, the longest he'd yet seen—slides quickly into her open, snarling mouth. Her beautiful dark eyes go wide. Her head jerks back violently, as if yanked by the roots of her hair. In the soft light of the desk lamp's glow, Tyson watches her neck bulge as the branch pushes past her throat, and down.

Within seconds, more strands are reaching out for her. They wrap around her thighs, her waist, her arms and neck. As Tyson stares in a sort of numb wonder, her heels lift from the floor, her back arches and her feet twitch, as if she were having a seizure.

One black high heel clunks down onto the hardwood as she spasms and shakes in midair, a dying fly caught in the milky glue of a spider's web. Her face lowers for one final moment, and Tyson meets the terrified eyes staring down at him. More strands of wood follow the first, plunging giddily between her lips, punching through her cheeks, so that her sagging, open mouth is filled with them, and he can't help wonder how many made it down her throat.

Diana makes thick, liquid, gagging noises. Dense strings of blood and saliva leak from her lips. Her body is still racked by spasms, and there are sounds of fabric ripping where the points of certain branches have pushed *out* from within, glistening black strands breaking free from her flesh through her stomach, her throat.

Mercifully, a final tendril, slick as oil, rises like a cobra, and flashes forward, piercing her right eye. It continues, pushing itself deeper, deeper, through brain and skull, until the tip of it can be seen exiting the back of her head.

After a few moments, her body stops its movement, her eyes drifting from afraid to empty, and she slumps, lifeless, like meat on a hook, suspended by the desk's army of limbs.

Then, just as quickly as they came, the tentacles retreat, uncoil, slip almost gently out of her body.

Diana collapses unceremoniously to the floor, legs askew, one arm folded beneath her, the other reaching for something it will never hold onto. The gun bounces against the floor, lands a couple feet away, and lays still.

Tyson watches her corpse for a moment or two, and then his world begins to fade, becoming illusory, as if his world was being swallowed by a dream.

Soon, reality is nothing more than a soft-hued, impossible fantasy.

He hardly registers the old man's face as it lowers into his field of vision, coming to rest only inches from his own, so close that Tyson can see the whiskers on his chin, the blackheads on the fleshy nose, the bulging eyes that stare at nothing, and everything. Close enough that he could hear the wheezing of his breath, smell the foul odor of his rotten mouth.

A strong, bony hand grips Tyson's own, pries open the fingers to reveal his palm, and place a phone receiver gently within it.

A minute later, and for the second time that week, a 911 operator receives a call from the Parks residence.

# FORTY-THREE

AS BILLY *dies...*

*Slumped against the wall, a bullet in his guts. A tug at his soul.*

*His brain takes over in the end, offering, as it will often do with violent deaths, a sideshow. A vision to distract the dying mind when the horror and the pain prove too much for a human to bear. Typically, these are comforting scenes.*

*Tunnels of light. Glimpses of heaven.*

*Sometimes, the brain is pushed other directions. Toward truth.*

*In Billy's mind, there's a blinding flash of white and...*

---

TYSON CALLS him into his office. The old boy has been acting strange lately, and not looking so hot. Billy's been worried. After Sarah's accident, he called Tyson to see if he could come by and have a drink, sit and chat about this, that and the other.

Tyson agreed and they'd spent the evening speaking about Tyson's new book, how William Morrow had increased their offer, and things were finally looking up. Tyson told Billy how he had begun writing a *new* book, and he was confident it would be a giant success.

Later, they go into his office, and Tyson says he wants to show him something.

Billy notices that the windows of the office are a bright crimson, the sky the color of blood. He finds it curious, but not alarming. When Tyson calls for his attention, he forgets about the windows altogether, because what does it matter?

"It's called *The Horror*, and I think it's going to really scare some people," Tyson says as he fiddles with the stereo behind the desk, humming to himself as he shoves in a compact disc. Billy stands by the bookcases, his eyes pulled to the books lining the shelves, reading but not registering the titles on the spines. After a few moments of this, he realizes he's purposely avoiding looking behind him.

He doesn't want to see that black desk, the one dominating the room.

"Rachmaninoff again? How drab," Billy teases, pulling out an early John Farris title. He studies the bizarre cover image before sliding it back into place. Finally, he turns to face Tyson—and the desk—fighting off a cramp of pain that stabs his belly. "Seriously though, quite amazing about Morrow. Sounds like Harry's got balls of steel. Who knew?"

Tyson nods, still humming, but says nothing as he listens to the music, sliding a hand back and forth along the top of the desk. Billy clears his throat, suddenly feeling too warm. Uncomfortably so. "Did you want to discuss, you know... what happened to Sarah? Or, hell, anything else? I'll be honest, buddy, I'm a bit worried about you."

Tyson moves his eyes past Billy, in the direction of the reading chair that rests at the far side of the office. He smiles oddly, and it looks as if he's about to say something—toward the chair—when his eyes dart back to his oldest friend. The smile falls, and he appears deeply troubled.

"I guess I'll show you now," Tyson murmurs, frowning. Pouting, even. Billy thinks he looks like a kid who's been caught stealing a dime store candy bar. "I gotta warn you, Billy. I don't think you're gonna like it."

"Okay," Billy replies slowly. Showing confidence he doesn't feel—*and damn if my stomach doesn't hurt like a sonofabitch*—he walks across the room to face Tyson, sets his drink on the top of the desk. The glass *clinks* against the stone. "So, show me."

Reluctantly, Tyson nods, then slides open the desk's middle drawer—the long, flat one that typically holds pens and paperclips, a roll of tape, a bright pad of Post-it notes.

"Should I..." Billy asks, gesturing toward the open drawer. Tyson steps to the side and Billy walks around the large desk to inspect whatever sits inside. *Goddamn, this thing is huge,* he marvels, and comes to stand next to his oldest mate, his best friend. "Okay, Tyson. Here I am."

Tyson points to the drawer, and now he *does* smile. Wide and toothy and feverish.

"Look," he says.

Thinking his friend has definitely lost a few cards from the deck, but deciding to humor him regardless, Billy sighs and looks down, into the drawer.

At first, he sees only black. Then, as if from far, far away, a bright spot of brilliant blue light emerges, like the flexing of an aperture; a pinprick that grows steadily larger as it spirals toward him, growing until it consumes the width of the drawer, reaching impossible depths of unfathomable distance. Billy suddenly feels like he's on an airplane, the bottom of which is made of glass.

*Or, no, that's not it. It's like I've jumped from the plane. Like I'm skydiving.*

As he looks more closely, and the scene beneath him becomes more vivid, his brain kicks into overdrive, as if he's just snorted two monster lines of cocaine. His heart speeds up, pounding in his chest hard enough to shorten his breath, make him gasp. He begins to feel faint. The pain in his stomach is suddenly *unbearable.*

But even worse than the pain is what he's looking at. He sees things down there... he sees *shapes* moving around this window to a nether world.

Tall, charred treetops, black oceans, an impossible sky. And... *creatures.*

"Oh God, what are they doing?" he moans, his face breaking out with sweat. His heart starts skipping, losing its rhythm. His head feels as if it's filling with fluid, like it's going to expand and expand until it explodes. "Tyson, what is this? What am I looking at?"

Tyson continues to smile, but his eyes are wide and wild behind the glass lenses, reflecting that horrible blue light from the depths of a dimension no man should ever see while still alive, let alone dead.

"I think it's hell!" he says excitedly, and lets out a deep, broken chuckle.

Billy begins to scream. His body stiffens, as if paralyzed, but his eyes never leave the open drawer, or the world which lies beyond. He screams and screams until his throat gives out, until something *pops* in his head and blood rushes into his eyes. His heart squeezes as if clenched by an iron fist until it finally comes to a hard stop, like a driver doing seventy-five down a city street before slamming into a brick wall head-on.

Billy's back arches, his fingers claw, his head jerks upward, but instead of seeing the office ceiling he sees an endless sky the color of a filthy white sheet, and the last thing his mind shows him in this life is his view from far, far below, looking up to where clouds should be floating, but are not.

Instead, it is the visage of a grinning Tyson spread across the canvas of sky, his eyes hidden by opaque blue lenses, sliding the drawer slowly closed… before killing the music.

# FORTY-FOUR

AS SARAH *dies...*

*On the kitchen floor, staring sideways at the legs of the kitchen table. She watches the blood from the wound in her head pool into her vision, a growing red lake breaking through the dam of her skull, spreading across a landscape of white tiles...*

---

THIS TIME, Sarah doesn't knock when she opens the office door. She's tired of these insane writing sessions that last entire days, often into nights—without pause, without break.

*It's unhealthy*, she reasons, and therefore blames her intrusion on her deep concern for Tyson (*not* her curiosity) as she pushes the door silently open, pokes her head inside.

She looks toward the desk... and clamps a hand over her mouth.

To stifle the scream.

Tyson's writing, but he isn't looking at the computer. He's staring straight upward, as if studying a cobweb arched across a far corner of the room, while his fingers move frenetically across the keyboard, pounding the keys with such force and speed it sounds like a stampede of plastic horses.

What truly frightens her, however, is his face—slack and deeply-lined as a walnut, as if he'd aged twenty years since breakfast, and a slick of drool stems from the corner of his mouth.

But his eyes are the real horror show.

Bulging and white as cue balls, streaked with red veins and smeared spots of dirty gray, blind and unnaturally wide, as if he's *watching* something that fills him with terror, something unspeakable.

Something only a blind man can see.

He mumbles to himself, as if dictating to the flying, obedient fingers. She hears strange phrases, strings of words that don't seem to be associated with the rapid movements of his hands. Part of some other book, perhaps. A different story he's hoping to tell.

"Ty?"

She takes another step closer, shivering with cold. She looks down at herself and realizes, with more curiosity than alarm, that she's completely nude.

*Now how did that happen?* she wonders, but then thinks no more of it. For some reason, it seems perfectly natural.

"Come inside, come inside," he says, never shifting those horrible eyes from the ceiling. "We see you."

The typing stops, and along with it the mad clatter of the keys.

The room is deathly quiet.

Tyson turns his head away from the corner and looks directly at her, scrutinizes her with those dreadful blank eyes, that trenched face. Three long lines run dark red along one withered cheek, bleeding as if freshly cut.

He smiles at her, a smile so broad that it makes the sides of his face stretch like rubber.

*Like a mask,* she thinks wildly. *He's just wearing a mask. Of course!*

But it isn't a mask, and she knows that, too.

And when he stands and walks toward her, she knows the truth of things: that it was *him.* Yes, it's Tyson, but it's also *him.*

*The other one.*

She stands frozen, unable to move as he comes toward her in fast, shuffling steps, that awful smile never lessening, those dingy cue ball eyes never wavering.

He clutches her arms in a fierce grip, leans down to put his wet mouth by her ear.

"We've been waiting for you."

He moves behind her and pushes her toward the desk. Gently at first but then, when she begins to resist, with more force.

She digs in her heels and yells for him to "Stop, please STOP!" because now the desk is not a desk at all, but a massive, monstrous *mouth.*

It splits open horizontally, a ghostly, blue-lit gap shines brightly across its middle. Wooden teeth, sharp as vampire stakes, ridge the top and bottom of the expanding breach, ready to chomp her up, chew her flesh and hair and bones and swallow it all down.

Eager to devour. She can sense its desire. Its *hunger.*

The stone top—*the altar where the sacrifices are laid,* she knows, feeling suddenly light-headed, feeling very strange indeed—boils like black soup left too long on the burner. The laptop and other accessories are gone, swept away.

The desktop has been cleared, just for her.

Tyson—or the thing that he has become—spins her around to face him and she screams as he opens his mouth and shows her the black gummy works within, tongue lolling over gray, chipped teeth, wild egg-white eyes rolling in his skull. She thinks he's going to push her into that blue mouth but instead he tightens his grip and lifts her high in the air, then *slams* her body down onto the amorphous desktop. The bubbling, gurgling surface sticks to her like thick glue, adheres to her skin with such strength that she knows if she tries to tug her arms or legs free it will rip away her flesh like an orange peel.

Tyson places a hand between her breasts and the other on her abdomen. He begins to push her *down.*

Sarah feels herself being slowly submerged into a hellish quagmire—a feeling more terrible than sinking into hot sewage or boiling tar, into a lake of fire. It *disgusts* her. It shames her. It's as if she is being baptized in the river Styx by the Ferryman, blind eyes replacing his hollow furnaces of fire, and she cries out for mercy.

As he continues to push her deeper, deeper, she becomes more enveloped, her body tingling as it sinks, her lungs squeezing, collapsing. Her stomach revolts, nausea rising into her throat. She struggles, gags, and curses; her terror combines with a violent survival instinct, demanding she get *FREE,* but the desk holds her fast. She can't move her arms, legs, feet, head.

Suddenly, the heat of the fluid around her body becomes icy cold—*so cold oh my god save me anything but this*—a frigid sea that seeps higher, swallowing her whole.

"Aaaahhh," Tyson says, an audible sigh of near sexual pleasure.

"No no no." She weeps denials of her fate as tears run from her eyes. "I don't want to die, please... not yet. I don't want to die... Tyson please... I love you."

For a brief moment, Tyson's rapturous expression relaxes, his smile smears into a frown like wet paint, but the firmness of his hands pressing down does not falter.

She thinks, before the end, he may have mumbled, "I'm sorry."

The icy black fluid blankets her legs, slides over her waist like a cold wet arm pulling her down from behind. Her ears are covered and the world falls mute. Liquid climbs past her temples, dips into the carved ravines that lead to her eyeballs... and pool inward.

She opens her mouth to scream one last time into the face of that smiling, dead-eyed visage of the man she once loved more than anything in the world. Flashes of her life—a child, a teenager in love, her parents, Violet as an adult, visiting her in old age, her husband holding her close—erupt in her brain, images of a life lived, of the life she will never live.

His blind eyes are the last thing she sees as darkness spills over her face, covers her eyes, her nose; slides into her gaping mouth and down her throat, filling her.

Then there is nothing.

Nothing but the corrupt, blessed dark.

# FORTY-FIVE

AS VIOLET *(almost) dies...*

*OH MY GOD! FUCK FUCK FUCK!*

"Violet, RUN!"

But Violet stands rigid, motionless, staring at the body of the woman she thought of as her mother; the woman who helped raise her, who loved her as her own flesh-and-blood for the last decade of her life.

Sarah lies on the kitchen floor, knocked off the chair by the force of the bullet that slammed into the back of her head and split it wide. A pool of blood pours from the wound and spreads out in a puddle across the floor.

Preposterously, Billy throws a dinner plate at the woman with the gun—*Diana, her name is Diana, and she had been sitting with them only a few minutes ago, drinking wine and telling them the most bizarre story*—and then he lunges at her. Violet sees the two of them disappear into the hallway. Billy slams her hard against the wall, struggling with her, grabbing one of her arms. He turns his head to yell at Violet to RUN but she can't...

Her father's voice bellows out from the office: "OH GOD, PLEASE STOP!"

Then two muffled shots erupt—*POP POP*—and she sees Billy's sport coat flip up the back like it caught a gust of wind. Blood sprays the white wall. He groans and slumps lifelessly against the woman, pinning her to the wall with his dead weight.

A moment...

Violet runs not for the front door but, inexplicably, for the upper floors. To her room. To sanctuary. She leaps over Billy's sprawled body, past the open office door, and pounds up the stairs. She sees the top and in a few more seconds she'll turn the corner and be gone, out of the line of fire, toward the second flight of steps and to her room where she can barricade the door and call for help.

The bullet catches her in the middle of the lower back. Her legs go immediately numb, as if erased from her body. Her strong young muscles turn to rubber, and she collapses.

*No more morning runs for you, we're afraid. So sorry. Still, life is precious, isn't it? Hope you enjoy it to its fullest.*

Violet lies on the stairs, groaning, in shock, helpless. She waits for that second shot, the one that will put her out of her misery forever. Even then, in that moment, she figures it would be a blessing. Yes, yes, a gift. Because part of her already knows—instinctively knows—that something very bad, something very *permanent*, has been done to her body.

But the second shot doesn't come.

Instead, she hears voices from her father's office. The woman talking to him, and then she curses and then... nothing.

Violet lies there, panting, trying to find the courage, the strength, to *move*, to go to her father, to call for help...

When someone begins to stroke her hair.

Violet strains her neck to look up at whoever has sat down next to her.

A very old man stares down at her with blind, bloodshot eyes.

"Daddy?"

"Not the way your story should have ended," the stranger says, then grins. "Not the way. It's all so... *horrible,* isn't it?"

He laughs as blood flows down Violet's body, fills the seat of her underwear and seeps down the side of her waist in warm tendrils.

*So much blood,* she thinks. *So much blood.*

Then consciousness, along with the old man's laughter, floats away, as if carried by a dark stream, to a great unknown ocean.

Part Nine

# THE END

*One Year Later*

# FORTY-SIX

TYSON SITS quietly near the middle of the long, glossy white table. He counts fourteen leather chairs, mid-century design, all white and clean as the table upon which he taps his fingers. At his request, the fluorescent lights have been turned off, but bright sunshine splits the vertical blinds which run the length of the room, creating enough luminosity to give the space a glowing, if somewhat hazy, ambience.

Harry sits opposite him, and Tyson can't help studying him from the corner of his eye.

*It's like we've switched places.*

Which isn't far from the truth.

In the year which has passed since the Horrible Incident, Tyson lost nearly thirty unnecessary pounds, mostly by doing nothing other than eating healthy (he hired a chef who prepares a week's worth of meals at a time, all of which are vegetarian and "heart-smart"), and continuing the strenuous physical conditioning he had to endure for ten weeks following the surgery on his broken hip (among other damage) done by the bullet. He'd converted Violet's third-floor bedroom into a mini-gym, purchasing a treadmill identical to the one at the physical therapist's office, along with a universal weight machine that allows him to do enough basic lifting to keep his muscles taut and well-toned.

Sarah might have fought him on this house alteration, but Sarah is dead.

And Violet... well, Violet won't be on the third floor ever again. Assuming she ever has a desire to visit her father, which seems unlikely given the downward spiral of their relationship. Regardless, he'd shed the heavy writer's belt he carried around most of his adult life, and reached the optimum weight targeted by his doctor, all within four months of the Horrible Incident.

He'd needed new clothes, of course, and spent lavishly on an updated wardrobe. He's currently sporting a Giorgio Armani navy pinstripe wool suit for the big meeting. In addition to his weight loss, he's also been seeing a dermatologist, who began treatment on his hair that energized and regrew many of his scalp's stagnated follicles. He's already noticed a good amount of new hair growth in the six months since he began treatments (needles in the scalp were a small price to pay for the luxury of using a comb again). Lastly, he'd changed optometrists, thrown out all his old eyeglasses and purchased sturdy Robert Marc frames for his new prescription. All this work combined to make him appear ten years younger than his actual age, and he figures it's more like a twenty-year swing from how he'd looked only a year ago.

Harry, on the other hand, looks like shit.

Nowadays, Harry always appeared disheveled whenever they met, but over the last few months he'd *really* let himself go. He'd put on weight, which gave his face a jowly appearance to go with his new potbelly. Tyson knows for a fact the guy drinks around the clock, and it's common knowledge he's become hooked on prescription drugs. Harry once told Tyson he needed them to "get up and get down," and Tyson believed it.

The guy looks like he hasn't had a good night's sleep in twenty years.

But what strikes Tyson the most about Harry are his *eyes*. They're dull and glazed. He'd lost that spark of quickness, of alertness. Energy. He reminds Tyson of a zombie. And not the fast Max Brooks *World War Z*-type, but more the old George Romero, shuffle-and-groan, brain-eating variety.

Tyson often considers firing him, God knows he doesn't need him anymore (not in his current state, anyway), but always decides against it. Besides, it's probably the necessity of having to read and re-read Tyson's most recent books that's knocked old Harry sideways, pushed him off his equilibrium. Ergo, he feels a little guilt, a little responsibility, for Harry's collapse. Not to mention that long-forgotten thing called *loyalty*, damn it.

Tyson is nothing if not loyal.

Loyal or not, though, he's growing impatient. They've been in this room waiting nearly ten minutes, and he's about to ask Harry what the fucking balls is going on when the conference room's glass door pushes open, and two men strut inside. The first is a young assistant in a black suit and bright red tie. He has a long, horse-shaped head topped by an oil-slick of black hair that would probably spring into unruly, boyish curls were it not cemented down. Tyson has never met the kid, and mentally dismisses him.

The second man is Jim Pruitt, the president of PMA, the fine agency Harry works for, the very same one that represents Tyson's interests and takes its fifteen percent off the top for doing so. Tyson *has* met Jim.

Once.

In the '90s.

"Hello, Mr. Parks, nice to see you again," Pruitt says primly, what remains of his white hair neatly trimmed, his gray suit tailored snug to his manicured body like a soft glove. Tyson knows the guy is pushing eighty, but he'll be damned if the old man looks a day over sixty-five. Tyson smiles and nods in return, but doesn't stand up to shake any hands, and none are offered.

*He acts like we do this every week,* Tyson thinks, but it doesn't bother him. He doesn't want, or need, theatrics. He wants to sew this thing up and get home.

He has work to do.

Tyson's most recent book did even better than anyone had dared hope, blowing past even the wildest global sales projections.

*Black Altar* had become a sensation.

It came out of the gate number one on *The New York Times* Bestseller list and, after thirty-six weeks, had yet to slip from the Top 10. Rights were sold in twenty-nine foreign countries, for a total upwards of two million bucks. It had been optioned by Warner Brothers for a feature film, with an A-list cast assembled to ensure it opened with a bang.

Tyson's star has never glowed more brightly.

His new book, *The Horror,* is currently being sold as part of a three-book-deal to the highest bidder, and Scribner (also known as the House of King) is currently leading the pack with a ten-million-dollar offer.

*And so... heeeeere's Jimmy,* Tyson thinks, fighting the urge to roll his eyes. *They must drag his wrinkled old ass out for all their top clients every now and again. I'll be sure to act impressed.*

"It's been too long," Tyson finally replies. "To what do I owe the pleasure? Is Harry not good enough for me anymore?"

Harry laughs shakily and wipes a hand across his mouth. Tyson sees beads of sweat on his forehead.

"Ha! Well, of course that's not the case. Harry's one of our best and brightest," Pruitt says, almost looking like he means it, then smiles lamely.

*He certainly used to be.*

Tyson grins. "Say, can I get a Coke?"

"Sure, sure." Pruitt turns to the kid at his elbow. "This is Tim Little, by the way. My assistant." Tyson imagines old Pruitt patting young Timmy on the ass every chance he gets. *Or a spanking in the sack,* he thinks, swallowing the mad urge to bust out in a fit of giggles.

Tim goes to a jet-black credenza resting along the glass wall, where an army of small bottles are lined up next to a leather-wrapped ice chest. Tim opens a bottle, dumps some ice into a glass, then walks glass and top-popped soda over to Tyson, who accepts it without a word.

"So, if I may..." Pruitt says.

Tyson holds up a *hold that thought* finger, and Pruitt clamps his mouth shut while Tyson slowly pours soda into the glass.

"These things are fizzy when you pour them on ice, especially when the soda is warm," he says, staring intently at the brown foam rising near the top of the glass. "Can't even sip the damn thing until it's gone down..."

In silence, all four men watch the glass, and the slowly shrinking head of foam, as it recedes. As seconds tick by, Tyson thinks he actually hears Harry groan, and is forced to stifle yet another giggle.

"Tyson..." Pruitt starts, but Tyson thrusts up a finger once more, eyes never leaving his glass.

"Ah-ah-ah..." he says, and Pruitt shuts up a second time, this time wearing a grimace.

Finally, Tyson sets down the empty can, lifts the glass, takes a long drink, then puts it down on the table, smacking his lips. "That's better," he says. "Please, go on Jim."

Pruitt clears his throat. "We're all very pleased with how your last book did, and the deal we are shopping now seems like it's going to be very, very successful for you."

"You mean, for all of us," Tyson says.

"Of course, of course..." Pruitt agrees, then seems to gather his courage. "Anyway, there is *one* thing we'd like to address. Get us all on the same page, as it were."

Tyson raises his eyebrows. He was expecting this, of course. Albeit not so formally.

"Oh?"

"Look, Tyson, I don't need to tell you the kind of world we're living in these days. It's a hashtag-fueled society. With the global movement going on for equality and inclusiveness, and the new PC-culture, we need to be sure we're stepping lightly and in-line with current... *beliefs*."

Tyson's eyes darken and he leans forward. "Beliefs..." He repeats the word slowly, rolling it on his tongue like sour candy. "Look, let's cut the bullshit and let this gorilla out of the box, shall we? What's your *concern*, Jim?" Tyson slides his half-finished glass to the side, crosses his arms on the table, and stares directly at the agency president. "Maybe you can spell it out for me."

"I guess I'll just say it," Pruitt starts, speaking quietly at first but then picking up steam. "And I hope we can have a productive discussion about the issues."

Tyson imagines the elderly man beneath the veneer of tailored clothes and a two-hundred-dollar haircut; the saggy-assed, worn-out piece of shit who probably just wants to be on a boat somewhere, fishing as the sun comes up, kissing grandchildren that likely don't exist.

*He's nothing but regret in a nice suit,* Tyson thinks.

"It's the book, Tyson," Pruitt continues. "More to the point, it's some of the *content* of the book. It's... well, to be frank, it's not going to fly. I mean, we don't think, with today's... uh... sociopolitical climate..." he trails off, looking around the room for the right word, the right phrasing. "Hell, come on now, you've seen the headlines. Even you have to admit some of the ideas, er... the content, that is. Well hell, it's a bit dated, is what it is."

Tyson lets the dropped shoe sit for a beat, then reclines casually. "So, you've read my book, Jim?" he asks, already knowing the answer.

Pruitt flushes and, to his credit, doesn't try to lie. He turns once again to his assistant. "Tim, why don't you..."

*Maybe I'm wrong,* Tyson muses, watching the two idiots interact. *Maybe it's the kid does the ass-spanking in that relationship.*

"Of course, sir," Tim says with the snarky, youthful exuberance of a recent ivy-league graduate who believes themselves the bellwether of the new world order. It reminds Tyson of a joke: *How do you know when someone has gone to Harvard?*

*They tell you.*

The sour grapes joke makes him think of Violet, who once had dreams of getting a master's degree at Harvard after her time at Brown, where she now goes from class-to-class in a wheelchair.

Tyson grimaces and shoves the thought of his daughter from his mind, does his best to focus on Little Assistant Tim, who is yammering away in a broken, high-pitched squawk. "To start with," the kid says, "it's way too gory. I mean, what is this, splatterpunk? Come on. Child abuse? Body horror? No, it's mainstream horror for the masses, am I right?"

Harry shoots Tyson a look of concern, but Tyson says nothing. His expression placid, attentive. A look that says: *Please, go on. I want to hear more.*

"Second, to be blunt, it's sexist. Completely tone-deaf. Describing a woman's breasts for a paragraph may have flown in the '80s and '90s, Mr. Parks, but in today's society we'll get crucified for this stuff. I won't even get into the extreme sexual violence. I mean, there's a reason Richard Laymon's novels were exiled to the UK."

*Read a lot of Laymon, have you Timmy? Lying shit.*

"Uh-huh," Tyson says.

"Last, and with all due respect Mr. Parks, the *language*. I mean, our editor counted 96 F-bombs, 88 shits, and, most shockingly of all, double-digit racial slurs, including use of the N-word. *Twice*."

"Sure, but not as an insult," Tyson says defensively, annoyed he's even responding to the little pissant. "Look, that's the way the characters speak. I mean, these aren't good people we're talking about. The characters, I mean."

Harry looks at him with growing concern, but Tyson ignores him.

"That may be," Tim continues, and even Pruitt appears uncomfortable now. "But your last novel, popular as it was—and still *is*—does not have a great reputation. People have reported feeling ill for days after reading it. Children have acted out violently against other kids—and adults—pointing to your novel as their inspiration. People complain about not being able to sleep at night. Twitter had a field day with it, and so did Reddit. The black altar hashtag was trending with hate groups and violent criminals, even sex offenders."

"Sounds wonderful," Tyson says with a smile. "I love *trending*."

"And then there's the rumors, Mr. Parks. More than rumors, the *allegations*."

Pruitt looks suddenly ill, and the room takes on a quiet breathlessness.

"Rumors?"

The assistant looks heated now, like maybe this was all about to get personal.

*Hell,* Tyson thinks. *Maybe it is.*

"Yes, the rumors. The claims that people are reading your books and acting out. Did you know that a family in Los Angeles was gunned down by their sixteen-year-old child? He wrote the name of your book on the wall, Mr. Parks. In his mother's blood."

Tyson waves a hand. "Black Altar? Kind of vague, don't you think? He could have meant anything..."

"He had a copy of your book on his nightstand," Tim says, his eyes locked in. "He fucking *highlighted* the section in your book where the teenager kills his family. Does that seem coincidental to you?"

Tyson lets out a breath, then takes another long sip of his Coke. He licks his lips, raises his eyebrows. "Are you done?"

But the assistant is now half-standing, leaning over the table like a prosecutor objecting to the judge. "There are suicides! Murders, Mr. Parks. All clearly connected to *Black Altar.* To release more of the same would be..."

"Dangerous," Pruitt finishes, eyes roving the tabletop, as if he's unsure how he'd gotten in this room in the first place.

*Senile old bastard probably thinks he's in the Bahamas.*

Little Tim, now red-faced, nods once to his boss, then sits back down.

Showing off a smile of newly whitened teeth, Tyson stands. "Well, gentlemen, this has been very educational." He smooths down his suit coat. "It's always good to have some face-time. Very interesting stuff all around. But, if you don't mind, allow me to respond for sake of clarity. Just so we're all on the same page. Sound good?"

Pruitt nods absently, even though Tim looks like he has more to say.

A *lot* more, Tyson guesses.

"First, I hear there's a movie deal. I want to write the screenplay for that and be paid accordingly. I also want an executive producer credit with points on gross. None of this net bullshit." When Pruitt opens his mouth to respond, he adds: "These are not suggestions."

"Second, make the Scribner deal. I like the idea of making a run at King. Let's see who's worth more money come next year. And last," he turns to the assistant, and the smile slides off his face like a snake slithering beneath a bedsheet. "If you, or anyone else, *ever* tell me what to put or *not* put into one of my books again, I will dump this agency faster than a whore with an Adam's apple, and you can shove your fifteen percent up your asses. I didn't go through some batshit fanatic killing my best friend and my girlfriend, not to mention putting my only daughter in a goddamned wheelchair, so I could sit here and listen to this shit-sperm with an MFA tell me how to write a horror novel." He points to Harry. "Harry, get that Scribner deal done, and let the studio know my terms."

"Yeah, you got it, Ty."

"And you," he says, turning back to the (now very pale-faced) assistant. "You limp teenage cock. If I ever see your face in this building again, I'll walk out the door and never come back." He flicks his eyes toward Pruitt, who looks like he's bit into a rotten apple, and is now eye-to-eye with a worm.

"I hear CAA would *love* to be in the Tyson Parks business, Jim. So don't piss me off."

Tyson puts on his smile again, then raps his knuckles on the table.

"Good meeting, gentlemen. Good fucking meeting."

# FORTY-SEVEN

SIX MONTHS to the day after his come-to-Jesus meeting with Jim Pruitt at PMA headquarters, the one where he made sure the suits taking a share of his income knew who—who, *exactly*—was in charge of this particular tour bus, Tyson stands naked in front of the full-length bathroom mirror, hair still dripping from a hot shower, the sodden towel he'd used to dry himself tossed onto the floor (the maid comes in the morning so there's no point in being tidy).

As he considers the naked body reflected in the glass before him, the instinct he'd developed over the last couple decades (the same reflexive action all men over fifty come to know quite well) to suck in his gut, is strong. But as he studies himself—turning side-to-side, looking up-and-down—he realizes there's no need. He hasn't looked this fit and trim since college. Hell, maybe high school. The writer's belt is history. The old spare tire deflated.

The gym has paid off in other ways, as well. Aside from a flat stomach, his arms, chest and legs are nicely toned, especially for a guy walking the back nine, as Uncle Steve might say. He won't be mistaken for Arnold Schwarzenegger anytime soon, but an early-aughts Kevin Costner isn't totally out of the question.

Of course, there are things that regular visits to the gym and a healthy diet can't explain.

His eyesight, for one.

He hasn't needed to wear glasses for months and can't recall the last time he searched for one of several pairs of reading glasses placed strategically around the house, an infestation that began in his early-forties.

There's also his hair, which is full and—he'd swear to this in a court of law—*darker* than it had been a year ago. The scalp treatments had helped, sure, but this was something altogether different. He never touched a box of hair dye, wouldn't know how to use it if he did. And when his dermatologist said he'd never seen a response to the treatment as vigorous as Tyson's, he thought it prudent to stop going in for treatments altogether.

In the months since, if anything, his hair had only gotten thicker.

*Very soon that thing is going to stop feeding you, and you will begin feeding it.*

Tyson shakes the stray memory away, shows himself a toothy smile, then steps closer to the mirror to study his eyes. He notices, with some concern, that the gold flecks are gone. The same gold flecks he's looked at in thousands of different mirrors over the course of his life, starting when he was probably no more than five or six years old.

"Huh," he says, and decides it's likely nothing to be concerned about. The molecules of the human body complete a total reboot every seven years (or so he'd read somewhere), therefore, biologically speaking, humans become different people every decade. *Literally.*

So, it didn't make sense to lose sleep over looking better, feeling younger. Having more hair isn't something to cry about, and the restored vision, he figures, could be put down to being more healthy—eating right and exercise, etc. (he thinks maybe he read that somewhere as well).

*Sure you did. And geese lay golden eggs and if you climb a beanstalk you'll go to a castle in the clouds and reach the domain of one particularly nasty motherfucking giant, one with a hard-on for human meat.*

Tyson lets the smile go and turns away from his reflection. He has no wish to see himself any further. Not today. Besides, it's time to get ready for the big rumpus.

*The Horror* hadn't sold as well as its predecessor, the much-maligned *Black Altar.*

It had sold better.

A hell of a lot better.

The movie deal had come through, and he got the terms he asked for, the ones he'd made no bones about sharing with Harry, Jim Pruitt and that little pissant assistant in the agency board room. *What was the kid's name again? Sam? Bill? No... Little Tim. Thaaaat's right.*

Little Tim had been canned right around the time the Scribner contract got wet with blue ink. Harry confided the information to him one night while out for celebratory drinks.

Harry had been doing a lot of celebratory nights recently—mornings and afternoons, as well. On one particularly strange evening, he called Tyson, hysterical, crying and raving like a madman. Talking about visions... no, that wasn't it.

It was nightmares.

Yeah, sure, good old Harry was having some real doozies. Once, he called Tyson stinking drunk (and most likely high on coke) screaming about Tyson's desk, of all things. Raving about a man who lived inside of it. Apparently, this man had been visiting Harry late at night. Threatening him, *warning* him. Making sure Tyson's affairs weren't left untended, that his priorities were right at the tippity-top of Harry's daily to-do list.

Tyson calmly told Harry to get some sleep and hung up on him as gently as he could. He had a barrel-full of problems to deal with, including an idea for a new book, and an estranged daughter needing tens of thousands of dollars in medical care. A drunk literary agent with a bad case of night terrors wasn't something he could take on. Nor did he want to.

Besides, it isn't like Tyson can do anything about it. What the old man did was up to the old man. No one else.

Harry apologized the next day, of course. Swore to get himself cleaned up, take some time off, and the rest of that whole song. Tyson told him not to worry, reminded him they were rich and getting richer.

And they are.

They're getting much, much richer. Still, there are hiccups... speedbumps on the road to Success and Happiness and all those other tourist traps the world sells you as being A GREAT PLACE TO LIVE!

Visit, sure, but live?

No thanks.

One of the problems being that, although the new books are selling like blankets in the arctic circle, what's not going so well is the critical reception.

More alarmingly, as Little Tim once put it: the *accusations.*

Tyson's used to negative reviews for his books. Hell, he's been getting them for decades, and horror is always an easy target for a snooty newspaper critic-slash-wannabe-poet, and his feelings aren't going to be hurt by a few scathing, one-star reviews on the internet.

No, it's the *other* stuff that niggles at him.

One *New York Times* opinion piece wrote that Tyson's last two books were "morally destructive" and "a blight on the landscape of genre fiction." Another withering piece from *Entertainment Weekly* even suggested that Tyson isn't the one behind the keyboard, that he's been using a ghostwriter, or—get this kids—a *staff* of writers to complete his books for him. They figured the speed of the books' releases, and the size of the books themselves (*The Horror* is what most folks refer to as a "doorstop novel"), is such that it would be impossible for one man to write it all. The same article also made references to the overall *style* of the writing, advocating that it was vastly different from Tyson's previous books. Therefore, the rest could be inferred.

"They're coming for you," a voice says, and Tyson spins around, finds himself looking directly into the mirror. He sees his own startled face... and something more.

A semi-opaque version of flesh, muscle and bone. And beneath it, hiding behind the eyes, beneath the skin, he can see the old man.

The blind bastard stares back, leering, like he did that day in the movie theater except...

Except...

*Except this time, he's not just looking at you, hombre.*

*He IS you...*

"Hogwash and bug spray," Tyson says out loud, not allowing himself to get worked up, not on this very important night. He turns his back on the reflection and enters the walk-in closet adjacent to the bathroom, picks out a cream suit, a chocolate-colored silk shirt, and the new Magnani dress shoes he picked up that afternoon.

He pretends not to notice the old man watching from the mirror. Who keeps watching him as he walks away, wearing that same wide, ugly grin on his pruned face.

*Doesn't matter. Doesn't matter.*

Tonight, they'll be toasting the release of his newest novel, and he plans to look dapper as hell for it. Nothing is going to stop him from enjoying this evening—not his doubts, not his memories, not his downward-spiraling sanity. If he's losing his mind, so be it. He'll still get what's coming to him. He's *earned* it, damn it.

He *deserves* it.

"Sure you do, Papa, sure you do," the old fart says, his voice filtering through the mirror as if transmitting from another dimension. "First you play, then you *work*. Yes? Much work to do. Now go play, go play. Then come back to me.

"Come back to *us*."

Tyson folds the suit over his arm and leaves the closet. When he walks into the bedroom, he ignores the hunched shadow in the corner, only slightly alarmed at the speed and ease with which the wraith seems to move through his world at will. No, he won't acknowledge the dull white eyes following him, tracking him as he crosses the room to lay the suit out on the bed.

"Tonight is a special night," he says, pretending not to hear the dry chuckle coming from the shadow. "Tonight's a special night, and I'm going to enjoy it. I've earned it."

As Tyson steps into his boxers, pulls thin socks over his feet, and buttons-up his silk dress shirt, he repeats the phrase to himself, over and over again, focusing on his words, his mantra, so that he won't have to listen to the voice from the shadows again. Won't have to hear that raspy, fingernails-scraping-cardboard chuckle one more time.

"It's a special night. I'm going to enjoy it. I've earned it. It's a special night... a special night..."

When he's done dressing, he goes downstairs to call the car service. While he waits, he treats himself to a swig of the good stuff.

He's earned it.

# FORTY-EIGHT

IT'S A full house at the Salon de Ning rooftop bar, a space where most New Yorkers couldn't afford an Old Fashioned, much less their famous Croque Monsieur, or even a melt-in-your-mouth order of Gotham Tiramisu. But hey, Scribner is footing the bill, so anyone who knows anyone with access to the VIP list is in attendance, gawking more ardently at the amazing view of the brightly lit Manhattan skyline than the giant posterboard book covers of *The Horror,* strategically placed on black easels around the patio. Tyson shakes hands and flows mercilessly through the crowd. Gauged by their affectations, it's obvious, to him anyway, that folks are more impressed at being on the chic peak of the Peninsula Hotel than with his book release.

Thankfully, there's a scheduled window for signing books that night, so at least he won't have to deal with every Dick and Jane who snuck in because their brother-in-law or best friend or some shit was an intern at the publishing house with access to the Excel file gateway. Still, he must admit it's easily the nicest release party he's ever been thrown, and that soothes his ego nicely, makes the smile-and-handshake and dozens of photo ops a little easier to swallow.

After the first couple hours, Harry pulls him into a VIP area inside a funky, glass-paneled geodesic dome the restaurant put up for the holidays. Tyson doubts Bucky Fuller's trademark invention has ever come complete with a leafless tree decorated by golden Chinese lanterns, not to mention a private bar stocked with the kind of booze you don't so much drink as admire yourself holding. Tyson orders a Yamazaki 18-year—neat—and nurses it for a while before Harry tells him to *drink up for God's sake* and hands him a second. Tyson doesn't like the idea of slugging down a hundred-dollar glass of whisky, but he agrees to speed things up a bit—happily so.

"You know what you're going to say up there?"

Harry indicates the glass-walled barrier between the (rather chilly) patio and the interior of the bar, where most of the guests are schmoozing, listening to a middle-aged, White-people version of a DJ, drinking from the "everyman" open bar and eating off the trays of passed hors d'oeuvres.

*Or whore divers, as Violet liked to call them, feigning a distaste for the fine things.* Tyson lets himself dwell on the memory a moment, before it turns black in his head. *Back when she still spoke with you, that is. When she would actually go places with you. When she loved you.*

*When she could walk.*

An image—long ago filed away in the early databases of his aging mind—plays like an 8-millimeter movie in his head: Violet as a pudgy toddler, wearing a blue dress that her mother picked up earlier that day at Baby Gap, taking her first steps across the great expanse of pine hardwood floor they had in the townhouse living room before he carpeted over it a decade ago.

*Da-dee,* she'd said. Arms outstretched. Practically bursting with unconditional love.

Tears sting the backs of his eyes, and he curses under his breath, flings back the entirety of the overpriced whisky like it was Jack Daniels, and refocuses his thoughts on the present.

"You all right?" Harry asks.

"Yeah," Tyson says. "And no, I don't know what I'm going to say. I'm not gonna read. You know that right? The publisher knows that?" Tyson looks around for someone he recognizes from Scribner—his editor, a PR person, an intern, any-fucking-one.

"No, of course not," Harry agrees, pursing his lips. "God, no. Just, you know, thanks for coming, blah-blah-blah. Tell your friends and family to buy my book, blah-blah-blah. The usual thanks-and-beg routine. Then we'll announce that you'll be signing, and get that circus started. After that, you can stay and find a young female sycophant to suck on, or you can skip out. Matters not to me, my man. Matters not to me."

Tyson gives Harry a sidelong stare, wondering how drunk he is. "So, should I go in now? You gonna introduce me?"

"Me? Hell no. We'll have one of the PR people do that. This is their show, bud. We're just the bears in tutus dancing on the dirt."

*Speak for yourself,* Tyson thinks, and feels petty for thinking it.

"That's what they have an emcee for," someone says. "Haven't you guys noticed that dude on the little stage all night? The one DJ'ing the music? He's also been telling terrible jokes. Pretty painful actually."

Harry throws a quizzical glance over Tyson's shoulder at the man who's just spoken. Tyson turns, and his eyes go wide with surprise.

"Hiya, Tyson," Ben Howard says.

Ben's wearing his usual garb of black raincoat, blue work shirt, khakis, and sneakers. His fisherman's hat is stuffed into a pocket, and he looks older than Tyson remembers him. In the subway, and outside the restaurant, he'd seemed like a kid. College student, perhaps. Now, slightly unshaven, eyes fatigued, hair grown out, he looks like the big brother, or perhaps even angry uncle, of the bright-eyed young man who'd asked him for an autograph in the subway car.

"Ben?" Tyson says, then follows it up with the first thing that comes into his mind: "How did you get in here?"

Ben laughs, then turns to Harry, extending a hand which Harry shakes, but not warmly.

"I have my ways," Ben says. "Anyway, just stopped by to say congrats on the new book. Personally, I wasn't a big fan of the last one. Seemed pretty bleak, even for a horror novel. I found it..." Ben eyes the stars beyond the glass panels of the geodesic dome, tapping a finger on his chin theatrically. "Hateful. Yeah, that's the word I think fits. It was hateful."

Tyson nods dumbly, mouth slack. "Well, everyone's a critic, eh?" he says, clearing his throat and looking at his empty glass regretfully. "Besides, it's just human nature."

"What's that?"

Tyson shrugs, the corner of his mouth twitching into a smile. "To be bad, of course."

"Yes sir, yes sir," Ben says, his smile not finding his dark brown eyes. "Regardless, may I say how sorry I was to hear about your family. That was a tragedy. A real tragedy. I mean that from the bottom of my heart. Thank God you weren't implicated."

Tyson bristles. *Not implicated, hell, they tried to dump the whole damn thing in my lap. Luckily the forensics were crystal clear as to who pulled the trigger, and once Violet recovered enough to recount events I was exonerated completely, yes.*

*For two of the murders.*

*Jesus, but it was touch-and-go for a while regarding the woman. The detectives saying the stab wounds were "out-of-context" with self-defense. After all, there were dozens. But enter one well-paid lawyer stage left, and my modest celebrity, to help win the day. Even if I was still lain out as a sacrificial lamb for all those social media fuckheads.*

"Is Violet here, Mr. Parks? I'd like to speak with her."

Tyson shakes his head, his eyes on his drink. "Not that it's your business, but no, she's not here. She doesn't read my books anyway, even though I always send her a signed copy, quite religiously, when I receive my personal copies from the publisher. I'm sure they're making a fine doorstop for her apartment, if she hasn't burned them all, that is."

Ben's smile slides away, and his eyes go distant. His playful tone turns sober, almost sad. "If I had known, Mr. Parks, I never would have..."

For a moment, he looks almost ashamed.

"Would have what?" Tyson asks, feeling a wave of faintness cloud his mind. Suddenly, it's as if the party has fallen away, the volume of the world around them turned down. Like they'd entered a place where only the two of them exist: the two of them, and a writhing black mountain of things unspoken.

Harry steps between them, puts a hand on Ben's shoulder. "You know what, dude? I think you should go."

Tyson almost warns Harry to be careful. He feels strongly that there is more to this particular man than his young looks and bargain-store raincoat, his ridiculous hat. Tyson thinks Ben Howard has many layers, some of them very peculiar, and some of them quite dangerous.

"It's fine," Tyson says, gently pushing Harry back a step. "He's an old acquaintance. Look, let's go make the damned speech, huh?" Tyson turns back to Ben with the formality of a professor at the end of a lecture-heavy class. "Thanks for coming, Ben. Hope you'll stay for a book. Let's go, Harry."

Tyson walks away, leaving the glass dome and heading for the small stage inside.

After a moment, Harry follows.

---

THE LINE winds nearly the entire circumference of the large room; guests stand three-deep along the walls, gripping their brand-new hardcover copies of *The Horror.* The publisher provided two hundred complimentary books for the night, and Tyson had been made aware they were all handed out. They could have likely gone double that number, but Scribner isn't *that* generous. And regardless, Tyson has no interest in signing books until midnight. So, two hundred, and no more.

*Thank God,* he thinks, eyeing the long line. His hand is already giving him shit, just fifty copies in—tight cramps in his knuckles, a dull soreness spreading in his wrist.

Still, he smiles and tries to say a kind word to each person he signs for. It's the way of things, after all. Thankfully, the guests have been told in advance that there will be no photo ops in the signing line. Slapping on a fake smile a couple hundred times is *not* something he's willing to do, not even for his own book party. Besides, he's taken plenty of pictures while mingling around, squeezing hands, saying "thank you" over and over again like a damn puppet.

"Hi Mr. Parks, oh my God, this is... wow... this is such an honor for me."

A book slides across the white tablecloth where Tyson holds court, a publicist on his left, Harry on his right. A security guard in a cheap black suit stands mute but visible directly behind him. *Just in case some crazy fanatic tries to stab me in the neck*, he supposes.

Tyson opens the front cover and smiles up at the man standing before him. The first thing he notices is how *sweaty* the guy is. The second thing is how incredibly *fat* he is. Not just round belly and full-face kinda fat, but the sort of obesity where there are thick rolls of fish-belly-white flesh coiled beneath his chin, below which a barrel-width gut squeezes out—the shadowed, single eye of a cavernous navel staring at Tyson eagerly—past the bottom of his black T-shirt like a beachball made from hairy bread dough.

*Guy's a caricature,* Tyson thinks. *They must drive these people around to every horror event in the world and unload them off the back of a truck, handing out tight black T-shirts along with some stink-oil to rub into their hair and skin before cutting these suckers loose on us poor writers.*

"That's nice, thank you. Did you want this inscribed?"

The big man grins so broadly that his eyes scrunch into slits, his cheeks flush red and his chin fat wobbles like an anxious turkey. He nods vigorously and Tyson notices, with his own idea of horror, that a few droplets of sweat have spattered down onto the open pages of the book, leaving gray speckles below the space over which his pen currently hovers.

"I'm Randy," he says, heaving it out as if it was his final breath. "I'm your number one fan! Get it?"

Tyson smiles gamely and nods, bent to his work. "Uh-huh. Great. To... Randy..." He signs his name with a flourish, ignoring the way the ink spreads like a fractal painting where it sinks into one of the particularly saturated sweat droplets dotting the page.

As he hands the book back to Randy, he notices Ben Howard standing right behind him.

Ben isn't holding a book.

"Thanks again," Tyson says to Randy, whose nose is buried deep into the crease of the open book. *Most likely studying the signature for authenticity.*

Randy steps slowly aside, and Tyson turns his attention to Ben, giving him a wary look. "No book, Ben?"

"Me? No, not this time, Mr. Parks. But I did have some ephemera I was hoping you could sign for me."

Before Tyson can respond, Ben lays down a few news clippings, or whatever you'd call an article printed off the internet these days. Two of them are printed from the digital back pages of *The New York Times* website, one is from the *Post* (according to the text header), and the fourth from the *Detroit Free Press*.

All feature gruesome headlines.

Ben lays a finger on the image of a smiling young lady on the *Times* printout. Tyson recognizes her, but can't place from where.

From the chair beside him, Harry mumbles *God damn it* under his breath.

"Kim Sullivan leaped out her apartment window last week. Fell twenty-three stories. You recognize her, right?"

*Now* Tyson does. He knows her. Of course he does. He's spoken to her on countless occasions, mostly over the phone. He only met her in person a few times, though... the last time she'd given him a cup of cold coffee and apologized for it.

Harry's assistant.

Tyson turns to Harry, whose fiery eyes are glaring at Ben.

Fiery, yes. Surprised, no.

"Harry? What is this?"

Harry's eyes shift to Tyson, then soften. Tyson wonders if he registers a degree of shame in those eyes. "We'll discuss it later, Ty. She had issues, okay?"

But Ben is already moving on. He shifts a page, rests his finger on the *Free Press* article. This picture is a bit more graphic, and troubling. "You don't know this cat, not personally, but a few weeks ago this Tyson Parks fan decided to fire a shotgun blast into his wife, teenage daughter, and infant son in the middle of the night," Ben says casually, as if reciting the paper's review of last night's Knicks game. He points a finger gun at Tyson. "Blam. Blam. Blam. Afterward, he's so distraught about the misunderstanding that he swallows the business end of the shotgun himself and blows the top of his head off." Ben pauses, looks up from the article to meet Tyson's eyes. "I keep thinking how the barrel must have burnt his mouth, you know? After all that blasting, it would have been hot, right? Hey, maybe you can use that detail in one of your books." Ben points to an italicized paragraph of the article. "See this? It's his suicide note. That's plagiarism, isn't it? I mean, that's word-for-word from your novel, Mr. Parks. Page two-hundred-thirty-one, I believe. You should sue his ass."

Tyson stares down at the article, the photo of small corpses beneath white coroner sheets. "What the fuck is this?" he says, seemingly more baffled about Ben's show-and-tell than angry. Ben ignores him and moves on, sliding over the *Post* article. "This dude was a junior editor at your publishing house. I did some digging and found out he was one of the editors who worked on *Black Altar*—one of many, I guess. Not really sure how all that works. But he also read the new one, the one folks are lining up behind me to have you sign for them. Anyway, it seems he isn't a fan, because he was arrested earlier today after pouring gasoline on a display of your new novel inside a Barnes and Noble. He was tackled by a security guard before he could get a match lit, but I think that batch is ruined, don't you? Hey, what was it you said earlier?" Ben's smile is gruesome as he snaps his fingers. "Oh yeah. Everyone's a critic."

Tyson stands, red-faced and pissed-off.

He notices two things right away: First, that his buddy Randy hasn't left the table. No, no... his new best friend Randy—*I'm your number one fan, get it*—has decided to hang out for a while. Chill with his favorite author. His chubby face, Tyson notices, doesn't look too thrilled about it, though. No sir. Tyson thinks Randy looks downright *angry*. His free hand, the one not clenching his freshly-signed copy of *The Horror*, is squeezed so tight that the knuckles stand out like white bolts. His cherubic cheeks are now patches of hot red, and his once-jovial eyes are hard as chipped steel.

And those hard eyes, Tyson notices with a degree of amusement, are fixated—locked in, you might say—onto Ben Howard.

*If looks could kill.*

The second thing Tyson notices is the quiet. It seems everyone—despite their drinking and eating and not being anywhere near the signing table—is now watching the drama as it plays itself out. Tyson even spots a couple assholes filming it with their phones.

"Ben," Tyson says, "I don't know what your game is, but I don't like it."

Ben stares back at Tyson, unflinching, all innocence. "But don't you want to see the last story? It's a doozy, Mr. Parks. It's right up your alley, in fact. See," he places the page on top of the others like a fourth Ace, points at the headline:

TEENAGER SENTENCED IN GRUESOME MURDER.

"Check this out, dude. It's about a teenage boy who did a little junior autopsy on one of the neighborhood kids. Right there in his garage. He used his dad's tool bench as a sort of surgery table, I guess. Anyway, he lures this poor little kid into the garage, knocks her out with a hammer, then slices the girl open while she's still, you know, breathing. Nine years old. Her name was Lisa, I think? Anyway, he has some fun with Lisa's insides, puts together some sort of... I don't know... I guess you'd call it a *diorama?* Using the girl's organs, of course. What's really weird, though? The police say he kept mentioning your book when asked about..."

"I never wrote any such thing!" Tyson roars, anger rising inside him like a storm. But he's more than angry, more than just nonplussed by this show-and-tell...

He's scared. No, scratch that.

He's fucking *terrified*.

The security guard in the cheap suit is at Ben's side now, gripping one sleeve of his raincoat. Meanwhile, good old number-one fan Randy is also moving in, getting in on the action, shoving a sausage-sized finger at Ben's face.

"WHAT'S YOUR FUCKING PROBLEM, MAN!" Randy yells.

Tyson realizes that things are getting quickly out of control, but Ben doesn't seem bothered. As a matter of fact, Ben wears the very last expression Tyson would have expected, given the circumstances.

He looks confused.

"Get out," Tyson says, and nods to the security guard who, likely delighted to have something to do, nods back brusquely, as if they'd just teamed up to collar the criminal of the month.

"Let's go, man," the guard says heroically. "Or I'm calling the cops."

"Mr. Parks," Ben says, almost curiously. "Jesus Christ. Do you really not know?"

But then Ben is yanked back, pushed away through the crowd. Tyson sits down, wipes sweat from his eyes. The news clippings, he sees, have vanished. Next to him, Harry is balling them up like used Christmas morning wrapping paper. "What an asshole."

"I don't even... I mean, my God, what's he talking about?" Tyson mumbles, not quite sure who the question is meant for.

"Who knows. The guy's a nutjob." Harry signals for one of the staff, most likely to ask for a couple more drinks. Tyson isn't going to argue.

"It's in *Black Altar*," Randy says.

Tyson, having momentarily forgotten about the guy, glares up at Randy, who's still standing by the table, cheeks still red, one fist still clenched. He's talking to Tyson, but his head is turned away, toward Ben's retreating raincoat. It seems he only has eyes for Ben.

"What do you mean?"

Randy turns back, and Tyson sees something in that puffy white face he doesn't care for. No, not one bit. The expression is hard as stone, the lips tight and bloodless. The eyes, so jovial one second and steely the next, are now hollow, as if all human empathy has been dug out and thrown away.

Deadly *is the word you're looking for,* Tyson muses, but tries not to dwell on it.

"Your last book," Randy continues in a numb, unsettling monotone. "It's what the priest does when sacrificing the little girl. Can't recall the chapter, but it's near the beginning." Randy's voice sounds robotic to Tyson's ears, and if the guy seemed like a joke before, he doesn't seem that way any longer. Right about now he's giving Tyson a nasty case of the heebie-jeebies.

"Oh, sure, that's right," Tyson says meekly, having no goddamn idea if it's right or not. Not remembering, of course, the events which take place in the novel. He'd read it, sure, but still... the plot points are hard to recall.

And of writing it, he has no memory whatsoever.

Harry plops a very full glass of scotch on the table. "For your nerves," he says, and swallows half from his own glass, also filled near the rim. "Now let's finish this. Next!"

A blonde woman in a red dress slithers in front of the table, pushing Tyson's novel toward him. "For Ginger," she says, and bends over the table to show a boxcar of cleavage and a hint of black lingerie peeking out from behind a cut of crimson fabric. "With love, if you don't mind." She giggles and Tyson slurps his drink, Ben quickly becoming a memory.

"Not at all, my dear," Tyson says, smiling broadly, and opens the book.

He hardly notices, or cares, that Randy, his self-proclaimed number one fan, is gone.

# FORTY-NINE

BEN ENTERS the elevator along with the black-suited security guard, who's more cordial than he would have expected for someone dealing with a young Black guy who'd crashed—and tried to ruin—a famous author's high-priced book release soiree.

"What floor, buddy?" the guard asks politely, half-in, half-out of the elevator himself. Ben notes the twisting cable and white earbud stuck into the guard's left ear, the small microphone clipped to the cuff of his jacket, and is grateful the guy hadn't felt the need to call for backup. All Ben wants to do now is get home, take a shower, and forget about all this bullshit for a while. Maybe catch the end of the Yankees game.

"I'm not staying here, so lobby is fine. I'll get a cab out front."

The guard nods and presses the 'L' button, lighting it up. He gives Ben a meaningful look. "You're done making trouble, right? Or do I need to ride down with you?"

"No man, it's good. I'm a private detective and that guy in there is on the hook for some bad business." Ben nonchalantly pulls his ID from his coat pocket, lets it flop open. "Just rattling his cage a bit."

The guard smiles and nods. "Gotcha. Ain't no skin off my nose, I don't read that shit. When you get to the front ask for Lucius, he's one of the door guys. He'll get you a ride."

"Thanks. Good night."

"Night," the guard says, and steps out of the elevator, letting the doors slide closed.

Ben leans back, thinking the big adventure of his night is over, when a vertical line of pudgy white fingers jam themselves between the two doors, thrusting through the narrowing black gap. The doors bounce back open, revealing the big guy who'd been getting his book signed while Ben confronted Tyson, the fat dude who smelled funkier than the nasty cheese folks were gobbling down at the party. His T-shirt, Ben notices, has some crazy occult design on it, a pentagram with goat heads and other nonsense all over it. The design is stark white against the stretched black fabric, bulging across his globular belly to give it an almost three-dimensional quality.

The man steps inside the elevator, glances at Ben for a beat, then turns his back on him, giving Ben a good view of the dandruff snowfall powdering his upper back. This time, the doors slide all the way shut.

Ben always had a gift for reading people, a hidden aptitude that had come in handy hundreds of times in his profession, an instinct that often makes him seem a much better private dick than he really is. Still, all's fair in love and war, et cetera.

So, for example, Ben knows that the guy he's riding to the lobby with—the insanely overweight dude clutching Tyson's book under one arm, while his opposite hand is stuffed pointedly into a deep front pocket of his cargo pants—is thinking bad thoughts.

Oh yeah, *very* bad thoughts indeed.

Another fun fact he pulls from his preternatural insight: harbored deep in Randy's pocket, clenched in one sweaty wet fist, is almost assuredly a weapon. By the curl of the dude's knuckles beneath the fabric, Ben's guessing a knife. Most likely a nasty-ass switchblade.

Ben wonders if maybe Randy has murder on his mind.

"You wanna press six for me, brother? I'm gonna stop at my room for a minute."

They're blowing past the twelfth floor when he asks, because he figures Randy would be quick. Getting off before the lobby is best-case scenario if Randy means him harm. It's much better for Randy, say, than following Ben outside and doing him in the street.

Randy huffs, as if the movement expends serious effort on his part (Ben thinks it might have done exactly that, based on Randy's apparent ignorance of the gym and the cornerstones of a good diet), and presses the button.

Ben hums a light tune as the car slows to a stop. A soft *ding* chimes inside the car, like the bell before the first round of a heavyweight fight.

As the doors slide open, Ben lifts his sneaker and kicks the back of Randy's leg, which promptly collapses beneath the bulk the poor guy has been hauling around all these years. Randy squeals like a stuck hog and drops to the floor like a sack of meat.

Ben kneels smoothly and grips Randy's elbow—the one linked to the hand still jammed into the front pocket—and pinches it.

He pinches it *hard*.

Randy screams in pain as his ulnar nerve compresses, freezing his arm and causing a tremendous wave of pain to course through his body. Ben coolly pulls Randy's lifeless hand from his pants pocket and plucks the un-sprung blade daintily from his loose, numb grip. Ben slides the knife into his own coat pocket, then releases Randy's elbow.

"I'll be damned, Randy, you packing, huh?" Ben says, using a tone he rarely employs, but comes in handy when he wants to intimidate someone. When he wants to make a *point*. "Now get the fuck outta my elevator before I shove this blade up your ass."

Randy tries his best to get up using the deadened arm, fails, and manages to slowly crawl his way onto the carpet of the sixth floor using a combination of knees and one good arm as support. The doors close on his waist, crunch against his body, then open with a warning *ding*. They close again on his legs, because Randy's not moving so fast, and again rebound smoothly, showing their irritation at the obstruction with the same, obstinate, *DING!*

Finally out, Randy rolls onto the hallway carpet, staring back at Ben not with rage, but despair, like a child who's just lost his lunch money to the school bully. Something Ben Howard could relate to.

"My book," Randy whines, eyes watering.

Ben looks down, sees the copy of *The Horror* lying on the floor, and kicks the thing out of the elevator, enjoying the widening of Randy's eyes as the dustjacket catches and rips on the metal ridges of the door track. It skids to a stop a few inches from Randy's nose as Ben taps the DOOR CLOSE button a few times.

"I'll see you again!" Randy yells, defiant now that the doors are closing and Ben has obviously lost interest.

"No you won't, buddy," Ben replies, looking up at the row of numbers above the door. "Your heart ain't what it used to be."

Ben is still humming along with the music filtering in through the elevator speakers when the doors open to the lobby. He tosses the cheap knife in the first garbage can he passes, then steps into the night, searching for his boy Lucius, and a ride home.

There's something still nagging at him, though. Some piece of vital information he isn't piecing together. Something that's almost certainly more important than catching the end of the game.

It isn't until his taxi is pulling away from the curb that Ben recalls Tyson's words from earlier, and he realizes what's been bothering him.

*She doesn't read my books anyway, even though I always send her a signed copy, quite religiously, when I receive my personal copies from the publisher...*

Ben's stomach churns. He pulls a frayed notebook from his coat pocket, flips through the pages in a rush. "Where are you?"

The steady strobe of passing streetlights illuminate the page he's looking for. Her name is written at the top, all her contact information scrawled below.

"Yes..."

An icy sweat breaks out on his forehead as he fumbles out his phone and dials, praying that someone will answer.

# FIFTY

AS VIOLET pulls the belt tight around her neck, she wonders what compelled her to open the damned book in the first place.

Three days ago, she received a package from her father, and knew immediately what lurked inside.

*The Horror.*

She'd left the sealed box resting on her table as if it contained anthrax, or explosives, instead of her dad's latest novel. She knew it would be inscribed to her, as always, from The Author. *With all my love,* it would say, just like it always did.

To date, her father has dedicated three books to her. The first was dedicated to her along with her dead mother—who had *not* been dead at the time—and Violet just a newborn. The second time she was conjoined with Sarah on the dedication page for *The Attic,* and the third time it had been just her. *To Violet.* That had been for *Crimson Skies,* his big bust of a historical novel about witches hiding out in Pennsylvania.

Along with millions of others, she'd never bothered to read it.

When she was very young, she thought it was neat her father was a writer. In her innocent, naïve way, she was proud of him. She loved seeing his face on the back cover, smiling as if he was looking at her alone, his only child, instead of the millions of readers he truly adored. She read his first book when she was only eight years old. He was thrilled, but she remembers her mother being upset. Worried about nightmares. But Violet didn't find the book scary, partly because she didn't believe in strange creatures and old curses, but also because her daddy had created it. What could possibly be scary about that?

When she turned nine and her mother died (tragically), Violet lost her taste for demons and monsters; for the macabre. Only one year later, Sarah entered the picture, and Violet swore she'd never read another one of his books. A promise she'd kept to herself.

Until today.

She doesn't know why, can't put her finger on the strange compulsion she felt to tear open the box and pull the heavy hardcover free from the brown wrapping paper. After all the hubbub over his last book, *Black Altar* (*Violent! Tone deaf! Sexist!),* she couldn't have been less interested in the follow-up. Especially when she knows he'd been putting down the final touches while she'd been getting spinal surgeries, while Sarah and Billy had been lowered into the cold ground. It disgusted her that he continued writing, that he so proudly revealed the cover and title of his newest, darkest opus on social media while his daughter was learning the hilarious ins-and-outs of using a wheelchair. Part of her thinks he might have been *using* the publicity of the horrific murders to raise interest in the book—every review, every article, referenced the tragedy of that night, forced her to play it over in her mind again and again. His use of the tragedy was one of the reasons she'd made another promise to herself: that she'd *never* go into that house again.

She'd since stopped reading the articles, ignored the trending hashtags *(#thehorrorkills, #tysonparksisthedevil*), and began to bypass the Books section of the *New York Times* website altogether.

And yet, despite it all, tonight she found herself, trancelike, slicing the taped seal of the box with a pair of scissors, opening it to reveal the paper-wrapped book, waiting to be consumed.

The cover was typical Horror Design 101—black cover, the graphic image of a woman screaming, clawing red lines into her cheeks with razor-sharp blood-red fingernails, the title bold and embossed, her father's name only slightly smaller along the bottom edge. She'd turned it over, expecting to see her father's visage staring back at her, as she had when she was a child (and he a much younger man), or perhaps a series of blurbs from other authors proclaiming the book's unrivaled excellence...

But it had been blank.

Plain, simple, black. There was the standard bar code, of course, centered along the bottom... but nothing else. No picture. No blurbs. No synopsis. She'd frowned when she saw that. It made the book seem somehow more ominous... as if it had just *appeared* out of the ether, unread, untouched, unseen.

She'd opened the cover, flipped through the front pages.

No dedication.

*That's a first,* she thought, and found herself, surprisingly, turning to the first page of text, the chapter heading a simplistic number 1 at the top left corner of the page.

Before she knew what was happening, or could raise any form of conscious argument against doing such a thing, she'd started to read.

She sat in her wheelchair, and read, and read, and read.

The aging light outside her window turned from white, to pink, to black. She urinated into her catheter without even realizing she'd done it. She didn't eat or drink. She didn't put the book down and take a break, or throw it across the room when the content grew so vile it physically repulsed her.

She simply kept reading.

When she turned the final page, she set the book neatly on the table next to the open shipping box, the one spilling shreds of bubble wrap like plastic guts, the nest from which she'd plucked the tome, and sat quietly for what felt like a very long time, thinking.

Violet isn't sure why, exactly, her thoughts began dancing along the lines they did, or why she'd started thinking that way at all. For the life of her, she couldn't understand why she wasn't already in her bathroom, brushing her teeth and getting ready for bed.

It was while sitting in the dim light of her sterile kitchen, with alarmingly little emotion, that she decided to take her own life.

After all, she was a cripple now. Her future stolen by a madwoman's bullet. All because of her father, because of what he represented to people, to the world.

Violence. Death. Rage. Despair.

She wheeled herself into the bedroom and opened her wide closet, then pushed aside some blouses in search of her old plastic rack of belts. She rarely wore belts anymore, there was little need, after all. Her pants weren't going to fall down, and not needing to wear them made things easier in many ways. She liked not having the restriction.

Violet fingered the straps on the cheap rack until she found a long cloth belt with a "pass-through" clasp, one that allowed her to cinch the belt loop as small as she needed. Humming a tune she did not recognize, she pushed the stiff black fabric through the buckle, then—with some difficulty—tied the other end of the cloth into a loose knot.

With an effort, and after multiple tries, she finally managed to toss the knot so that it slid down the crease between the door and the doorframe, snagging on the higher of two sets of hinges. She pulled the excess belt toward her until the knot caught, then she closed the door, making sure it clicked shut securely. She positioned her chair next to the closed door, and the hanging belt (now looped loosely at one end), then slipped the noose over her head.

Now, here she is, still humming the strange tune as she pulls the slack through the pass-through buckle until the fabric is tight around her neck. She doesn't think before she does what happens next, she just... *does* it. It's as if she's been planning the thing for weeks, using diagrams and physics equations and measurements, rather than it being a spur-of-the-moment impulse, like buying a purse she doesn't need, just because it's on sale.

Gripping the black handles of the armrests, she shoves the wheelchair backwards and lets her body sag forward, falling out of it, toward the floor.

Her knees hit the carpet first, but she of course doesn't feel the impact, and the muscles don't resist as the weight of her body continues to bore downward.

The coarse fabric of the belt tightens like a vice around her neck, just below the jawline, collapsing her throat. Squeezing it shut.

She begins to suffocate.

On the nightstand behind her, the cell phone rings.

Violet hears the loud chirping, and it's like a slap in the face; as if the sound was not a phone but a shrilling alarm, shattering early morning silence, blowing her dreams apart. The effect, however, is the same:

Violet wakes up.

*OH GOD! NO! PLEASE NO!*

In a rush of panic, Violet tries desperately to breathe, to take in air. Her mind demands that her legs start *working*, that they answer her body's call, to please just—this one last time—to please *STAND UP*.

Instead she hangs, gagging, fighting… choking.

Realizing her legs won't magically respond, her hands fly to the belt pressed deep into the flesh of her throat, now hard as taut rope. Despite her grappling efforts, she can't get even a single finger beneath it, between fabric and flesh. Her face tightening from the blood trapped there, her vision tunneling from lack of oxygen, she moves her fingers to the back of her neck, to the hard metal buckle straining against the door. She grabs at it with desperate fingers, clawing at the fabric, at the buckle, trying to figure out *some way* to loosen the tension.

Nothing works.

She spins her body awkwardly, the belt biting savagely into her neck, her mouth hanging open, gasping, desperate to take in air. Her tongue swells, the tip pushing past her bottom lip. The pressure behind her eyes is tremendous, and there are hard knots at her temples. Her heart beats so hard and fast she thinks it will soon burst, popping like a squeezed water balloon behind her rib cage.

For a moment, she swears she sees an old man sitting on her bed.

Watching. Leering.

She *knows* him.

*Not the way your story should have ended. It's all so... horrible, isn't it?*

Violet ignores the vision, the nightmare, whatever he is, and turns her bulging eyes toward the sound of the phone, and the nightstand it rests upon. She reaches a hand toward it, as if answering will somehow save her, somehow turn back the clock to the moment before she'd closed the closet door, slipped the makeshift noose around her neck.

But something is obstructing her ability to grab the phone. In its desperate, frantic struggle for life, her hysterical mind isn't thinking right. It's lost its ability to reason, like a frantic drowning victim pulling a lifeguard down with them, forcing them to die beside them, beneath the waves.

Something is in her way...

*The wheelchair.*

Raging with panic and raw terror, she claws with numb, panicked fingers, desperately reaching for the chair.

It slips out of her grasp as her tunneled vision begins to narrow, until she's looking at the world through a pinpoint, the rest already hazy, and black.

She finds the chair with one hand, pinches the lip of the seat, pulls it toward her...

The chair is jammed awkwardly against the wall, and the small front wheels have turned crosswise, preventing it from moving. With a feeble last effort, she pulls with all her strength, but her fingers slip from the leather seat, fall lifelessly to one of the metal footrests.

The phone stops ringing.

Darkness crowds her vision, erasing the light.

Her arms are slack, weightless. Dead.

Her oxygen-deprived brain begins to spark wildly, sending out signals of panic and calls for survival that are as bright and explosive as Fourth of July fireworks.

Ignoring the orders from above, her thumping heart slows. Her eyelids flutter, and start to close...

---

**BEN CURSES** as the cab honks at another taxi that cuts into their lane, missing their front bumper by inches.

He looks at the phone, thinks about leaving a message, then hangs up.

They go another block, make a right turn, and stop dead in a sea of red brake lights.

"Sorry, mister, it's like this everywhere since the construction on the bridge..."

Ben lets the cabbie talk, his own mind racing. Something's wrong, he can *feel* it. He raises his phone once more, hits REDIAL.

It rings once, twice, three times...

"Damn it," he mumbles, about to give up hope.

Then the ring tone cuts off.

It's followed by a click and a heavy silence.

"Hello?" he says too loudly, sitting up in the cab. "Violet? I'm sorry to call, I..."

A hoarse voice interrupts, whispers something inaudible.

"What? I'm sorry, I can't hear you."

The voice comes again, slightly stronger this time, but still sounding like a secret being told via two tin cans joined by a long string.

This time, however, he understands what the voice at the other end is telling him.

He holds the phone away from his ear, presses his face to the sheet of plastic separating the backseat from the driver. "Can you forget the address I gave you? I need to get to Penn Station right away. Please, it's an emergency."

The cabbie lifts a hand in a gesture of accommodation, then hits the left-turn blinker and edges over into traffic, ignoring the protesting horns as he does so.

Ben leans back, speaks hurriedly into the phone. "Violet? Are you still there? I'm on my way."

But the connection is dead.

Ben doesn't know if he should call the police. He isn't entirely sure what's going on, or how urgent the situation is. His mind is racing, and he can't slow it down enough to think clearly. He looks at his watch, tries to organize his thoughts.

If things go his way, he can be at Violet's door in under four hours. He thinks about calling her back, but something stops him, an intuition that there is nothing more he can do, other than get there as fast as possible.

He leans forward impatiently as the taxi crawls through late-evening traffic, replaying in his mind what he'd heard through the phone. The words that came soft and strained, as if under great pressure. She only said two words, but they'd been enough:

*Help me.*

"Damn it," he says under his breath, and dials 911.

God willing, he isn't too late.

# FIFTY-ONE

TYSON ARRIVED home later than he wanted.

Full dark had fallen like a final curtain on the day's drama. *Make your way to the exit folks, the show's over,* he thinks sourly as he climbs the steps to his empty house. *You don't have to go home but you sure as hell can't stay here—har-har.*

Tyson groans as he turns the final bolt and pushes through the door. Aside from the strange confrontation with that obstinate Ben fella, the launch party had been the usual bore. Scribner had gone all out, though, and it was nice to see some fans, and a few friends.

Still, he can't help feeling a sense of resentment from some of his colleagues, many of the very ones who'd cheered him so grandly at his birthday party. Instead of cheers and slaps on the back, most of them now offered nothing but curt hellos and cold shoulders.

*Jealous,* he thinks, letting hate and resentment have its way, shield him from his hurt feelings, his dented pride. His great sense of loss.

He'd slipped out after signing the last copy of the book, leaving Harry in charge of whatever groupies remained, shitfaced enough to have lost their best decision-making capabilities. By the time he left, Harry had blown by that particular stop sign himself.

*Harry's next stop? Blackout Station.* He chuckles and locks the door behind him, turns to examine the dark, empty townhouse.

Even after being alone for more than a year—secluded from the rest of society, from the ghosts of the past—he still finds his house vacuous. He misses not coming home to the glow of lights, to Sarah's voice, the smell of her perfume; the sight of her curled on the couch reading a book, on the phone with a friend, prepping vegetables for dinner. In some ways, he misses those dinners most of all. Those were the times during which they'd formed a habit of always preparing the meal together, talking about her job, his writing, Violet's future, *their* future... all the mundane things that emerge in the lives of two people who share an existence, a life.

But Sarah is gone. And, in a way, so is the man he'd been while she was alive. At times he misses both of those people, now lost forever.

Tyson sighs wearily and goes upstairs to change. He's had enough of the suit (and the hard-ass persona that comes with it) for a good long while.

# GOTHIC

WHEN HE returns downstairs (having shed the sport coat and tie), he grabs a light beer from the refrigerator, goes into to the living room and flips on the gas fireplace.

He leaves the other lights off. He prefers it this way, his private purgatory of flickering orange and inky dark. In the dim light, he sips his beer and contemplates his career, his next steps.

After finishing *The Horror,* he'd been able to stop working for a while. The old man and the desk had gone relatively silent, seemingly assuaged for the time being. It had grown so quiet, in fact, that he soon began fiddling with his *own* ideas, outlining a novel to write as a follow-up to his old smash-hit, *Dangerous Dreams.* Or maybe a sequel to *Blood Moon,* an idea he'd long toyed with.

He tells himself that the next book will be *his* ideas, that it'll be *his* words on the page. Tyson Parks doesn't need ghosts or haunted desks to write a great novel, he's been doing it for decades!

"Enough is enough!" he blurts out, then settles heavily on the couch, staring at the fire, taking a long swig of beer. "From now on, I'm in charge around here," he says, his directive delivered to the dancing flames.

Cold hands run through his hair.

"Christ!" he yells, leaping to his feet. He spins, lips and chin wet with the beer he'd spit out in surprise, eyes wide in the reflection of the fire. He stares, slack-jawed, unbelieving.

"Sarah?"

She stands between the couch and the kitchen beyond, as if she's just wandered down from the bedroom to find him napping. She's smiling—a knowing, cunning smile—and wears a simple white dress, one he does not recognize. It's semi-translucent and fitting, but unadorned, low cut, sleeveless, and tied with a string bow at the throat. She wears no shoes.

Licks of orange and yellow lap her bare skin, turn her hair a fiery gold, make her teeth shine. She looks beautiful. Healthy and unharmed.

Alive.

Even in his shock, Tyson can't help but recall the sight of her body sprawled on the kitchen floor, the back of her head popped open like a split pomegranate, red and pulpy from the gunshot. He wonders... if she were to turn around, would he see that patch of red in the firelight? The moist sheen of blood? The hot pink of brain nestled within the jagged white teeth of splintered skull?

"Hiya babe," he says shakily.

She spreads her arms wide. "What do you think? An improvement, right?" She walks around the couch and approaches him. He takes a half-step back from her, and she stops.

"Yeah, sure," he says, fighting the impulse to take her into his arms, knowing very well what she really is—that she's not Sarah at all, but something horribly different.

An old muse in a new form.

A welcoming form.

An *inspiring* form.

"Don't you think it's time for you to get back to work?" she says. "We have *one* more book for you to write, baby." Her lips curl into a sneer, showing teeth. "To be honest," she says, laughing lightly, "we're a little fucking tired of seeing you lap up all our glory. Even *we* have egos, you know!"

She laughs loudly, abruptly, and—quick as a snake—grabs his hand with her own.

Her skin is ice-cold.

"I've done everything you've asked. I've given you what you want, haven't I?"

The muse says nothing for a moment, as if considering whether the question merits an answer. Finally, she says, "The question of *what we want* is not for you to ask. Our desires are boundless and ever-changing. In some ways we're like you, Tyson. Greedy, I mean."

She leans close, puts her mouth by his ear. "But mostly," she whispers, "we're *hungry.* We crave so much that it feels, at times, we can never... get... enough."

She pulls away, still gripping his hand, squeezing tight.

"Come on, big guy." She gives him a heavy wink. "Let's have us a palaver."

# FIFTY-TWO

JUST UNDER four hours later, a few minutes before 1 A.M., Ben approaches Violet's apartment. He hasn't seen any police cars or ambulances outside and sees no sign of emergency personnel in the hallway.

He isn't sure if that's a good thing or a bad thing.

Assertively, but not so loudly as to bring out neighbors, he knocks on Violet's door.

He had the address of her new (more wheelchair-accessible) apartment, along with her phone number, in his notepad. On an earlier page was the email address she'd given him that day at the museum.

It took him fifteen minutes to get from the Providence train station to her apartment, and he'd jogged the second half, leaving him hot and sweaty as he waits in the carpeted hallway for her to answer. Praying for her to answer.

He knocks once more. "Violet? It's Ben Howard. I called?" He waits, listening, then continues, voice lowered, mouth close to the door. "We met… *before*. At the museum?"

He hears something move from inside. The sound of furniture—a table or a chair—being pushed across a floor. The locks on the door unlatch, the knob turn, and the door is pulled inward.

Violet looks up at him from her wheelchair, looking small and young and fragile. There are starbursts of broken blood vessels on her cheeks, and one of her eyes is a gory dark crimson where there should have been white. Ben's investigator eyes move immediately to her neck, where he can see the flesh-rubbed imprint of a burn, as if from a rope.

*Like she's been hanged, or strangled.*

"You," she says in modest surprise. Pleasantly so, he hopes. The word is barely a whisper, but more than loud enough in the quiet of the late-night hallway.

"May I come in?"

She nods, wheels her chair backwards. He follows inside, closes and locks the door behind him. She's pushing her way into the kitchen, and he walks in behind her.

Without asking, she pours coffee from a fresh pot into two mugs. Her eyes indicate a chair at the table. As he sits, he notices, with a pang of sorrow, there is only one.

She sets the mugs on a dish towel laid folded on her lap, and he fights the urge to stand and help her. Instead, he sits and waits as she slowly wheels across the linoleum floor and sets one mug, then another, onto the table. He pulls his over to himself, takes a greedy sip.

"Thank you."

"You're welcome," she says, her voice raspy and quiet, but much better than it had sounded over the phone. In addition to the marks on her neck, and the blood behind her eye, he can tell she'd been crying. She looks worn, rung out as a washrag, and it hurts to see her in such a terrible state. "Should I wonder how you have my number?" she asks, voice scratchy and slow. "I don't recall giving it to you after the museum. We exchanged emails, but..."

He nods, removes his floppy hat, folds it, sets it neatly on the table. In the stronger light, he notices additional abrasions beneath her chin, and puts together what she'd done. Or *tried* to do. He keeps his educated guess to himself and instead concentrates on holding her eyes with his own. "I can explain, but I hope you know that, whatever else I might be, that I'm a friend. And right now, I'm worried about you." They both let his words settle. She doesn't ask for more explanation, so he continues. "You feel like telling me what's going on? I called nine-one-one..."

"I know. They came and I sent them away. I'm fine. I mean, I'll be okay. It's just..."

Her eyes fall to the table, then she sits up and reaches for a book that's resting there. Ben had been so focused on her—on her wounds, on trying to figure out what had occurred—that he hadn't noticed the volume with the plain black dustjacket.

When she turns it over, he recognizes the familiar cover, the title. After all, he'd just come from seeing it blown up grotesquely on poster board signs, repeated in a line of two hundred party guests, clutched tightly in their excited grips.

Violet pushes it toward him, and he instinctively pulls back. She smiles a little, the side of her mouth curling delicately upward. "You're right to be scared of it. The fucking thing just tried to kill me. If I hadn't been able to get back in my chair..."

Ben looks at her, wide-eyed, then settles back, huffing out a breath. He looks around the kitchen in an attempt to gather his emotions, redirect his anger into something more productive.

"You believe me," she says, sounding astonished despite her thin, wounded voice.

Ben rubs a hand over his face. "Yeah, you bet I do. There's something wrong about all of this. I didn't know what I was involved in... I mean, who could have thought... your father, the books, what's happening to people. What? Because of... because of a..."

"A desk," she finishes, nodding. "Yeah, I know."

Ben shakes his head, as if the subject disgusts him. "Listen, do you need a doctor, or..."

Violet sips her coffee and winces.

"Wow, coffee was a bad idea." She smiles again, more easily this time, and Ben notices how beautiful she is, how the combination of vibrant youth and deep-seated pain birthed something new in her features; how it darkened her eyes, gave her soft youth the polish of experience. He wants, in that moment, to do nothing but take care of her. To protect her, help her in any way he can, any way she wished. He can't help feeling all of this has been his fault, or, at least, *partially* his fault. What happened to her. To Sarah Foster. To Diana.

He'd put the gun in her hand. Told her where to point it.

"We need to stop it," Violet says, interrupting his thoughts. Her eyes are hard, determined. "We need to stop *him*."

Ben thinks about it a moment. He remembers how confused Tyson seemed when he'd shown him the newspaper clippings. How he hadn't remembered writing the scene described in the article. He'd told Ben he had written no such thing, and Ben believed him. Believes him still. He debates how deep Tyson is; how much of the man is pawn, how much of him is king.

How much of the true him even remains.

"I agree," he says finally. "But it could be more complicated than that."

Violet tilts her head, waiting.

Ben sighs, continues. "I'm not sure your father is the problem, or whether it's something, *someone,* else."

Violet shakes her head. "I'm not following."

Ben leans forward, folds his hands on the table. "I think the evil we're talking about is something we haven't seen yet. And, I'm sorry to say this, and I don't mean to frighten you, but I think your father is in over his head. I have a feeling that his usefulness is finite."

"I agree. I think I've seen it. That evil. Or, I don't know... part of it. Okay, so... what? I mean, I don't know what we can do. What we're supposed to do. Do you?"

"Honestly? No, I have no idea," Ben replies. "But I think we should try. Together, if you'd like."

"Maybe after we can go back to the museum. Look at some art."

Ben smiles, nodding. "That'd be nice." He pauses a moment, gathering his thoughts. "Violet, can I ask you something? What did it look like? What you saw?"

Violet's eyes fall to her wringing hands, her numb legs. She recalls the events of that awful night. Remembers being shot, bleeding out on the stairs. And how, just four hours ago, she was hanging by her neck, twisting for the phone, seeing the strange figure hunched on the bed, watching her die.

When she answers Ben, she can't meet his eyes. "It looks like my father."

Ben doesn't know what to say, where to begin. He decides he'll just wait a bit. Stay with her. For now, they'll stay still, and let the future come to them.

Beneath the dim circle of light inside the dark apartment, they sit together in a companionable, if troubled, silence. Outside, the great chamber of night eclipses their world, oblivious to the menace which runs swiftly through its black halls, rides the wind to points far and wide, aiming for distant horizons.

# FIFTY-THREE

TYSON SITS at the desk and wiggles the mouse. The large screen of his brand-new PC springs to life, the pages on the monitor every bit as white and large and imposing as a physical page would be. Tyson figured the upgrade would be good for his eyes long-term (no more squinting at a laptop screen), and the mechanical keyboard he purchased along with the new computer allows him to type faster than ever, the clackety rhythm a meditative balm that soothes away his anxieties while creating a new piece. The reflexive keys also mean less wear and tear on his fingers and wrists, which is nice.

*Less blood as well. Fewer broken fingernails? Always a plus.*

The only other light inside the office is the faint flicker of firelight coming from the living room, barely bright enough to illuminate the back wall of bookshelves and a patch of hardwood floor. In the dark, Tyson's skin shines ghostly pale in the glow of the bright screen. His hands are curled into fists on the desktop, defiant.

"I have some ideas..." he says. "For the new book, I mean. Perhaps..."

Sarah stands off to the side, just outside the light of the monitor, a rippling shadow nestled within the heavy dark, a hazy patch of white against the muted reflections of firelight.

"Oh," she says. "I don't think so."

Tyson feels a sharp pinch in his leg. He looks down but can't see below his waist. The monitor is too bright, the dark too dense.

"What... again?"

Another needle-prick slices his forearm, slides beneath the skin.

A third stabs his neck.

He winces and sucks air, raises his fingers to his neck, presses them against the thin tendril of wood that has stabbed through his flesh. He feels the pulse coursing through the wood as it drinks. "Shit. That one hurt," he says, laughing uneasily.

"I'm afraid," Sarah says, "this will be our last project together. This form was difficult for me, but I thought it was the least I could do."

She steps close to the desk, the monitor's light luminescent against her plain dress, her chalk-white skin. Tyson's eyes move up from her waist, past her belly, to the bumps of her breasts, then higher, to her slender neck... resting below the deep shadow of her face.

She bends over, her features blunt in the harsh light. He recoils, sickened.

Her eyes are the swollen, cloudy blind eyes of the old man.

"As you well know, sweetheart," she says, her red mouth grinning. "All good things must come to an end."

He sees them now, curling up from the edges of the desk.

Twenty, thirty... *more.*

They dance and wave, their needle-sharp points and long leafy limbs glinting with the distant light of the living room's fireplace.

"Wait," he whispers.

As one, they fly at him.

The tendrils punch into his flesh, then push *inward*, deep into muscle and organs, scraping bone. The pain of a hundred wasp stings burns his nerves like acid.

Tyson cries out as they spear him again, and again, puncturing the fabric of his pants and shirt, slithering past the skin, burrowing into veins. He feels white-hot pricks in his calves and thighs. His cock is pierced, and he gasps, mouth wide in shock, as the prickly wooden stem slithers up the shaft like a catheter. Before he can cry out again, a dozen more stab mercilessly into his stomach, hip, chest.

He wonders if they are winding around his heart.

Slowly, as if his body were submerged deep beneath a black ocean, his arms float upward as long strands of wood weave themselves into the tendons of his forearms. Fingernails split and fall away as the branching tips push through the ends of his fingers.

He watches, horrified, as the blood-smeared stems curl and flex his fingers and hands, getting used to the controls.

More tendrils plunge into his neck, then his cheeks and tongue. They worm into his ears, perforate the drums and slither along the bones of his jaw, holding his head in a vice-tight grip that forces his gaze straight ahead, at the screen, the blank page, the blinking, taunting, cursor.

He screams then. Screams so loudly that it tears his vocal cords to shreds. Screams his throat raw, and then keeps right on screaming. Sarah laughs like a demented schoolgirl as he does, pausing only when she drops to her knees to lick the pooling blood at the edges of the desk—sensually, hungrily.

When she thrusts her face back into his vision, her lips and teeth are smeared with blood, her chin dripping red.

She opens her mouth wide and laughs.

His eyes roll up into his head, and he has visions—bright flares that soar like falling stars across the darkening night of his mind.

Of his sanity.

In his mind's eye, he sees an image of himself sitting at the desk. The windows are filled with the crimson color of a dying day. In this vision, as the sun is bursting like an overripe cherry, he's nothing more than a sunken-eyed husk, the flesh of his face so dry that his bloodless lips have withered to dead skin, pulled away from the teeth to expose a wide, joyless grin. His eyes are panicked, desperate. As if he's imprisoned inside his own body.

Then that vision slides away, and another replaces it.

He stands on a great plain. The horizon is fire, the sky bleached the color of old bones. He walks forward, seemingly forever, but hears nothing, sees nothing but that distant horizon of flame. He hopes to find the ones he loved, to one day be forgiven. If not by God, then by whatever is left in the world to forgive, by whatever runs things in this place of pale skies and blazing horizons, of endless steps.

He doesn't like this story, and desperately wishes he could think of a different ending.

When that vision passes away, he returns to himself. The windows are no longer the color of blood, but have turned black, soaked in midnight. He looks down at himself, or at least the parts he can see by roving his eyeballs.

His head is held fast.

"I'm sorry to say goodbye," the old man says. Tyson can just barely make out the spirit's bodily form in his peripheral vision. "He's coming, you see, and I'd rather not be here when he arrives."

The old man shuffles across the room one final time, leaving the office without a look back, and closes the door behind him. Tyson tries to swallow, but it proves impossible.

His mouth is full of wood.

With the dim light of the room, it might have appeared to an outside observer that, from a certain distance, Tyson is sitting in a great chair, one boldly arched on all sides with fine woodwork, bowed outward into complex, concentric wings around his body. A seat of honor. A throne.

And when the desk begins to glow, the false image of his regality increases ten-fold.

A low hum fills the room, and the stone of the desk brightens to a dizzying, translucent blue, a window to a world no human can ever look upon and still retain their sanity, their humanity.

From deep below, as if rising from the bottom of a great sea, something is rising toward the surface. A leviathan emerging from the depths of a different world, an alternate plane of existence.

Tyson watches it come, and shrieks in tear-drenched horror, from deep in his throat he murmurs guttural protests, begging, then he cries out once more, for the last time.

The ends of the desk split apart with the *CRUNCHING* of splitting trees, of shattering bones. Two majestic horns slide out from within and rise high into the air, their surfaces slick as oil, covered in the fluid of birth, like the skin of a newborn child.

They continue to push out, curve upward, thick as a man's thigh, drenched in blood. Like the barbs of a great bull, they taper at the ends into glistening tips that gouge the ceiling.

Tyson moans through a torn face pierced with thorny wood, his wild eyes flicking incessantly from side-to-side in his immobilized head, searching desperately for escape, for help, for a savior.

Instead, the branches which breach his flesh *push deeper*, and his body is slowly bent forward, forced into the maw of the beast. The monitor, wrapped in vines, tilts precariously before him, a dull glow shining through the branches. Before it, like a holy offering, lays the keyboard, now slightly recessed, as if it has become part of the stone itself.

As Tyson stares in horror, the sharp wooden splinters of his new fingers begin tapping, faster and faster. *Madly.* His reinforced hands fly with an impossible speed across the keys, the words on the screen zipping left-to-right in a blur, blackening the partially obscured white pages with words and ideas. With shocking twists, and heart-stopping scares.

With a story.

# EPILOGUE

HARRY NODS at his new assistant—some nerdy kid who can't be more than a week out of Columbia's MFA program—as he passes by. Sinatra is softly crooning *Summer Wind* through the office's ceiling speakers.

*...those lonely days, they go on and ooonnn...*

He goes into his office, shuts the door... and stops short when he sees a thick package, wrapped neatly in brown paper, resting on his desk.

Part of him knows immediately who it's from, and what it likely contains. His stomach clenches, and he swallows a knot of fear.

*Not sure how much more of this I can take.*

But he also knows the pills will help.

They help everything.

He sits down, gently places his mug of coffee to the side, and lifts the heavy parcel. Across the front, in precise handwriting he knows all too well, is his name.

He's perplexed, however, at not seeing an address. No messenger's receipt. No postage.

*Hand-delivered?*

He debates asking his new assistant about the package's arrival, but decides he doesn't really give a shit. It's here now, and he'll just need to deal with it.

*Thing must be 800 pages,* he thinks, turning over the thick bundle. He hasn't seen or heard from Tyson in weeks, and although this new arrival isn't at all expected, Harry isn't really all that surprised, either.

"All right, damn it. Let's get this over with."

He tears open the brown paper to reveal a dense stack of white, type-filled pages. On the top is a blank page made from a heavy cream stock, the kind you might use as a cover.

Harry debates retrieving the flask and the bottle of Xanax from his desk drawer before digging in, but curiosity gets the better of him (he is a literary man, after all), and he scans the thick cover page at the top of the stack.

Scrawled across the page, in bold, black ink, is a handwritten message from the author:

Do this in remembrance of me.
- T

"Uh-huh," Harry says, stroking his lower lip with a cigarette-stained fingertip. He taps his fingers against the top of the stack of paper, debating.

"Screw it." He sits up, flips over the cover to reveal the name of the book:

GOTHIC
By Tyson Parks

He stares at the page for a moment, ignores the chill that runs up his spine, the sick feeling of darkness that floods his mind. He licks his lips, lets out a held breath.

*Shitty title*, he thinks.

Then he turns the page over, and begins to read.

*More Books by Tyson Parks*

Ne'er Do Well
Blood Moon
Kill You Down
Dangerous Dreams
The Storm
Midnight Whispers: Collected Stories
The Quiet Neighbor
Deep in the Night
The Man in the Bowler Hat
The Attic
The Night Plow
Missy Darling
Crimson Skies
The Last Witch
Black Altar
The Horror

## ABOUT THE AUTHOR

**PHILIP FRACASSI** is the author of the award-winning story collection, *Behold the Void,* which won "Best Collection of the Year" from *This Is Horror* and *Strange Aeons Magazine.*

His newest collection, *Beneath a Pale Sky,* was published in 2021 by Lethe Press. It received a starred review from *Library Journal* and was named "Best Collection of the Year" by *Rue Morgue Magazine.* His debut novel, *Boys in the Valley,* was published on Halloween 2021 by Earthling Publications. His novel *A Child Alone with Strangers* was released in August 2022 by Talos Press.

Philip's books have been translated into multiple languages, and his stories have been published in numerous magazines and anthologies, including *Best Horror of the Year, Nightmare Magazine, Black Static, Dark Discoveries,* and *Cemetery Dance.*

*The New York Times* calls his work "terrifically scary."

As a screenwriter, his feature films have been distributed by *Disney Entertainment* and *Lifetime Television.* He currently has several stories under option for film/tv adaption.

For more information, visit his website at www.pfracassi.com. He also has active profiles on Facebook, Instagram (pfracassi) and Twitter (@philipfracassi).

Philip lives in Los Angeles, California, and is represented by Elizabeth Copps at Copps Literary Services (info@coppsliterary.com).

CPSIA information can be obtained
at www.ICGtesting.com
Printed in the USA
LVHW041359140223
739375LV00005B/99

9 781587 678400